Angle of Attack
An Adventure in Aviation, Love, and Crime

Lee Baldwin

DEDICATION

For Sherri, with gratitude for the wisdom of your heart, and your dedication to good drama.

TITLES FROM LEE BALDWIN

Angle of Attack ~ An Adventure in Aviation, Love, and Crime

Next History ~ The Girl Who Hacked Tomorrow

Lance Sidesaddle ~ Tales of an Old West Private Investigator

Halcyon Dreamworlds ~ The Robot Cries in the End

Savage Genesis Book One ~ Rescue and Asylum

Aliens Got My Sally ~ UFO Pulp Fiction for the Modern Mind

Beauty Pill ~ Drowning in her world of lies

COMING 2020

The Hidden Perils of Suicide ~ Sex and Death in 2099 California. (Stay glued at Baldwin-Books.com)

ACKNOWLEDGMENTS

With regard for two Mustang pilots I was honored to know: Captain Robert J. Love, the Korean War's 11th jet ace, and Colonel Charles W. Reed, who flew prop and jet combat in WWII, Korea, and Vietnam.

PHOTO CREDIT

Mustang P-51 cover image by A. Syed. Cover design, Lee Baldwin.

CHAPTER 1
A QUESTION OF BALANCE

I AM INNOCENT. The news blogs refer to me as Cicero Clay, glider flight instructor and paroled convict. But I didn't do it. I can prove it. And no, you don't want to call me by my first name.

I am Clay.

Far below me lie patchwork fields of Hollister, California. Alone in this long-winged sailplane, nothing disturbs me while the radio's off. I know I should keep the thing on but I enjoy quiet sometimes, so shoot me.

Wave lift over Fremont Peak has been decent this morning. I'd coaxed the glider to nearly 19,000 feet before my toes numbed with cold. You would love the view, snow-capped Sierra and Monterey Bay.

I flip the radio on, and no surprise, hear the insistent voice of Julie, our gliderport manager, asking me when the hell am I gonna get their aircraft back. I pull the oxygen mask from my face and key the mic.

"Eight-Seven Romeo. Hey, Julie."

"Clay, mind using your damned ears? I'm wearing out my jaw down here."

I'd rate that at least eight on her fed-up-with-Clay scale. I say nothing. Julie worries too much. I always get back on time.

"We need that glider in three minutes. Where the bleep are you?"

"About two minutes away."

I can imagine her perplexed scowl. Yes, I do stretch Julie's patience with my occasional antics. Left to me, I'd stay up here as long as lift holds out, practice acro maneuvers. But there's one stunt I can try and still keep everyone happy by getting back to the gliderport, which is directly below me. From this altitude, the crossed runways of Hollister airport glare at me like a gunsight.

"Okay," she says. "FYI, I'm getting chatter from the boss."

Since we're on an open radio band at a public airport, she's speaking code: Stacy, the gliderport owner, is getting impatient with my envelope-pushing behavior.

"And your one-thirty student wants to move to three this afternoon."

Arrgh. The bane of an independent flight instructor. "Negatory there, Julie. I have to be in San Jose at 4:30."

"Ah. Of course." Julie knows, as do most of the gliderport folks, that I have a regular appointment with my Deputy Parole Officer on Wednesday afternoons. What she doesn't know is I'm being moved to a new DPO. Doesn't fill me with joy. The new dude will likely take me back to square one, ask every single question about a crime I did definitely not commit. And for which I served three years in State lockup. Worse, rumor is he likes everyone wearing the GPS anklet, which will put an end to my flying. And a chunk of my income. Not going to be a fun afternoon at County.

"Well in that case he'll book for next week," Julie says.

"Eight-Seven Romeo." Tail number of this glider. I'm telling her bye for now. The radio band is silent.

Scanning the wide horizon, my well-worn thought replays: What if I leave right now? The idea has echoed in my head since my disaster of a trial four years ago. But where can you go in a glider, with no power of its own, how can you get away? Patience, I tell myself. I'll fly away soon enough. And not in a glider.

Get back in three minutes? Sure. My first rule of flying survival is simple: Know every detail about every ship I fly. And I want to know something about this ancient Schweitzer 2-32 sailplane. Specifically, will the airbrakes stay attached when I point the nose straight down?

I bank into a steep turn. Watching below for other aircraft, I'm cranking the elevator trim full down. Deep breath. Why would I do this, besides the endorphin high? A hurricane pilot once told me that the 2-32's airbrakes could hold the glider below redline in a vertical dive. Redline, you know, speed beyond which pieces of airplane start to fall off. Always curious, today I'll find out. I pull the airbrake handle all the way toward me. Outside the transparent wraparound canopy, in the middle of each wing, the brake flaps extend.

I push the control stick hard forward and I'm weightless, nosing into a steep dive. The shoulder straps yank me forward and the craft howls down the sky. Unbidden, a newspaper headline appears in my mind:

Misguided Felon Becomes Decorative Lawn Dart

Standing on its nose, the sailplane screams toward patterned earth three miles below. The airspeed needle jerks frantically in its glass face. My nutsack contracts. Don't try this at home, says the little announcer voice. I don't care how many stunts you've flown, going vertical will get your attention.

But the airspeed holds steady at an indicated 147 MPH. The legend is true. Every four seconds, I'm 900 feet closer to the ground. The vario is pegged negative, altimeter's unwinding like a berserk clock. Things in the cockpit are shaking around me and the airbrakes deliver a moaning thunder that's the last sound some pilots ever hear.

Alone in the sky and pointed straight down, I make a face at the canopy release. Didn't wear a chute this flight, and though sanity has already bailed out, jumping for me is no option. If something breaks coming out of the dive, my legacy will be a fleeting viral snuffer on YouTube. I'm below 7000 feet now and the runway's visibly larger. I can see dark tire smears near the runway two-four numbers. Again the little voice comes: Don't say *smear*.

Radio's still quiet. No aircraft in the pattern. The altimeter whips past 4000 feet. I ease the stick back and G-load pulls at me. The glider's nose lifts to a more normal flight attitude, she groans but nothing snaps. Not going to die today.

I release the airbrakes, bring her level in a whistling glide over the airport at about 140 MPH, plenty of altitude. For the hell of it I do a lazy roll, take a couple deep breaths to relax.

Below on the end of runway 1-3, black-and-white California Highway Patrol cars slalom through orange cones. The usual Wednesday drill. And today there is a fire truck on hand to wet the surface. One car, tiny as a toy, zigzags through the cones in a cloud of spray.

I key the radio. "Hollister traffic, glider eight-seven Romeo, midfield crosswind two-four left traffic, Hollister glider."

Automatically my mind steps through the landing checklist: radio, gear, flaps, speed, trim, airbrakes. Already tested those. Lined up on final, I ease left on the stick, push the right rudder pedal all the way in. The glider slews right until she's crabbing sideways, and begins to sink. Passing beneath is the typical weekday scene for Hollister. Gliders tied down along the taxiway, my faded-blue El Camino among other vehicles on the dusty access road, a glider lifting on tow behind a Piper Pawnee.

Crossing the threshold now, the two-four numbers pass below me. I'm still in the sideslip, waiting for the glider to settle in. Five feet up I center the controls and ease the stick back. A bump and subdued chirp from the single tire beneath me, and I'm down. In prison they always insisted we follow the yellow line, and on this runway I can do that without resenting it. I steer the centerline with rudder pedals, turn onto the empty taxiway, slow, full brakes, drop a wing.

Stop.

Soon as I'm out of the cockpit, another instructor and his student rush up to help. Together we push the glider toward its tie-downs. Grateful for the warm breeze on my face, I shrug out of my parka. It was cold up there this morning.

Julie, in cutoff shorts, tee shirt, and oversized dark glasses, walks toward me from the shade of the parachute-covered patio with her handheld radio and clipboard. She fills me in about the afternoon schedule.

"Your acro student is here. And the K-21's back." She waves the radio toward a graceful white sailplane at the far end of the taxiway. The Schleicher ASK-21 twitches eagerly in the wind.

"Did you hear that noise a few minutes ago?" she asks. "Sounded like landing gear falling off a jet."

I chuckle, reaching into the cockpit to disconnect the radio battery. "Trying out the dive brakes on the wreck here."

She gives me an appraising look over the rim of her dark glasses. "We assume your hull insurance is paid up." Finished, she turns away. I catch a view of her tail section as she strolls among the quiet sailplanes.

Under the parachute canopy, amid the instructors briefing students on their upcoming flights, I shake hands with short, bulbous Martin Roswell, who hands over his logbook. Roswell speaks with a clipped European accent. Wearing a heavy jacket zipped to his pudgy chin, his cheeks have a sheen of sweat. I can't read the man's eyes behind the dark aviator shades.

"Have not flown acro for over a year," Roswell explains. "There's a contest at Minden this weekend. Therefore I rush." He chuckles nervously and wipes the back of a hand over his cheek.

I send him out to preflight the K-21, and walk to my ancient El Camino. The interior, already too warm, smells of greasy car parts and too many miles. I feel beneath the dash, my hand on a burner phone I keep there. Touching it I get a stab of impatience. I need to call a certain brother about a certain missing airplane. A valuable missing airplane. But no, this is not the time for that conversation, with all the complications my older brother brings. Wade and I are beyond ready for his pilot friend to show up and fly the hidden airplane out of our lives. It will change everything. My hand comes back empty.

On the flight line, Roswell is doing his preflight. As he walks around the K-21, checking control surfaces, inspecting hinges and attachment points, I page through his logbook. Leather-bound and fancy with gleaming brass corners, the logbook shows years of flying in many gliders, at many locations around the world. Not only gliders, but he's checked out and flown multi-engine aircraft, plus some WWII warbirds including the Texan AT6 and the Mustang P-51, which many pilots argue won the air war over Germany. My eyebrows arch appreciatively. Roswell is very well prepared. I wonder if the man actually needs an aerobatics lesson.

Why do I think that? For one, there's my unwelcome notoriety. Visiting pilots occasionally schedule flight time with me just to say they'd flown loops with a local felon and getaway driver. Occasionally someone brings an ancient DVD for me to autograph - *Police Chases Greatest Hits*.

Roswell calls out he's ready. The sheen on his cheeks makes me ask, "Hey Martin, you really need the jacket?"

"In case we go high."

I drop it. Maybe it's what he plans on. Roswell will decide where we fly today, unless I have to pull him back from some mistake.

I inspect the canopy release handles in both cockpits. Red-tipped for visibility and safety-wired to guard against accidental release, they've never been used on this glider. Clamshell canopies are enormously expensive.

I read aloud from the engraved metal placard on the instrument panel: "This glider requires a minimum front seat weight of one hundred fifty-four pounds. Do you weigh that much?"

Roswell nods, grinning. "Ja, with some to spare."

Just for drill, I ask, "And why is that important?"

Roswell considers briefly. "The placard front seat weight is the minimum to keep the center of gravity ahead of the wing's center of lift. Otherwise, the glider would be uncontrollable."

I nod. "Uncontrollable how?"

"Tail-heavy, impossible to bring out of a stall. You could never get the nose down to increase airspeed," Roswell answers. "By the way, the radio doesn't check out."

I look in the forward cockpit. The small black radio battery, strapped to its floor receptacle with bungee cord, is not connected. I point this out. Roswell somewhat sheepishly inserts the connector and keys the mic to call for a radio check. From somewhere out in the sky, a pilot's voice in the speaker: *Five by five, K-21.*

I hit him with other random questions about glider airworthiness and flight dynamics. He gives me quick and substantial answers. Satisfied, I use the cockpit radio to call our tow pilot. Across the runway, a Piper Pawnee turns its prop. The engine sound reaches us faint on the wind.

Together, Roswell and I push the K-21 along the taxiway to runway center. As he clambers into the front cockpit to strap in, I walk to the flight line patio and hand his logbook to Julie.

"Possible shear line toward the coast," I tell her. "Back in a couple of hours."

Julie grins. "Do bring her back in one piece, Clay."

Like I say, Julie worries too much.

On the wide concrete runway, I'm connecting the Pawnee's towline to the K-21's belly hook while Roswell, clumsy in the bulky jacket, reads out the takeoff checklist. I stuff my parka behind the seat cushion. Not planning to be that cold this trip. The afternoon is warming, cumulus clouds are popping all over the valley at 8000 feet. Perfect day for soaring.

I step into the rear cockpit, close my half of the transparent canopy, strap in and adjust the rudder pedals. Roswell completes the takeoff checklist aloud.

"Controls free, pedals adjusted, wind down two-four at ten, canopy locked, belts secure, altimeter set for..."

"Two three zero," I supply.

"Ja, that's two three zero feet, radio set, canopy closed, brakes on, we're ready."

Our wing runner holds the glider level as the Pawnee taxis slowly forward, taking up towline slack. Roswell eases the brake handle back as the line pulls tight.

"We're ready and we're leaving," Roswell says, giving a thumbs-up and waggling the rudder. Ahead, the tow plane's rudder moves in response. The engine roars and both planes start to roll. The glider lifts off quickly into the headwind. Hands and feet light on my own controls, I follow Roswell's movements. He's keeping the K-21 in perfect match to the tow plane, using only minor movements of stick and rudder. Although the climb is bumpy, he holds us steady in the high tow position, watching the Pawnee out front for sudden lift or sink.

"Thirty-three hundred feet," Roswell says over his shoulder. "We should be able to find lift from here."

"You're flying," I reply, not wishing to provide any information. From long habit, I want to assess the other man's skills, not show off my own. In a cockpit, the smallest detail can become vital in a heartbeat. I notice that Roswell has both fresh air vents pointed at his face.

Roswell eases the glider slightly above the tow plane's altitude, then enters a shallow dive. As the towline goes slack, he pulls the release handle and the line drops away without a sound. Gotta admit, he's smooth.

"I see the line falling, I'm clearing left and turning right," Roswell calls out. As we separate, the tow plane turns back toward the airport, trailing its long line. Solid bumps from below signal more lift. "This could be your shear line," Roswell adds.

I stay quiet. Roswell has already trimmed the glider for 60 MPH, and in minutes he places us firmly in the wall of rising air and we're climbing above 4500 feet. Headed west toward the ocean, we see scattered cloud over Monterey Bay, flooding into the coastal mountain ridge. Roswell controls the glider skillfully, finding lift by instinct. The man is a respectable pilot.

"Get us another couple thousand feet," I call out from the rear seat. "I'd like you to start with an Immelmann, then get back your altitude and do some loops."

"Fine," Roswell says, banking to center in a thermal. "May I ask you a question?"

"Knock yourself out."

"Just between me and you, are you planning any more TV appearances?"

I hear the humor in Roswell's voice, and grin wryly. My sole TV appearance, if you would call it that, was the only successful escape ever televised on *Police Chases*. On the road to California's Mt. Baldy Village, there are two tunnels.

My car had flashed out of the first one in full view of two police helicopters, veered sharply off the road, and crashed down a ravine in fiery and spectacular fashion. The fact that I was no longer aboard was not revealed by any cameras. It was only thanks to my so-called employer that police showed up at my house two days later to take me in.

I don't usually hear such questions from the soaring crowd. Most locals know I've been in the joint, and that glider flight instruction is considered my 'rehab' by the authorities. Occasionally someone at the gliderport will ask me to get in their selfie, and thankfully that's about it. But what Roswell says next jolts me.

"Did you hear that McIntyre may soon be released from prison?" The man's tone is taunting.

I scowl at the back of Roswell's head, for this is truly bizarre. The drug kingpin Mick McIntyre, my former 'associate,' is cooling his jets at Lancaster State Prison on an extended basis. I am instantly alert. Anyone who knows the gang boss can be dangerous.

"He's down for major drug trafficking," I reply carefully. "Eight to twelve."

"True enough," Roswell says, turning his head fractionally toward me in the tight cockpit. "He's been given an appeal." I can see how the butthead's grinning.

Wherever this is coming from, I intend to pound it out of Roswell when we get on the ground. If McIntyre gets an appeal, I need to be in the mix. He has major payback coming. From me.

But enough of this random crap.

"Alright," I order him. "Show me your Immelmann."

"Looking right, clearing left," Roswell calls out, banking the glider steeply. Both of us search below through the turn, watching for any aircraft that could pass underneath. Roswell finishes the turn, pushes the K-21 into a steep dive. As the sailplane accelerates past 160 MPH, he pulls smoothly back on the stick and the G-loading builds to 4 gravities. We're in a fierce climb, nose straight up. At the top of the climb, we level off inverted, then Roswell performs a slow roll so we're again flying level at 55 MPH.

"Hammerhead," I tell him.

He pushes over into another fast dive, then begins a vertical climb.

"This glider is not stressed for tail slides," I call out above the slipstream noise, "so cheat early with the rudder when airspeed hits about sixty."

Roswell's reply is to push in a bit of left rudder as we lose airspeed. We're weightless, the sailplane sliding backward flips sharply and plummets straight down. "When I bring us out of this," Roswell calls over his shoulder, "I'd like you to show me a full loop. Zero G on top."

"Alright," I say, beginning to be impressed. The man can talk and fly at the same time. And I know something else. He doesn't need an aerobatics lesson any more than that heavy jacket.

As we dive out of Roswell's maneuver, I say, "I have the glider," and take the controls, putting us into a steep descent. I watch the airspeed build toward redline, then pull the stick smoothly back. The K-21 hurries upward. Watching for the earth to come around as we go inverted, I glance at Roswell, outlined above me against blue sky. Oddly, the man is hunched forward in his straps. My mind is on other things, but he's definitely not watching the maneuver he asked for.

Just as we come upside-down at the top of the loop, three things happen in quick succession. Something hard bangs into the top of the forward canopy. A forward canopy which blows away in a sudden howl of wind. And with no goodbye, Roswell falls out of the inverted cockpit and disappears.

The ship hesitates as though stunned. Working to bring the stumbling glider into the downward arc of the loop, I see a brief and distant flash beneath me... sunlight glinting from the falling canopy. Upside-down, the K-21 is twitchy, no sense of direction, like it's not an airplane anymore. Howling wind buffets me. Picked up from the floorboard, tiny grains of dirt pelt my face. Quickly I scan for my falling ex-passenger but see nothing. Against the vast pool of clouds below, a human would be a flyspeck.

The glider starts its downward plunge. In the empty forward cockpit, Roswell's abandoned shoulder harness lashes wildly. Out of balance with no one in front, the glider wants to nose up sharply and G-loads build dangerously. I feel myself blacking out and shove the stick hard forward.

The glider comes level, then climbs, which would be great if I was in control, but it's not flying right. Airspeed's dropping too fast, I can't push the nose down! I loosen my shoulder straps, leaning my weight as far forward as I can in the rear cockpit. It doesn't help. Refusing to dive, the K-21 shudders like a gut shot buck. There is a moment of silence as the slipstream quiets.

Full stall.

With a sickening lurch the sailplane drops a wing and falls into a fluttery spin. I kick in hard opposite rudder and hold the stick all the way forward but the glider hangs in a flat spin, rotating ever faster and uncontrollable as a falling leaf. My mind sorts wildly through my dwindling options to not fall out of the sky.

Altitude 7000 feet. Three thousand feet below me, a river of cloud pours into a wilderness of steep ravines and eroded slopes. Losing 300 feet with every gut-wrenching rotation, I have little time for action. But I know one thing as the glider lurches downward toward the waiting clouds. There is a single, impossible act that might possibly save me. And I totally hate it.

I release the rear cockpit canopy, which blows away with a roar. Flopping helpless in my loose harness as the craft gyrates downward, I reach for the flailing shoulder straps Roswell vacated moments before. Holding tight, I grit my teeth and release my harness buckle. An overpowering sensation of spinning vertigo grips my brain as I haul myself out of the rear cockpit and toward the front, pulling myself along the straps, fighting to hold myself low against the cyclone of my descent.

Everything's spinning and twirling, wild forces try to slam my head into the cockpit margin. Flung out over the wing, I glimpse a whirling cloud mass reaching up to swallow me. Holding tight to the harness, a useless thought forces its way through: Roswell's fall was deliberate.

The glider thrashes in its spin, trying to fling me away with each violent lurch. I grab a hip strap and pull myself down into the front cockpit, find the right rudder pedal with a flailing foot and kick hard. Gripping the straps fiercely with one hand, I shove the stick forward.

And the glider flies! Again in balance with my weight in the front cockpit, the glider obeys the controls and noses down, gaining airspeed. I halt the spin, fly it out of the dive, and point it up to regain altitude. From here, I can fly straight and level toward the fields of Hollister, 25 miles distant. With luck, I'll find lift and make the airport. My cap is gone, but the aviator shades still cling, protecting my eyes from a wind so suddenly cold.

Fumbling to secure my hip belt, I scan the cloud cover below. There, a scant thousand feet below, I spot the pale green of a high-performance parachute.

Roswell.

Rage mounts on instinct. Reflexively, I push the K-21's nose downward toward the colored blossom below. Only after that automatic response does my thought surface: I knew the sudden rush of events had been no freak accident with an inexperienced pilot. The loop, the battery, the canopy. Roswell's jump was meant to spin me into the ground!

My certainty hardens. Roswell's insinuating questions about Mick McIntyre were a gesture of bravado from a taunting killer before the act. And I know, surely and deeply, that I will not allow the man to get away. I can guess the reason for his heavy parka. It had concealed a parachute and possibly a flotation device. But who is he? And why the hell does he want to kill me?

I grit my teeth against the howling slipstream, crouching low in the cockpit to aim over the K-21's bare nose.

"Just you and me, Roswell."

Cockpit agape, the sailplane screams toward the floating parachute. Airspeed tops 180. I point the glider's nose directly at the middle of the drifting nylon, watching the puffy airfoil expand in my vision. At the last available instant, I pull back hard on the stick. The K-21 groans as the parachute passes scant feet beneath her howling wings. If I am close enough to Roswell's parachute, my wing turbulence will blow his chute inside-out.

Climbing, I bank steeply away and look over my shoulder, pulling around for another pass. But no second attack is necessary. For one mind-bending instant, I catch a fluttering green wisp vanishing into clouds. Then, I'm alone in the infinite sky.

Trembling from shock and adrenaline, I let the glider climb from its furious dive until it runs out of energy, scratching for every foot of altitude. I level off and trim for minimum sink speed. I must stay in the air as long as possible. It's a blessing the radio battery is gone, I need time to calm my nerves and sort out the rush of events before I speak to anyone. Seconds ago I'd been flying a routine loop with another pilot aboard. Now this!

Altitude 3800 feet, only a few hundred feet above the clouds. If I fly into them I'm a dead man. I search frantically ahead for signs of lift, hoping to locate the shear line, or a thermal. From this altitude the K-21 can fly nearly 15 miles, if I encounter no serious sink leaving the mountains. I take my hands off the stick and will myself to relax. In perfect balance now, the glider floats serenely at 47 MPH. Hands folded in my armpits, it comes to me that I am very cold. Glancing toward the rear seat, my parka there seems infinitely far away. Shivering, I close my eyes as the glider soars peacefully, and replay in my mind the rush of events.

Roswell asked me to fly a loop with zero-G on top. With no G-forces holding him in the seat, he could easily jump out. Inverted, the safest way to avoid hitting the tail. And the battery! On our way toward the top of the loop, Roswell was bending forward, doing something I couldn't see. Next instant, the radio battery is bouncing around in the forward canopy, which then blows down and away. Roswell falls out of his harness, leaving me inverted at low speed in a glider that's instantly un-flyable.

You dumb sick bastard, I think, shivering with cold and rage. Grimly I see that my instant reaction had been right. The split-second I'd seen Roswell's parachute, I'd calculated my single chance to repay the haughty assassin in kind, and had sent the man falling to his death. Why the hell not? He tried to kill me.

I know what he'd been thinking. Without the radio, I could not Mayday, the glider would have vanished into a ravine or beneath the waves of Monterey Bay, never to be found. Searchers would conclude that we had crashed together and there the trail would end, though the mystery would remain. I groan aloud. Someone wants me to disappear. Well, it's what I want for myself, but nothing like this.

Where is a cop when you need one, I'm thinking, with a bright flashback of that wild police chase years earlier. But thoughts of cops lead me to the most threatening realization of all. My current parole officer has been helping me stay alive, literally. Professional yet sympathetic, Parole Officer Yamamoto has helped me stay in the cockpit and out of the joint. But what will he conclude about this Roswell thing? If he writes me up for this I'm back in prison, no discussion. Back inside where Mick's dudes can find me, and that will be the end.

Then it hits me again, it won't be Yamamoto. It'll be the new guy, starting over from square one, no personal rapport, only sharp suspicion. I've got to leave this tarnished existence forever.

Chimes from my shirt pocket. Working my phone with stiff fingers, I look at the name. A student. I can't talk to anyone until my mind is in control. I ignore it.

Cloud cover below gives way to tree-dotted slopes. Bumpy air signals the presence of lift, and by pure instinct, I find myself centering a thermal, climbing the invisible column of rising air. The practiced moves give my mind an anchor, reassurance that the world is possibly sane. I'm breathing again yet still I tremble, and not merely from the cold. I've experienced many tense moments in aircraft, but have never felt so threatened. As I work my careful way homeward, my mind wears a groove in the impossible sequence of events.

Now less than 10 miles from the runway, I plan what to do next. The radio is out, and landing without it will be dangerous if I'm unable to hear traffic calls or announce my presence. Fortunately, there is an alternative. Stiff fingers fumble with my phone. It's cold in this wind! I speed-dial Julie on the club's line.

"Julie! Clay."

"Clay? What's up?"

"Well, first of all my radio's out. Can you relay my pattern calls, and let me know about other traffic?"

"Say again? There's all sorts of noise, I can hardly hear you."

I hunch forward to shield my phone from the blast of cold wind coming over the smooth nose, and yell this time.

"No problem" Julie says. "What's that racket?"

"Problem with the canopy," I tell her.

From miles away, on the ground, Julie's voice registers concern. "Are you guys alright?"

"Yeah, we're flying okay. We'll enter the landing pattern in about ten minutes. Any traffic?"

"The active is two-four. The tow plane just left with the Grob. You may see them on your twelve at two thousand. Right now it's quiet."

"OK, thanks. And someone better come meet us when we get down. We may need some help pushing back."

"Do you need to declare an emergency?"

Declaring an airborne emergency means a mountain of paperwork, risk of my instructor's rating, and many unwanted questions. There will be enough without that.

"No effing way," I tell her. "Leave it."

I wish again for my parka, to be warm. Flying straight now on final glide to the airport, the placid agricultural scene floats beneath me. Gliders quiet in their tie-downs, parachute billowing over the club patio. And CHP cars in slalom practice at the end of runway 1-3.

On my phone, with Julie relaying my pattern calls from her handheld radio, I set up for a crosswind landing, heading toward the police slalom area. On downwind I'm surprised to see a restored P-51 Mustang fighter taking off on the intersecting runway, but have no time to process that. On final approach, I put the phone away and adjust my aim point, not to the 3-1 numbers closest to me, but much farther, beyond the runway intersection.

As I float five feet above hard concrete, inquisitive faces in the club patio swivel to watch me go by. Usually, gliders are on the ground well before the intersection. Usually, gliders return with their canopies. Usually, gliders come back with the same number of pilots as at takeoff.

A tow pilot, watching beside the gas truck, jumps in and follows me down the runway. I glimpse his grim expression.

I let the K-21 sink to the runway, a chirp from the belly wheel. Keep the wings level with the stick, with rudder pedals guide the craft along the center line, toward the cluster of black and white police cars lined up for slalom practice. Several officers turn as I roll up. I haul back on the brake handle and bring the glider to a stop ten yards from the nearest cruiser. I feel the warmth of the sun.

At least it will be easy to find a cop.

CHAPTER 2
OLD GIRLFRIENDS

I DON'T GET THE TREATMENT I wanted, but perhaps what I deserved. The California Highway Patrol guys are first quizzical, then official. They listen to my story, cuff me, listen some more, then un-cuff me. They want to know how I can return from a flight minus my passenger without somehow committing murder.

This Q-and-A soon collects a clump of pilots and gliderport people around the K-21, which sits on the concrete runway looking forlorn without its canopies. All are trying to convince the cops that my tale is believable. Somewhere in the middle of the proceedings a CHP captain decides that an airborne crime, be it murder or suicide, isn't exactly their jurisdiction, and calls Hollister Homicide. When Short Detective and Tall Detective arrive, the whole thing rewinds for a remix.

Fortunately, everyone shuts up and listens to Stacy lecture the cops on flight characteristics. She's the owner of the gliderport and a Class A lady on the side. She and I go back.

"It's one of the basic things we teach all our pilots," she tells them. "If an aircraft is not in balance, it will not fly. If the weight is too far forward, it won't pull out of a dive. If the weight is too far back, the glider stalls and spins to the ground. Either way, you crash."

Short Detective wants to sit in the front seat of the glider. The other one sees what he's thinking and lowers himself into the rear cockpit I had occupied. It's a tight fit for even the smaller of the two men. Stacy comes over.

"Of course you realize that you have to be strapped in," she says, and helps the cop in the rear seat fasten his 5-point harness. Reaching forward as far as he can in the tight straps, Tall Detective finds he can't extend his hands beyond the instrument panel, much less reach through to the front seat.

"I know what you are thinking," Stacy says quietly to the two men. "Someone back here can't reach anyone in the front. The pilot in back would have to release his harness to even try. It would be very tough to reach through that narrow space, with the canopies closed. Nobody can release the front canopy from the rear seat, period."

"What about some kind of weapon?" Short Detective wants to know.

Stacy thinks about it. "That's more your specialty, but it would be hard to use a club, not enough room to swing it or even thrust it. A gun or a knife would leave bloodstains. And the front pilot would still be strapped in." Both detectives look glum. They had already checked the cockpit for blood or signs of a struggle. Canopy missing, radio battery gone, pilot missing. It's no crime scene they've seen before.

"Also," Stacy continues, "Suppose someone did purposely get the front pilot out of the aircraft. They still would be in the rear seat of a glider that was about to crash. There is no guarantee they could do what Clay did and fly the glider back. Clay wasn't wearing a chute. He could have hit his head, lost his grip, any number of things. Really not worth it as a way to murder somebody."

"Couldn't he have thrown the chute away, after he got into the front?" Stacy nods yes, that could be right.

"You do know Mr. Cicero Clay is a convicted felon, on parole," the other one says.

At this point one of the kids speaks up. He was the wing runner when we took off and saw me hook the towrope. He tells them I wore no chute when I got in. Tall Detective gets his info.

"Yah, we know about that," Stacy goes on. "Clay took his basic glider instruction here twenty years ago, he's been a flight instructor with us for ten years. We trust him, we're glad to have him back." Stacy's tone indicates she disbelieves my involvement in any crime. I shoot her a grateful look. She looks like she wants to go on, but stops herself.

The CHP guys thin out, shaking their heads as they turn back to driving practice. I don't fit the mold of somebody to arrest, for the moment at least. Although I'd now have to admit I'm guilty of murder, I'm keeping quiet about my duel with Roswell. The detectives lift themselves from the cramped cockpits, staring at me critically. I resent their prejudice. I'm a private citizen minding my own business, a victim even, and as soon as they find I'm a con, they want to slap on the cuffs. For about the hundredth time, I'm itching to just disappear. I was innocent, damn it. At least as charged.

"So you're saying the man in front jumped out deliberately," one of the detectives says to Stacy.

"Look at the fact that Clay saw a chute disappear into the clouds," Stacy replies, spreading her hands. "It was no suicide. The guy wearing the chute was the one who tried to hurt somebody, not Clay. There is no way anyone in the rear seat could stop that from happening. The canopy goes away, the front pilot falls out. Gone. No warning, no time to react. There was Clay, upside-down, in a glider that wouldn't fly. We don't train for suicide leaps. And look at the guy's logbook. Roswell. Hundreds of glider flights. He was a pro pilot. He knew what he was doing. Look for him over there you'll find him."

"He didn't need a stunt lesson," I throw in.

"Unless this is fake, like a fake passport." Tall Detective looks again at Roswell's logbook, fetched from the flight line when the discussion began. Page after page of hand-written entries, flights all over Europe, North America, Hawaii.

"Yah," I add, "and he wasn't showing his parachute when we took off. He was wearing a bulky coat. He intentionally concealed the chute. He was sweating." I don't mention my high-speed dive, the collapse of Roswell's chute, my guess that he's dead on a distant hillside.

"Suppose I buy that," Short Detective says. "Then why would someone want to kill you?"

I can think of a few reasons, but have no intention of opening that kind of convo. Anyone from that part of my life would probably just shoot me, if they aren't dead or in prison. I keep my face blank, shaking my head. "No idea," I reply.

Short Detective looks at Stacy, then at me. "Do you have anything that can verify where this happened? We need to start a search."

Stacy turns to me. "Was it turned on?"

I nod. "Every flight." From a Velcro flap of my parka I lift out my GPS unit. "This records the glider's position, altitude and speed for the entire flight. It's still recording."

Tall Detective takes the small unit from my fingers. "How do we see what it says?"

"We have a computer in the office with the software," Stacy tells him. "Come with me and I'll download the flight trace and print a copy."

Short Detective checks his notes, looking at me. "If you think of anything..."

I wave the white card the man hands me. "Right."

The plainclothes cops turn away. I am fuming at the rotten luck. I've kept my nose hyper-sanitary not only through three years in prison but my entire parole. So now they have new reasons to mess with me. I didn't do it. I have a life, dammit, and it doesn't include sitting still for this.

Jason, the senior flight instructor, turns to me. Behind the oversize dark glasses, his face is impassive. "What is it you do in case of an accident?" To me it sounds like a flight school pop quiz.

"Notify the NTSB."

"Under what regulation?"

I think for a second. "Article two, I think. If any required crew member becomes unable to carry out his duties."

Jason nods. "That will do. Got the number?"

Tiredly, I wave my phone and walk toward the fence. Several students begin to push the glider back to its tie-downs. It will be a long roll.

I slip through the wire fence and start back alone, walking the dusty road that borders a cornfield. My El Camino, parked with other cars near the gliderport's blowing parachute, is a small dot in the distance. The long walk gives me time to call the regional National Transportation Safety Board office in Gardena, California. I have to wade through the same incredulous reactions all over again, first with the admin, then with the base supervisor. Finally the names of the Hollister detectives, the CHP sergeant, and my instructor rating convince the NTSB people that my report is credible.

At long last the call ends, with promise of follow-ups by mail and phone. An NTSB investigator will be in the area tomorrow, to overfly the accident site and interview witnesses. I promise to be available.

I'm nearing my car when Stacy returns from the flight office. A paper in her hand flaps in the stiff breeze. I take it from her fingers. My GPS flight profile. The plot shows outlines of main topographic features, faint lines of latitude and longitude, and a wiggly orange trace, the path the glider followed over land. There is also an altitude trace. I stare incredulous at the peak of the last loop. I can almost see the glider hesitate at the moment of Roswell's jump. There is also the spin, the recovery, and the plunging dive that had cast Roswell to his final reward. Oops. I'll need to cook a story about that part.

"My unit?" I ask.

Stacy shakes her head. "They're keeping it to download on their own. Evidence."

"Figures." I turn to my car.

Her voice from behind me. "Clay?"

I stop. She is looking at me kind of funny. "Just between us, is there anything..."

"Stace, I don't know. He jumped. He wanted to kill me."

She looks at me a long moment. Watching her face, my mind serves up a sampling of private things we might have said to one another, if prison had not interrupted that budding friendship years ago.

"Alright, then." She sighs, turning back. Sadly I watch her go, her every step a stab of wretched defeat.

I'm settled in the El Camino's tattered seat when a dark car rolls up, trailing clouds of dust on the rutted dirt. The car's windows are opaque black. Two men in suits get out. One stands beside my door, motioning me to roll down the window. He pulls out a Federal ID case.

"Cicero Clay? We're DEA. We need to talk to you."

Oy.

So that was a while ago. Two hours to be exact. Because of my various past lives, cover stories and lies, I am never sure when talking to DEA or local law enforcement what they're after. But in this case I am safe. They aren't here to talk about a certain grow operation. Just want me to walk them through, again, every detail about today. Then they have to go through all the steps of my so-called former crime, leading to my arrest for drug possession, which I again insist I'm not guilty of. They shrug that one off with matching contemptuous smirks. I hate that more every time I see it. I had nothing to do with any dope. Directly. I was a fast driver with some electronics skills, carrying only money.

They go through everything. E-V-E-R-Y thing. But this time they focus their drug-besotted views to ransack every step of my flight with Roswell. Was I transporting any contraband? How much money was onboard the aircraft? How many pounds of drugs will the aircraft carry? And so forth, to which I keep pointing across the field where the K-21 sits tied up under a blue tarp. No propeller, see? No motor. Flying gliders is an art form, see? Not like a taxicab, you don't get in a sailplane and commute to Mexico. Completely dependent on the weather. Not like a powered aircraft, see? Besides, I don't have power training.

...et cetera, all to no avail.

Finally, what gets them off me is my probation appointment. Gotta drive all the way into San Jose, and it's getting to rush hour. So now after all that, including a flatbed trailer loaded with bridge parts trying to smear me at the Highway 880 exit, I am sitting in this institutional hallway on West Hedding in company with the usual run of luckless characters who, like me in certain ways, have been strapped to the wheel of life in various uncomfortable positions. I see a dude from my old lockup, guy who'd been in for smuggling and minor racketeering. We notice each other but don't make eye contact. What's his name, Salermo? I regularly see guys here I've crossed paths with, or know about. Small world? Nah. All your local felons come through here.

A clerk pokes her head out a door and calls, "Cicero Cassius Clay."

A woman glances up with a smirk at the name. I return a threatening glare as I walk by. For the millionth time I make a mental note I'm getting it changed. Not only that, I plan to disappear. I'm pointed into an office where I sit in front of a polished wooden desk. The chair is uncomfortable, smaller than it needs to be. The name placard says H.R. Harrison. Mr. Harrison is not with us at the moment, so I take a deep breath and look around.

Wait a minute. This Harrison's a woman. I can tell.

First, under the desk there are some girly-type running shoes. Second, a few post-it notes on the desk have flowing curlicue handwriting. So I cool my jets for what seems a long time. Finally the door opens.

I turn to look but only see the back of someone. Well actually it's a pleasant view. While she leans against the door jamb talking to someone in the corridor, I have a chance to take in the slim fit of her tailored slacks and the womanly posterior pointing my way.

She has carefully-styled dark hair, smooth skin, dangly earrings with light pinkish stones. On top she's wearing a custom jacket which fits her well, and almost hides her shoulder holster. Slim waist, I can tell she works out. She is talking in a stage whisper to someone outside in the hallway. Can't hear much, but what I do pick up suggests one of her parolees is having a very bad day. The woman she's talking to compliments her new jewelry, to which she responds with an easy laugh, *it's only costume*. That laugh is creepily familiar, but I don't place it. Yet.

I get a chance to think maybe my parole status is looking up. My previous parole officer is a grizzled old Japanese guy who chain smokes, so maybe he's died since my last weekly visit. He must've thought throwing me all sorts of little speed bumps was fun and appropriate. However I have to say that he was cooperative, because I've kept my parole tidy and there is not one single thing anybody can fault me on. I am due to be off pro in another seven months and I'm totally looking forward to that day. So I am ready for a well-deserved frequent flier upgrade.

Woman shuts the door, walks around the desk and sits. I'm just taking in her pleasing face when my nutsack goes into involuntary contractions for the third time today. I know who this is. Apprehension rises further when she lifts her face and looks at me coldly. A flat, dead stare from heavy-lidded eyes. She knows me, too.

And I know her. Damn. I haven't seen her in 20 years, but we were best friends in high school, mostly below the waist. But I lost track of my classmates after leaving school, owing to the fact that my dad died before grad and my mom became very ill.

Now this striking woman levels her dark eyes and regards me with open disdain. I try to hold my gaze steady as the thought goes through my head that will define this moment in all its nefarious glory:

Oh. Fucking. Hell. It's Montana.

My new parole officer is no promotion. This is a ticket to the innermost circle of Hades.

"Cicero Cassius Clay," she says, not quite looking down at her laptop. I try to remember what terms we were on when we parted company. Boyfriend-girlfriend at one time definitely. We'd been all over each other through senior year, then she became unavailable and later I heard she'd gone away. Had one letter from her. Ah, those quaint days before e-mail, on paper in an envelope. No return address, just a light perfume, nothing about I miss you, just some rambling sorry-for-her-lot-in-life spiel with no detail, vague regret. I saved that letter for a while. I'd been missing her back then.

Nice jewelry, earrings and a gold chain set with pinkish sparklers around her neck. Too big for diamonds, maybe fake ones like she said. No wedding ring, which surprises me for a second. And then again it doesn't. For around 38 she's still a knockout, but the vicious gaze she aims at me now reminds me there are other sides to her personality. If you can call it that.

She looks at her laptop. I have a second to watch her dark eyelashes flick as she scans my file. She leans back in her high swivel chair and gazes at me coolly.

"Hollister Homicide says you tried to kill someone today. Is that right?"

I look back at her without expression, thinking cops must go to school to act like morons. Everybody in the system tries to bait you into a lie if you are the slightest bit bent. I'm counting, if I go through this with her, how many times will it be today I've tried to explain glider flight characteristics to a cop?

I summon all my wit and eloquence for a deft reply.

"No."

She scowls at me with haughty disdain, like she's waiting for a bug to crawl off her plate.

I sigh and continue, trying to be brief. "My student jumped out all by himself. He had a parachute. I did not. It was only by great good luck I was able to keep from crashing. He wanted to kill me."

While this is coming out of my mouth I'm watching her eyes and wondering when she's going to cop to the fact that she knows me. Up to now she's acting like we just met. She's watching me intently, waiting. I'm waiting too. I don't have anything to say right now.

"I know more about you than what's in this file," she says, looking at me coldly. "Suppose you just tell me why you're here."

"Okay Montana, let's cut the pretense." Her eyebrows ratchet up as I utter her high school nickname for the first time in at least 10 years. Friends had occasionally asked about her, but after I got set up on this bogus rap and did a three-spot in the can, I haven't exactly schmoozed with my high school crowd.

"You do know more than what's in my file," I tell her sternly. "And you better be talking to me off the record about that for reasons you well understand. Why am I here? This is my regular weekly appointment. With you, it turns out. Why are you here? Why was my case moved from Officer Yamamoto? How long have you been a parole officer?"

"Parole Agent," she spits out. "Agent, not Officer. There's a difference."

It dawns on me this is her career now. I can see she's really proud of her position, and I'm curious to know how she got to this point. She and I did risky and illegal things when we ran together in school. Part of me feels like congratulating her. But the other part, the 98% part, says forget it.

"I need to ask you the same question," I say coolly. "Exactly why am I here? I have been letter-perfect every day of my parole. I intend to keep it that way till I'm out of the system."

She laughs from the side of her mouth. It's not a friendly laugh, but the way her eyes sparkle takes me back for a sweet second to warm summer nights long ago. I roughly shove the beguiling memories aside.

"You'll never be out of my system," she practically snarls.

I don't blink but I take a beat to contemplate that she uses 'my' instead of 'the.' She could've said 'my' because she feels a certain ownership for the parole system. Or, she could've said 'my' because she still feels a connection to me. Looking at her now, I recall how once I was so hooked on her. I begin to remember why, in semi-lurid detail.

Watching her face I can almost see similar thoughts parade through her mind. For an instant I notice a hesitancy that tells me whatever she believes she holds over me, she knows that I hold the same over her. And given my career as a felon, and hers as the well-regarded public official, she has much more to lose. Kid stuff back then, but what I could say now would be taken very seriously by her management. I speak up, letting impatience into my voice.

"Care to tell me why I'm here?"

She waits a beat. For the moment she can't meet my eyes and looks blankly at the laptop. I begin to recall things about Montana from back then, the way she is. I didn't know what a narcissist was in those days, but today I'm clear that she is one. Her mental self-image is about power, and being attractive. It was the lure of power that first pulled her away from me, a powerful older man when we were in high school. She totally believes she is better than other people. In the last few minutes I've been reminded twice that she doesn't understand that other people have feelings. She appears tough-minded and unemotional, but I know she's easily hurt. And if that happens, oh boy. Hell hath no fury.

Her eyes come up and that beautiful face is different. When she speaks her voice is not so snarly.

"This meeting is routine, as you say. However, when a parolee is found at a crime scene the Parole Agent has to intervene. I took your case from Yamamoto for that reason. We're going to have weekly meetings until this matter is cleared up. Any discrepancy we'll see you back on the tracker."

Please, not the anklet again. Yamamoto wrote me up twice simply because the damn things lose contact above 2500 feet. If flying is your living, the tracker is unemployment. It near cost me my job at the gliderport a year ago, before I was able to explain things well enough so they would listen. Stacy went to bat with Yamamoto and they took it off.

But Montana's face is softer, her voice more feminine in tone, which tells me I'm starting to work on her. Which is a good thing. Up to a point. Control, I tell myself, not involvement.

"Okay I can accept that," I reply. Now I have a question for her, the same one I'd pestered Yamamoto with the whole time I've been on parole. "You do know I was framed? I want to reopen my case."

Now she looks at me as though I'm something she needs to scrape off her pointy-toed boots. "You are joking, of course. Cicero."

Dammit. Cicero is Montana-speak for really pissed at me. But like a fool, I plunge ahead.

"No, this is legit."

"You are referring to…"

"Look Montana, I was in jail for three weeks before I was accused of possession with intent to distribute. My public defender was an amateur. How did I get convicted for possession when the cops found nothing at my house?"

She's not looking disgusted anymore, merely bored and faintly entertained. She knows I don't have the financial clout to hire an attorney to take on the State of California. For the moment at least, she is right.

"Take it up with your legal counsel. I have work to do."

Oh sure. Now she has some stock interview questions to put me through. I am sure she'll call it 'processing' in her report.

"What's your employment status?"

"You know I'm working. I have a schedule at the gliderport every week. It's kind of random, depends on when students book to fly. I've had that job more than ten years, except for my paid vacation as guest of the state. Also I have an aircraft parts business that I run from my house. It's profitable. So I do have obligations. But I'll be available when you want to talk. By phone sometimes if that's more convenient?"

"Take a card," she says, tilting her a head at the little card tray on the edge of her desk. "No wait not that one."

She reaches her purse from a bottom desk drawer and hands over a different card. Our fingers brush as I take it, sending me a tiny zap of woman voltage. Her surprised blink tells me she gets it too. She remembers.

"Living situation?"

"Rent a house in Felton, address is in my file."

"Housemates, girlfriends? Boyfriends?" She says the last word with a mini-leer, somewhere between insult and private joke. You're so witty, Montana. She damn well knows I'm not the boy-boy type.

"I live alone." What I won't go into is, I am tapering off on social contact leading to the day I can drop out of sight where dolts like you can't find me.

"Marriages, divorces, any kids?"

"None of the above."

"What is your evening life? What do you do when you're not at work?"

My mind is saying, Wha-a-a-t the heck? Never heard that question in all my years in the system. I shrug, "You know for a parolee to be caught in a minor traffic stop it's like a four alarm fire. Drinking away from my residence is therefore out, as is partying with people who do drugs. I stay home a lot, people visit, I keep to myself."

She seems to consider this for a minute, makes a notation on her laptop. "The report I got from Hollister Homicide," she says, all official again, "seems quite complete. They've handed over formal decision until the NTSB concludes its investigation." She looks back at her laptop. "I'm scheduling you in for next Wednesday at two o'clock."

I flip through my Commando. "Hold up. I've got two lessons that afternoon. It means about 600 bucks to the school and a couple hundred to me. Any way we can make that later, say five?"

She looks again at her laptop. "Check in with me by phone at five o'clock next Wednesday. Use the office number for that." I haven't looked at her card yet but my guess is that her personal cell is on it. Hah. Maybe she is thinking with her crotch again. Still.

The first line of a rap tune emanates from her purse.

"S'cuse," she says, taking her phone out. When she picks up, a lovely smile transforms her face. And transports me back to a time I remember as damn special. She swivels away. I can't see her over the chair's high back. She's talking quietly and giggling. Uses a cute name a couple times. Don't know if that's who she's talking to or talking about. Montana never had any trouble getting the guys, her only problem was the kind of trouble the guys brought home. I wasn't the worst bad boy she liked in school.

I spend the time flipping through my phone looking at text messages. The twins are back from their Los Angeles run, which is good news, we need to get together. Message from a student who's completed his pre-solo exam and wants to go over it with me.

But all of sudden it hits me again what happened today. Roswell. Who in the flock is Roswell? Who is he and why would he want to kill me? I ransack my memory, players I knew in the slam, people I met in business. But nothing comes. Blank. As a murder attempt it's an extreme way to off somebody. Unless it means something else. I think if I had done it, what would I be trying to accomplish? If I survived the parachute landing on rough terrain in fog, it would be an excellent way to break a tail. My mind spins out on the word tail. Montana.

Hormones, shut up. I remember this babe far too damn well.

While we're waiting for her to get off her smoochy call, you might as well know a little about me. I was born in Manhattan Beach California 38 years ago. My name, Cicero Clay, has to be a spelling error. What I think happened is my mom wished I was going to be a girl and she liked the name Cecily. Anyway both my folks are dead, my dad in a highway crash before I left school, my mom of cancer five years after that. My brother is four years older and went away to the Navy. He is mentally unbalanced, and I'm only half joking. When he left the Navy, he dropped out of sight, no phone or utility accounts in his name, everything in his ex-wife's name, he's strictly under the radar. Don't hear from him that often, he doesn't want any connection between us that can be traced.

What I look like in case you are taking notes or stalking me is I'm almost six feet, in good shape from mountain biking, blue work shirt I wear with sleeves rolled up, color that brings out my eyes, gray green to piercing blue. Wheat-colored hair that can grow out fast if I don't get it cut once a week.

I was arrested for supposedly dealing drugs four years ago. Yah I was connected with it but never touched or saw any product. It was so weird. I got away. But the cops showed up like magic at my crib. I did three years medium security at California Men's Colony in San Luis Obispo, place they call the Country Club, and am now out under supervision. Good behavior. Ankle bracelet for the first couple months.

I'll finish my parole in less than seven months, which is why this Roswell incident is so damnably inconvenient. There I was all under the radar, now I am a fat juicy blip to them. I work teaching students to fly gliders, and buy and sell vintage airplane parts on the side. Plus a few other activities I don't want any cops to know about.

When Montana spins her chair around she's dewy-eyed and shiny. She must really like someone. And I notice that inside I'm happy for her. She has a career, clothes, a guy. She seems okay.

A knock comes to the door. It's the clerk poking her head in to remind Montana about her next case. "One of yours is getting impatient. Salermo." I was right about the name. It's the dude I saw waiting outside.

Montana stands up, all business, our meeting has ended. "Next Wednesday then by phone. Call me if anything changes. Meanwhile you are not to leave the county."

"Well, Hollister's where I work, that's in San Benito County. Right here we're in Santa Clara County, plus which I live in Santa Cruz County. Which one am I not leave?"

Now she looks mainly insulted. "You know what I mean, Cicero," she says tersely, dismissing this lowlife with a distracted wave, "Keep yourself strictly between home and work." I leave her office without another word.

So she's pissed. As I recall she was frequently pissed at me. I allow a small sigh. Only seven more months of this up with which I have to put. As I start down the corridor I see her next appointment on the way in. Dude stares past me without recognition.

Crossing the parking lot it's nearly dark, the air is cooling. After six pm. Just grand, I'm in time for my most un-favorite sport, crush hour heading out Highway 17 for the coast. It's gonna take me forever to get home.

CHAPTER 3
AN UNINVITED GUEST

SO I MAKE THE DRIVE out Highway 17 palatable by killing an hour in the Los Gatos Brew Pub. Yeah, it's against my parole all right, but I gotta think luck's on my side today. I'm alive. So it's well after dark when I park the El Camino under trees beside my hacienda, an overgrown place in a redwood grove at the end of a dirt road in the Santa Cruz hills. Felton. Yah, sure, rhymes with felon. And okay, so I don't actually live in Santa Cruz, you got me.

I like that the old two-story bunkhouse I rent from the Grant kids stands well above the main house down by the road. I especially like the old swimming pool farther up the hill, hidden in the trees. Behind the bunkhouse, miles of wooded slopes and redwoods. And the bike trails, where I spend as much time as my schedule allows.

The Grant kids don't care what I do with the place, so long's I don't burn it down, a sore subject around here. In a few years they will likely sell it off to some developer. It's all part of the Old California, destined for better or worse to become the New. I plan to be long gone before then.

I'm walking up the wooden porch stairs in pitch dark, telling myself for the thousandth time to get a sensor light that works, when I trip on something heavy draped over the steps. Someone is lying there, too dark to see. Flopped out on its back, head resting a couple steps down. I can't tell who it is. I poke it with my foot and nothing happens. Dammit! After all the cops I've seen today, here's another load of shit.

How insensitive of me! Here this poor dude lies dead at my feet and all I have for him is irritation at how he's about to mess up my day for the second time.

I lean close to the guy's head and listen. No breathing I can hear. Hackles on my neck stand up, I'm not going in the house. Whoever slugged this guy could be waiting. And I'm definitely not calling the cops. Yet. Standing by my car I think hard. I need an alibi. I take out my cell phone. Who can I call, to make like we discovered this together? Not the twins. Fresh from the swimming pool, they'll smell like pot. Wait. Don't want to call from here anyway, the cell towers will have my location. Back into the El Camino and down the road as quiet as possible. I curse having to use headlights driving by the Grant place but fortunately the windows are still dark.

Several miles down Highway 9 I pull into a tree-lined turnout. Still ransacking my brain for a plausible witness, I dig out Montana's card. At first it seems stupid, but then it becomes the most reasonable choice. She'll hate it but she's the only person who can help me in this situation. When she picks up she sounds out of breath.

"Who is this?"

"Montana! Don't hang up! It's Clay."

"What! Who?" I get a momentary impression of her world tilting on its axis.

"Montana I need your advice. Want to be sure I don't get a violation."

I'm trying to talk in code. Can't say over the phone there's a dead guy on my porch and I need her for an alibi, so I improvise. I'm still expecting her to hang up any second saying this is improper contact, but she listens and it seems that she gets it. She's marginally over her shock at hearing my name but her talk is disjointed, still breathless. Finally she tells me to meet her at a bike trail in San Jose. Oh hooray, I get to drive back over the hill. That alibi is plausible enough, my beater trail bike is in the El Camino.

But I stop her. There's a better idea. I have to show her. She has to be here.

"You need to come here. Meet me outside the Chinese place in Felton." I click off to show I mean it. Then there is nothing to do but wait. Chinese place. Reminds me I'm growling hungry. I turn back toward Felton and park down the main drag, call Chopstix and order takeout for two. Waiting a block away, I dig the burner phone out from under the dash, dial a number from memory.

"Hey. We going fishing?"

On the other end, I imagine a guy older than me, in a clapped-out farmhouse 100 miles from here. Broad fields, flat for miles around, deserted wide dirt roads. He's probably wearing a beard. Cool guy. My brother Wade.

"Hey yourself," Wade says. There is a pause. Then, "I'm still waiting for your friend to show up with the fishing tackle."

It's always some phony topic. Fishing gear, car parts, telephoto lenses... just in case someone is listening we gotta sound all normal.

"He's not there yet?" We're counting on Wade's Navy pilot, Pete.

"Well the guy lives in his own universe. But he'll be here. Then we can take off for the Sierra. Talked to him a couple days ago. Was trying to scrape some cash together."

"Yah. What you said before. Is he for sure reliable, or should I bring my own?"

A wry chuckle from the other end. "He can be a major trickster. But he has the gear you were asking about. The fishing will be good."

"K, I'll call ya."

I punch off. There's always lots more I'd like to say to my big brother. We've been apart a long time. Family shit. Plus which, a major eccentricity of his keeps us at a distance. Can't use his real name anymore. We don't use names on the phone. But if our plans work out, I'll be living in the same world as my disappeared brother before long. To make that work, we need someone who can pilot a vintage fighter plane.

So I'm sitting in my car chomping on a spring roll when a Jeep wagon goes by slow toward the restaurant and parks. Wow, she made good time over 17. I start up and turn away toward the intersection. At the light, I call her.

"I see you at the restaurant. Turn around and take a left at the light. I'll be going slow up the hill in a blue El Camino. Follow me."

There is a long pause. "You better have a real good reason for this shit." Her voice sounds normal now, composed, icy. Angry? So what, I don't care. I have a very good reason. A few minutes later headlights are behind me and we're turning up my dirt road. The main house is still dark, to my great relief. Grant kids gotta be away.

In the clearing by the bunkhouse we get out of our cars. She pulls out a small flashlight, shines it around and toward the house but we can't see the porch from here. Her light trembles.

"So," she says, sounding completely normal. "Exactly WTF is up?"

"I get home tonight, and there is a person lying on my steps. Dead I think."

"Cripes. Did you touch anything?"

"Nada. Left right away and called you. After what went down today I don't need any more cops breathing down my neck. I needed someone to be with me when I find this."

"And you picked me for your alibi. My lucky day." Then she says, "What have you been doing since you left my office?" Always practical, first she wants us to get our stories straight.

I think a sec. "Nobody saw me. The drive home was slow. Lotsa traffic, house down below was dark when I came in. Tripped on this guy, left right away, called you. Got takeout. This could get me arrested."

"Shit," she says, scowling while she concentrates on something. "So the story is you and I were somewhere together. What have we supposedly been doing for the last two hours?" Her voice puts hard ice on *supposedly*.

"We were talking in your car, old school friends, that sort of thing." If it were truly like the old days, it would be something other than talking.

"That will do. I haven't seen anyone since I left work. So where is this guy?"

I start for the house. As we approach, Montana's flashlight reveals the dark shape on the steps. She lights up the face of the corpse, who already looks gray and stiff. Now I see a single neat round hole in the forehead. And blood. Which has dripped down, covering one plank step and starting for the next. I stare at the face in shock.

"Holy shit, it's Roswell."

Now this shakes me up. At first I am relieved, I'd been thinking it might be a friend from the neighborhood. But even as that passes, I can't say any more for the moment. My brain is officially in overload. First the guy tries to kill me jumping out of my glider, now he shows up extinct at my effing crib. Was he here to finish the job? Knowing where I live means he knew too much about me, such as who I am, where I work, where I go. Who else knows? I'm starting to feel paranoid.

"Who is Roswell?"

"This is the guy jumped out of my glider today!"

"What!" Montana looks at me hard. "You're positive?"

"Hundred percent. The gliderport people can identify him. Actually this is great in a way cuz it proves my story." Meanwhile I'm thinking it also proves that Roswell had a second chute on him. Either he thought the first one might fail, or he anticipated I might dive on him if I got the glider back fast enough. Either way, he planned that attack in crisp detail. But what for?

Montana pulls a dark gun from the holster inside her jacket. It reminds me that whoever did Roswell could still be around, after realizing his mistake and wanting to fix it. My hackles stand up.

"Who do you know, Montana? Who's the best person to call, instead of me just calling 911?" I'm thinking what's the number for Corpse Busters?

She pulls out her phone. "Wolfe," She says crisply. In a few ticks she has someone on the call.

"Hey it's Harrison, Santa Clara County Parole. I just rolled up at a friend's house here in Felton and we have a possible 187." She listens a minute. "No we just drove up. Guy is on the front steps, GSW forehead. My friend tripped on him. We haven't cleared the scene, too dark. Possible shooter still in the area."

They go back and forth like this for a minute, she sends her current GPS location, then clicks off.

So now I reckon it's OK to go in the house, if we avoid making bloody footprints. I switch on a few lights and start a fire in the woodstove. Montana is looking around at my officially bare existence. I take a couple Fat Tires from the fridge, pop them open and flop on the large beater sofa in the main room. With the Grant kids' permission, I'd knocked out most of the walls on the ground floor. The space is large and open, with a square coffee table in the center surrounded by the sofa and a couple overstuffed chairs. Woodstove in a corner. Now, only the bathroom and my bedroom have walls and a door. Stairs to the second level, bathroom and bedrooms up there, use them for storage.

Near the double sash windows stands a scarred wooden desk, early Goodwill, with my laptop, wires, gadgets, flying gear, and miscellaneous pieces of semi-functional electronics. An old telephone handset rests on the floor, not connected. A cluster of decorative holiday lights hangs from the ceiling in a corner, among them several lights that mean things, tell-tale indicators from my totally homebrew intruder system. One orange light in this scraggly arrangement tells me the swimming pool is occupied. The Desmond twins, finishing the day. I badly need to talk to them but it will have to wait.

The swimming pool reminds me how little I need more cop attention, and my fury at Roswell glows red. Dead or alive, I would still like to strangle that asshole. Why did he want to kill me and who the hell is he hooked up with?

My stomach reminds me I have Chinese takeout. "You hungry?"

Montana, who seems far off within herself, nods enthusiastically. I bring the bags to the coffee table. It is odd enough, eating out of white paper bags with someone I haven't seen for 20 years, but how many reunions are graced by a fresh corpse on the front porch? I'd have preferred a potted plant.

In spite of the situation, or maybe because of it, we find small talk possible. Montana is evasive about her life since high school, but talks about her career and her plans. She has ambition, going to have a life like her sister has, but without the dipstick husband. There is a boyfriend vaguely in the background, and her career in law enforcement does not sound like her main focus. She keeps it hazy with few details.

I'd heard Montana left town right after grad, but Dad had recently died and Mom was having health issues then. Wade was on his aircraft carrier being a jet mechanic, so I was on point at home. Montana alludes to living a few years with someone she really liked, with whom the relationship was interesting, but marked at the end by something black. *Complications* is how she put it.

Now she's coming at me again with everyone's question number one, but not like a cop or a Parole Agent, more like an old friend. Kind of refreshing, given everything.

"Who is Roswell? Why did he want to kill you?"

So I'm telling her some of this again. I understand little more than what I'd told the cops, and her as well, all afternoon. The local gangs know nothing about me, my past, or my current income source. I'm not connected with any locals. Yes I have a grow, I sell in L.A., not the Bay, and the twins take care of those runs. The people involved at the time of my arrest four years ago are all dead except for me and McIntyre, who in spite of anything the late Mr. Roswell might have claimed, is still enjoying Lancaster on a 12-year spin cycle.

Wait a sec, I caution myself. Is McIntyre connected to Roswell? In spite of the high stakes that go with any drug deal, my part had been minor. Delivery driver for the cash. No drugs with me, only the money, which I stashed in a secret location as planned. I'd have paid a fine or spent a few months in a County lockup for failure to yield to a police siren, exhibition of speed, reckless endangerment, and so on. Misdemeanors, yes, but still mere traffic stops. Except the cops thought I should give someone up. The only person I could give them was already in custody. McIntyre.

"I got nailed only because someone ratted me out. I was in jail three weeks before they made any charges," I tell her. "Why's it take the cops that long to bring a possession charge if they have product? Something fishy." Thinking about it pisses me off again. I know someone will pay for that someday. "I never handled any dope."

My getaway was clean. Brilliant even. But there was no one to brag to, and because I got caught there was no point. I disposed of the car per the agreed original and fiendishly clever plan and arrived quietly home by bicycle. It was only upon the arrival of the Hollister Police two days later that I became a criminal in their eyes.

Mick McIntyre is the name that comes to mind. I could mention this to Montana but hold back. She knows him, far too damn well. And that's another score I have to settle with him. And with her, for that matter.

She listens halfway, couple times looks like she's about to say something. But I can feel her persona wobbling from cop to friend and back again, and I hark back on all the mixed feelings we had for each other. Loathing and lust. Great name for a punk group. It was weird, how we were in school. We'd been in the same classes coming up, and when the teener hormones kicked in we found one another funny, smart, adventurous, and insanely hot. Deadly combo for kids that age. We were lucky to survive.

But underneath it there was something that bothered her about me. She didn't think me macho enough. And I'd thought her slutty, too flirty with the guys. Even during our good patch I had no exclusive on her. Told myself I hadn't cared, it was mutual. Besides at the end I was twisted up because of Dad.

My head jerks up. Bright lights shine on the house. Two cars come fast in the dust and darkness, scuff to a halt near the porch. Car doors slam.

We step out onto the porch. Montana holds up her ID.

Two uniform cops with bright flashlights take a look at the inert bulk on the steps, walk in opposite directions around the house, shining their lights into windows and among the thick trees. Wolfe, the investigator, stands over the body taking pictures and video. Medium height, tending to a paunch, high hairline, Wolfe would be the perfect TV detective. He asks us about what we did leading up to finding Roswell there, and our stories match well enough. The look that crosses his face tells a tale of suspicion: *Oh right, Harrison, the district playgirl. Now she's hanging with a parolee.* Montana picks it up and I feel her go rigid next to me, but fortunately she clamps down and says nothing.

Before long the Medical Examiner arrives, and guess what, I am being asked the same questions as all freaking day long, why Roswell would try to kill me, what would be his motivation to kill a complete nobody, how well did I know him? I can give them nothing new. And I don't divulge the fact that I'd blown Roswell's chute inside-out with a savage dive in the K-21. Hell, I shouldn't have wasted the altitude. Roswell, with a spare, was ahead of me all the way. It cheers me slightly that the NTSB might find his discarded gear.

Wolfe is sitting across from me at the kitchen table. He's starting for the third time on the same list of questions he's been asking.

"So how do you know this Martin Roswell?"

"Who?"

"The dead man's ID shows him to be a Martin Roswell, from Sand Point Idaho."

"Matches what's on his FAA license and logbook," I say defensively.

"Indeed."

I'm feeling I could punch this guy, but keep it straight. "The point is, detective, I don't know Roswell. Like I've been telling everyone all day long, first time I saw him was today at the gliderport when he showed up for the acro lesson."

"Acro?"

"Acrobatics."

All of my ID, driver's license, FAA pilot rating and CFIG license, parole card, social security card, library card, an ancient DVD rental card, lie on the table between us. Wolfe nods. "So the first time you saw him was today?"

"That's correct."

"And after he jumped out of your glider did you see him later?"

"Yes I did."

Wolfe looks interested. "And where and when was that?"

"On my front porch about an hour ago. He was lying on the steps just the way you found him."

"So he was dead when you next saw him?"

"I didn't see him. It was dark, I tripped on him as we were coming up the steps."

"What you mean by we?"

"Me and Mon – Agent Harrison."

"Did you and Agent Harrison arrive at the same time?"

"Yes, she followed me in her wagon."

"Where were you coming from?"

"A jogging trail down West San Jose, runs beside the canal."

"So you both were jogging?"

"No she'd been out for a run and I came to meet her. We were talking in our cars." Looking across the room at Montana in her tailored outfit and neat hairstyle I feel a burn of foolishness. Out for a run. Did she tell me that?

"Mr. Clay, isn't it a bit unusual to meet with your parole agent outside of business hours?"

"You're right of course, but we were friends in high school. I happened to be assigned to her today as my new case agent."

A deputy comes to the table and announces they need a residue check on my hands. I sit silent while he opens an Instant Shooter Kit, rubs my hands and forearms with a small fiberglass swab, and pushes the cloth through a membrane in a container of clear fluid. Sixty seconds later, he shakes his head at Wolfe and walks outside. I notice the deputy skips doing a kit for Montana, although he gives her figure a complete visual frisk on the way by.

Taking another tack, Wolfe goes on. "So who do you suppose killed Mr. Roswell?"

"I don't know. But suppose they were actually here to kill me? If you look at the fact that Roswell tries to kill me by jumping out of the glider, in case I survived he might have come here to finish me. Or maybe there's someone else wants to kill me too, and mistook him for me in the dark."

"The Medical Examiner says that he's been dead less than two hours," Wolfe says. "Which would put it 6:30 pm or later. Where were you since 6:30 this evening?"

"I'd say I was talking to Agent Harrison in her car or just arriving at the jogging trail."

"You were sitting in her car?"

"Actually we were pulled up side to side."

"So who can you think of would be angry with you?" Wolfe asks.

"Detective, I have absolutely no idea." Whatever ideas I do have I'm not sharing with this individual.

"Could it be connected to the drug sale you were arrested on four years ago?"

"I didn't know it was a sale," I point out, as I had been doing since the day I got arrested. "I was asked to drive a car. Deliver some cash. I suppose there could be some connection. But Roswell wasn't part of that scene. I never carried a gun. Not my style. And somebody planted drugs at my house weeks after I was arrested."

"I shall look into that, Mr. Clay. Do you have any firearms in the home?"

I shake my head. "Never owned a gun. Never borrowed a gun. Haven't shot a gun since I was a kid." This last was definitely a lie.

"How about in your vehicle or the grounds?"

I shake my head.

"Have you ever had any firearms training, Mr. Clay?"

"My dad took me to a shooting range when I was ten. He had a .22 - .410 over and under."

"How can we contact your father now?"

"I guess a séance or Ouija board might do it."

Wolfe cocks an eyebrow at me.

"He died 20 years ago leaving me and my mom."

"We corroborate that with your mother?"

"She's dead. Cancer. Fifteen years back."

"Sorry for your loss Mr. Clay." Although Wolfe must've spoken that line many times in his career, I have the sense he means it.

The man from the medical examiner's office comes in and whispers to Wolfe that they're taking the body away. I hear the man say that Roswell has an armed forces-issue sidearm on him. Wolfe looks at me.

"Mr. Clay thank you for your time. Here's my card, if any other details occur you, please don't hesitate to let me know."

I hold tight on an inner celebration. They're not arresting me.

"Detective Wolfe, can I have your candid assessment?"

"What do you mean?"

"How does this look to you? Does it really look like I'm involved here, besides simply a victim?"

Wolfe appraises me for a moment. "Right now I don't see any connections. Most capital crimes occur between people who know each other. But it pays me to keep an open mind."

I nod glumly, not knowing whether to be encouraged or not. Wolfe picks up his iPad and stands, heading for my front door. On the porch he turns.

"Mr. Clay, we need to search the premises thoroughly. It would be better if you stay away for couple of days. Also safer for you as I'm sure you understand. In case others are connected."

"I understand," I say, not really thrilled about it. But it makes me happy my grow room is 5 miles away on a separate property. His use of 'others' is ominous.

They had separated Montana and me for a lot of this. I hear her on the phone explaining to someone she is going to be late and to make dinner and yes your friend can stay over. The good little career mommy. How old is her son I wonder. She'd said little about him.

Finally they are wrapping up. Montana, much to my surprise, tells me I can crash at her place one night if I don't mind the sofa. Odd setup, but it will save me a hundred bucks. Either that, or I get to explain this scenario a couple more times to talkative friends. And I admit to feeling a certain crotch-level gravitational pull when I look at my new case officer.

One of the uniform cops smirks knowingly. But this time she doesn't let it pass. She gets up in the cop's face and in a vicious whisper rips right into him. Big as he is, he is no match for the stream of logic, profanity and wounded female pride that she hisses in his face. Her jiggling boobs keep him docile. Use what you got.

So they're all gone now leaving me and her standing on the porch. I've been watching her reactions since we arrived, and I must say it's a mixed bag. She goes from seasoned pro to concerned friend to frightened girl in a blink sometimes. Now we're alone, she says she's so so sorry. She gives me a hug that includes definite pubic contact. My hands lightly touch the contour of her slim waist. I ask why she's sorry and get a shrug. "Well it could have been a friend of yours, coming to see you, ya know?"

So I follow Montana's Jeep back over the hill to San Jose. Why do I agree to go home with her? First of all, underneath all her official demeanor I feel she's still my friend, and right now I can use being around someone who knows me. Plus which there are other possibilities that might have occurred to her as well.

South of Camden off 17, we wind through curving residential streets, lots of trees, RVs parked beside garages, no more than a couple Chevys up on blocks. Her place is all lit up, hip hop music playing from the first room in the hallway, the door of which slams as we come in. Montana walks around switching off lights and cursing about the power bill. She opens the bedroom door letting the music get loud then goes inside. For a second I get a glimpse of a Monroe poster on the wall in there. Montana's kid has taste.

Alone, I have a minute to look around. Suburban living room, adjoining kitchen separated by a high counter and some bar stools. TV, not a large one, on a low bookshelf, entertainment center, not fancy, couple dozen DVDs, plus stacks of books. Botany, biology, entomology, marketing, Web design, Photoshop, InDesign, a couple dozen on similar threads. Makes me think junior is in school, college I reckon, given these topics. I gotta give Montana props as a single mom.

On the door of the kid's bedroom a printed sign: Actual Parent Wanted. On the floor by the sofa there's a scuffed electric guitar case covered with band stickers, a trashed-out skateboard. Place isn't too neat, not dirty either, looks like ordinary life. No parole officer shit that I can see.

In the kitchen where most people would have a toaster oven is a small aquarium. Glass looks clean, bubbles coming up from a small fake diving suit, a dozen medium-sized fish in it, some quite colorful with long streamers from tails and fins. On the fridge is a chore list headed with the name Thor. Hah! She named her son after a Norse God. Or it's a nickname. Door off the kitchen leads to a stoop, steps, a concrete driveway. Garage in back, door's down, garbage cans, recycling, a tall hedge. Welcome to your American life.

Music comes up as the kid's door opens. Montana makes a few closing remarks on their conversation and shuts the door. I manage to ease over to the sofa so I'm sitting there all innocent when she turns to look at me.

"Kids," she says shaking her head. "Want something to eat?"

"I'm fine really," I say. She disappears into the hall, I hear her rummaging through a closet. She comes back carrying an armload of sheets blankets pillowcases and tosses them on the sofa. Whoop dee doo, looks like I get to sleep in the middle of Grand Central Station.

"What time the kids get up?"

"Seven," Montana replies. "I'm usually gone by then. She grabs a remote from the coffee table, presses a couple buttons and some music starts. Lush jazz singer, Jackie Ryan. I wonder if Montana's setting a mood. She plops down on the sofa, at the other end. Deep breath. She turns to me, a smile.

"Excuse the official layer in my office. If I don't keep that steely glint, people walk all over me."

"The job."

She nods, "Yes."

"Looks like you have things well in hand though. I was thinking earlier, you've got it together."

She smiles, looking at her hands, a little flustered. "I try. I have tried." She looks at me, for a second I see her lip quaver. "I have tried so goddamn hard. To make it all. Come out right." After a moment of softness, her face is a mask again. Full lockdown. But her voice stays soft enough. "What have you been doing Clay? Not what's in your file."

I look at her. Sincere? Playing me? Oh well.

"After Mom died things were rough. No idea what Wade is doing anymore. I trained up in gliders, I teach flying now. After I got out, the school hired me back. Things have been smooth enough until today."

She glances at me, searching, then guarded quick away. "I sometimes wondered about you. Those first few years. I almost got married. He was an asshole, I moved out. Seems there's never a good man around when you need one. Or when someone needs a good dad." She nods imperceptibly toward the kid's door. Guitar, skateboard, college books, kid must be interesting.

"Montana?" She looks over. "Why did you invite me here?"

She laughs like I'd lobbed an easy one. "We'll you're always broke, aren't you? The cops turfed you out of your place. Sorry there's no guest room, I need my home office."

"You work home hours too?"

"Seems like. We all get up early and leave. You'll sleep right through it. Wolfe will let you know when it's okay to go back to your place tomorrow. He'll text me."

"Montana, I never heard from you when Mom died. You must have been around. It was right before the reunion." I hadn't gone. Didn't hear from many who did.

She starts to look at me but doesn't manage it. "Yes. Well. It had been so long, with nothing. I thought I might be intruding."

"You're the one who disappeared."

"Well maybe it's because I felt my company no longer desired." Tone of her voice somewhere between Desperation Alley and Fuck Off Street. Couple minutes of dead air, we're both staring somewhere on the wall, seeing nothing except ghosts of sweet memories that died long ago.

Abruptly, she gets up. "Want something to drink? I might have beer."

"I'm good, I say. Water would be great."

"Cooler in the kitchen. Grab a glass from the drainer."

She disappears down the hall, past the kid's room. I hear a door close. I take it that's her way of saying goodnight.

I snoop a bit more then start arranging the blankets. The music from Thor's room gets loud for a while. I hear thumping like a fist on a wall. The noise goes down somewhat. The jazz singer finishes. I get horizontal on the sofa, but it's a long time before sleep comes. The house grows quiet but my mind is buzzing. But at least I'll see no more of Montana today.

CHAPTER 4
BUSINESS WITH PLEASURE

IT WAS THE LAST TIME I saw Montana that day. But not the last I saw of her that night. I'm sleeping along solid enough here on the living room sofa. Whoops. Something presses down on the cushion by my knees. Stray light from the fish tank in the kitchen gives me her outline. Gotta be after two a.m.

"Can't sleep," she says. "You awake?"

"Mph. If you say so." I am generally disagreeable when someone wakes me up. But my mind takes quick inventory of everything that happened yesterday just to put it all in order. Then I'm awake, for sure.

"What are you doing?" I mumble.

"Lying in bed thinking it's so sad. About that poor guy. Some poor nobody in the wrong place." She focuses her gaze on me, her voice takes on more steel. "And what an asshole you are."

"Doesn't take much brainpower," I point out helpfully. "You mean right now, or before?"

"Then. Now. Oh shit."

She falls across my lower torso like she's hugging me through the blanket. Then she's kind of shaking like she's crying, squeezing tight, but silent. I remember that about her, how she can be mega sad and totally hold it in. I get the picture that she and I have been having a whole convo inside her head the last couple hours. Then she sits up and starts hitting me in the stomach with both fists like I'm her new punch toy.

"Hey!" I'm trying to grab her arms. We're fighting but not being too loud cuz her kid and his friend are asleep in the other room but meanwhile she is majorly wailing on me from some deep reservoir of anger or regret she's stepped on over the years. Hissing out of her mouth are words like asshole, dumb fuck, shithead, and worse things you wouldn't want your mom to hear you say.

"Why'd you come back," she's asking, "why are you in my goddamn life? Everything was fine now I'm in a big mess with you just when everything was going good. I hate you I hate you I always hated you I always will hate you! Just go away go away gothefuckaway!"

Of course knowing Montana, she's a complete stranger to any notion she's responsible. She didn't have to take my parole case, did not have to pick up when I called, did not have to give me her personal number for any reason, didn't have to come to my house, or invite me to hers. But no matter, merely the workings of female logic.

I finally get both her wrists, holding so tight she can't hit me anymore. Make no mistake Montana is a strong woman and she hits the gym. This pulls her face right up to mine, shaking and pointing her stink eye stare right at me. She's wearing a long pink tee shirt that says Hello Kitty on it, and panties. Or not. Enough light in here to make out her expression. Her face is feral, full of anger desperation loathing, teeth bared in a snarl. So why does it cross my mind she is the most beautiful woman I've ever seen? And that's when I get it she is afraid. She is scared shitless about something.

"It could have been you, Clay." Her body shudders. The hard desperate look bleeds away then we're just gazing at each other in disbelief, all those years gone by. She stops pulling away. On some mutual signal we lunge at each other, open-mouthed.

What happens after that is not really suitable for a family publication. You can look it up online if you want. However I will say that it was just like the old times only way better. We're both more experienced, more mature, and had learned in two decades how to be more inventive. But deep down, the groundswell of lust and distrust is still there.

At least it is with her. All the pleasure we're feeling, seems like she's trying to pummel me to death with her hips. Which is probably why I wake up this morning with that sweet kind of all-over ache, like a zombie, alone in a strange bed that's funky with bodily fluids.

I lie here for a while going over yesterday. Non-stop excitement from end to end. Then, how it was the last few hours, with her. Mated up so tight, completely wrapped together in that sweet refuge of love, we were whispering all the hot delirious things we'd said to each other years ago. No connection with reality, the cold looks she gave me in her office, the shock in her voice when she heard me on the phone. It's like I've known for years, sex is a form of temporary insanity. But these images of all that certainly wake up my junior partner. Hey go back to sleep you're insane!

I look around for my jeans. No dice. I pull apart the sheets, scrounge around the foot of the bed, nothing. And me not a stitch on. Dude where's my drawers? And what time is it? I have to be at the gliderport at ten for a student. I open the bedroom door, listening intently. The place is still. I peek down the hall at the kid's door, it's closed, with its sign, *Actual Parent Wanted*. Something to think about later. Asleep or gone, I decide.

Ears alert, I creep softly toward the living room. I can see the sofa, sheets and blankets on the floor, my jeans and blue work shirt wadded up in the mess. Walk through, reach down and pull out my jeans. Stepping a leg in, that's when I notice I'm not alone. Two young women, peer at me from bar stools in the kitchen. Since I'm halfway into one leg of my pants when I notice this, it's no time for introductions so I forge ahead, although soon's I get that foot through I pivot away from them, step into the other and get them all the way up. I reach down for my shirt.

"Sorry," I say. "You guys were way quiet."

They don't say anything, just stare at me all expressionless. One's a blond, the other kind of auburn haired. I'm about to think that blond one's definitely datable, then I notice she's looking at me with something that could be smoldering resentment. I have a couple stray thoughts. First, where is Montana's kid, second, who is this chica giving me the stink eye? I know one thing for a fact, whoever she is, strangers walking out of Montana's bedroom in the morning could be par for the course. Then I feel damn embarrassed. About last night, the whole thing. Whatever you do, never bring the kids into it.

The auburn haired-one blurts out, apropos of nothing, "Think I've seen you somewhere." She smiles a little. Pretty. But given the circumstances I'm not sure what she finds familiar. Features, or fixtures.

Nevertheless I look right back at them. Now I've got my shirt buttoned, I start folding the sheets and pillowcases one by one, putting them in a neat unobtrusive pile with the blanket. Last item at the bottom of the tangle is a pair of pale green lace-trimmed panties. How nice, I think to myself. I get an arm under the pile of bedding, snag the panties in, and carry everything into the bedroom. Stack the whole thing neatly on the corner of the bed, close the door and walk back in the living room.

They're still looking right at me, motionless as deer, completely silent in front of bowls of what's maybe granola. Not being one to run and hide, I come right up to the kitchen counter where they're both sitting.

"I'm Clay," I say. "Sorry to come in that way. She said you all were leaving early. The place was way quiet."

Up until now they could've been statues, but now they move. I notice a couple backpacks by the door.

"I'm Twyla," says the auburn girl. After a couple of beats she smiles again, bigger, putting her eyes into it. My apology may have fixed things up some. She is still looking like she's trying to place me.

The other one is still staring at me, stony-like. "I'm Tharcia. I didn't know my mom was having guests last night."

This explanation sounds to me like there's an agreed household etiquette: don't bring dates home when daughter is here. Or at least, not in front of daughter's friends. The only thing escapes me now is, where's the kid? Thor. But then a couple of my more functional neurons rub together and produce the suggestion that maybe the sign on the refrigerator doesn't say Thor at all, but Thar, with an A. So Montana's kid is actually this blonde teener. Nice.

I smile at her. "Would you be Montana's daughter?"

She looks at me head-cocked. "Who is Montana?"

"Oh right," I say. "Old nickname we had for her. Hannah."

Comprehension comes into the girl's clear blue eyes. "You must've been friends a hella long time ago. Nobody calls her that." She looks at me levelly.

"Ah. Right. We know each other from high school."

Now it's her turn to look shocked. She shakes her head minutely from side to side like she's trying to get a ball to drop in a hole. Her blonde hair, long but pulled up in a casual-messy runway model look, follows the movement.

"You know my mom from high school, from maybe twenty years ago?"

The other girl is smiling, "Nineteen years, Thar."

"You know her from then?" the blond one repeats.

Now it's my turn to be confused. This Tharcia baby doll is looking at me with even more intensity than before I put my pants on.

"Yeah," I say. "Lost track of her after grad, though. Just ran into each other yesterday."

Now she looks really disappointed. "And so the two of you just had to…"

Her voice trails off, but her meaning is clear. She is not impressed with her mother much, or with me.

"Would there be such a thing as coffee?" I ask, hoping to derail this spazz convo. The way these two girl-women are staring at me makes me wish I'd looked in the mirror once and maybe even washed my face. I can see behind them on the counter there's actually a coffee maker with a couple of cups. But I wait.

Finally the blond one, the daughter, says "I'll get you some." All family manners now, but it's just a veneer on what she's thinking. Swings herself off the stool and walks to the cupboard. She moves her hips just like Montana, only slimmer. Hip hugger skirt over black stretch tights, killer.

"Milk and sweetener?"

"Black, thanks." She sets the cup down and sits. So now were back in our stiff but lifelike little tableau. But at least I have some life-restoring fluid in front of me.

"You guys go to school together?"

The auburn one, Twyla, nods, working on her granola. "We have classes together on Thursday so were driving together."

"In Twyla's hot new car," Tharcia says. What, can this mean she's actually thawing?

"What classes?"

"This morning it's Journalism and New Media," Twyla offers. "This afternoon it's study group then internship seminar."

"What school?"

"San Jose State."

I'm watching the blond one, now it's me thinking I'd seen someone before. At the same time Twyla is checking me out like will I ask for a date. Expectant look on her face. Yah right, she already took inventory. Tharcia jumps off her stool and takes her dishes to the sink.

"Move your butt, Twy."

So I get a chance to sip my coffee while these two bustle around collecting odds, ends, backpacks, out the door. I check my phone and see it's just after eight. Time to find a breakfast place and get over to the gliderport. I definitely need to catch up with the twins. And I need a shower. Been trying not to scratch too obvious with ladies in the room but now it's game on.

The door bangs open and Twyla comes rushing through and into the daughter's bedroom. On her way out she stops to ask with a smile if I'm going to be back tonight.

"Doubt it," I tell her. Her face registers faint disappointment as she turns to exit but she keeps smiling.

"Later," she says gaily, and out she goes. She's taller than the daughter and has a nice...but hold up pervo, I warn myself, these girls may be underage. Even if not, one of them's your parole officer's daughter. There would be no question about Montana murdering me.

Over on Bascom Avenue I've just found a small diner, sipping coffee waiting for my eggs and country fries, when my phone goes. Number I don't recognize.

"Mr. Clay?"

Oh shit I know this voice. Wolfe.

"Hello Detective. Did you find out who Roswell is?

He doesn't quite say he'll ask the questions but neatly sidesteps to ask me one.

"Mr. Clay. Last evening you told me that you and Agent Harrison were talking at the jogging trail in West San Jose. About what time was that?"

I groan silently. We'd gone over all that. I have to be careful, this guy thinks he's on the trail of something.

"That must have been about six to seven thirty. Give or take. Why?"

"And then she followed you to her place?"

"You mean my place? She followed me to my place. Ummm not exactly. She'd never been there so I said meet me in Felton. She had something to do before she left."

"Thank you. And did you reach her by phone while on the way?"

"Yah, I called, said meet at a restaurant there. I picked up some takeout."

"Of course. And so you talked to her how many times, was it once?"

Mentally, I bust a valve trying to think. Of all the stuff going on last night, I wasn't keeping tabs on my phone traffic.

"I think at least once. Excuse me if I don't recall everything, yesterday was packed."

"Certainly. So when you spoke to her, where were you?"

"San Jose. Actually I had left the park and was driving up Highway 17."

"Recall what you spoke about?"

"Kinda. It was about where we would meet. That's when she said she would be a little later."

"And would you know where she was at that time?"

Boy I am not liking this one bit. Hundred bucks says he's already snagged our phone records.

"I would imagine she'd be in San Jose still."

"Interesting. The fact is, Mr. Clay, that you talked to her twice. Both times you were in the Felton area."

"Sure. Means my memory of the times is off. Like I say, yesterday was pretty random."

"Indeed. You might find it interesting, Mr. Clay, that when you spoke to Agent Harrison, she was first in Santa Cruz, later in the Felton area. She was not in San Jose for those calls."

He waits a while. I hear airwaves stretch between us like a singing nerve. The waitress sets down my plate and sloshes coffee in and around my cup. Not sure I have an appetite anymore. For a bit of self-punishment, my mind picks this moment to offer another morose headline:

Lying Felon Handcuffed by Smart Phone App

"Well you've got me. I guess you will have to speak with her about that." And I'm thinking that soon as this idiot hangs up I'm calling Montana.

"Yes. I spoke to her five minutes ago. For the first call, she said she was in San Jose, which does not match the phone records. For the second, she claimed she was in Felton, which matches."

"Now that is just plain weird," I say, trying to put some cred juice into my voice. But Wolfe has already let the air out of my argument. Damn. I do need to talk to her, but not on the phone! Need to use my burner, see her face to face.

"One other thing," Wolfe says. My heart sinks into my gut. He has more?

"Did Agent Harrison change clothes at your place? Did she shower there?"

"No. That's how she was dressed when she arrived."

"You stated she was out for a run."

"I didn't see her on the trail. Pulled up and met her at her car. Not sure how she was dressed really."

"Alright. Mr. Clay, if you think of any explanation for these anomalies, please do let us know."

"Absolutely Detective. Not a problem. But what did you find out about Roswell?"

"And who is Roswell, Mr. Clay?"

This is so weird I am practically sputtering. "Roswell. It's him, the guy who jumped, my student yesterday. The guy lying dead on my porch. That's Roswell."

"Mr. Clay, I should inform you we found only false identification on the body. Searches for a Martin Roswell fitting that description have no match in our system. We are awaiting fingerprint results."

"You're saying Roswell may be someone else. He showed us an FAA glider rating with that name on it."

"And the school has records of that?"

"Talk to Julie or Stacy at the soaring club. Hollister Homicide. They have his logbook."

"I intend to do that Mr. Clay."

"Naturally. Find anything else at my house?"

"Aside from the victim and his backpack, we found a single shell casing and a number of cigarette butts, on the porch and in the dirt. Boot heel imprints. You are not a smoker, Mr. Clay?"

"Never."

"Nevertheless, we will attempt a DNA match with that evidence. It suggests someone waited for perhaps an hour at that location. You will contact me soon about my earlier question?"

I tell him yah yah sure and hang up. Well that blows. I'm staring at my congealed eggs and asking myself again, why was Montana so easy about coming to meet me last night? What the hell could she possibly get out of helping me with an alibi? And why did she lie, to me then Wolfe?

Then I get a bit of an ah-hah moment. Maybe she wants an alibi for herself, for something else. If she is lying to Wolfe about her location, then what? Business meeting? She isn't married. Multiple jealous boyfriends? How did she get to my place so quick? And why was she so surprised to hear me on the phone?

What stinks though is that the cops have caught us in a lie, and my alibi has gotten worse not better. Thanks to her. She's a cop, practically, and she lied to another cop, Wolfe, who will rightly think she is ass deep in something with me. Old school chums. God damn it. But then I think, why the hell would she be in Santa Cruz, tell me she was in San Jose when I called her? Makes no sense. None.

So after that phone convo with Wolfe, this day is a distracted blur. I teach a lesson at the gliderport and head over the hill to my place. Feeling paranoid, I take the battery out of my phone before I leave. Screw Wolfe, there's too many freaking eyes on me now. Driving slow past my place I check out the fact there's an unmarked car halfway up my driveway, beside the Grant's house. Empty. I take a side road up through scattered houses and park at a familiar trail head.

I unlock my beater bike in the El Camino's bed and ten minutes later I'm riding slow past the swimming pool, giving it a good look. In a secluded location I open a plastic cover on a hidden panel that shows a few colored lights. All the lights are normal. Shows no one is inside, meaning the twins are gone, and no one but me is in the area. Back at the swimming pool, not a pool anymore since I disguised it with a fake top, I open the door real quick, slip on paper coveralls booties and hood, and step into my underground concrete grow house. The lights are on, which is right. The place is noisy with fans and blowers, things that go drip. Sixteen tall green plants reach up to bright lights that shine 12 hours a day. A brief note in pencil tells me where I can find my last payment. Also that things are fine, we can talk when I want to, and what was all the commotion at my place last night?

I close up, wad the paper coveralls and note into a container of solution that will soon dissolve them, ride to a spot where there's a certain flat rock, take out a Ziploc bag containing a fat bundle of cash, and make a mental note to stop by my Union Bank safety deposit down on Graham Hill Road.

Several stops and errands later it's getting on toward evening, and I'm back in San Jose. I stop for some Thai takeout, pick up six entrees and some rice, etc. The battery is back in my phone and there are the usual messages but nothing from Montana, so I don't call her I just go there.

A short brunette with a neck tat answers the door. She eyeballs my armload of white food bags.

"Are you guys sure about the address? We didn't order anything."

I laugh. Now I'm a delivery driver. "I'm Hanna's friend. I knew Tharcia had some friends so I brought lots."

She opens the door for me and yells out "Guys, Thai food!"

Montana calls out from her office, "Back here Clay."

It's like swimming upstream getting there, because Tharcia, Twyla and the neck-tat girl are stampeding toward the takeout on the kitchen counter as I'm trying to get into the hallway. Montana sits at a desk in her office working on her laptop. She has a glass beside her.

"Come in and shut the door." She sounds light and happy, maybe a little snockered.

"What's that?" I ask.

"Oh just some Gin. Want one?" She has her flirty-sexual look for me.

The office is nice, organized and professional. Gleaming dark oak desk, bookshelves, a file cabinet that locks, a framed print of desert rock formations on the wall. I remember her bedroom at the family home was always neat. We banter back and forth a bit, a couple of long kisses. My hand under her sweater, no bra. Nipple pinches, blood flows in us. She sighs, eyes closed, savoring my mouth.

"Something we need to talk about," I tell her, hating that I have to say this now.

She pulls back looking kind of dreamy and superheated, like why talk now. "Oh yea, what?"

"Wolfe."

She is instantly all business. "That sodding prick. I told him I had a good reason for being in Santa Cruz when you called me but he didn't buy it."

"Well then what's the deal? I based my whole alibi on you being in San Jose. Like you told me. If he puts me close to Felton for those two hours then he'll try to hang Roswell on me. Motive, he tried to kill me. Method, anybody can get a gun. Opportunity, those two hours you fucking well tarred me with."

She snarls back, not the least bit daunted. "And everything was fine until you came into the picture. Loser."

"Montana that is all your doing. You're the one transferred my case."

There is more like that, back and forth, same old logic-free shit we used to sling at each other. Meanwhile through the light sweater her nips are standing at attention. She may be the enraged female, but her body has another agenda.

Maybe I should take time out and explain the undercurrent here. She is hiding something. We both are. Back in the day, for reasons I'll get to later, I was planning to pop a guy. You might think of it as urban kid stuff, but it was a paying job from a major dealer. Montana knew what I was up to and insisted on coming along to watch.

How did she know about it? Because like any hormone-addled machismo teenager, I felt that bragging to my fave babe was totally appropriate. Came down to it, she was popping uppers that day and there we were in our secret perch waiting for the guy to show and she insisted on pulling the trigger! I'd never seen her that way, totally lit up, nostrils flared, wired, ready to kill someone for sport. So I'm just taking careful aim and she tries to help by grabbing the gun then it fires and misses, The guy yelled really loud then ran off. Imagine me, age 18, thinking I'll be a hit man. Then Montana goes and fucks it up. Not that I wanted to kill anybody and it did bring me to my senses. We yell back and forth at each other for a while but get nowhere.

"Get the fuck out of here," she hisses. "Tell Thar to come in. And you stay away from her!"

"Anything. You're certifiable, you know that?" I walk out steaming. Whatever she says about a secondary alibi being better, it is worse for real and our cred with Wolfe is shot. Hell, he could arrest me tonight, right here, simply for lying.

In the kitchen, Tharcia, Twyla and their friend have done a job on the food. Growing girls. I hope there's some left.

"Your mom wants to see you," I say to Tharcia. "Take her some of this."

The look she throws me says it all, *Your lover's quarrel wasn't private. Keep it to yourselves, you're supposed to be the grownups here.* Tharcia walks off with a bag and some chopsticks. Watching her move, I find myself thinking, *a friend's daughter, bad juju.*

I peer in the bags and find one still has food in it. Settle on a stool, deciding I should just leave, drop in on a friend over the hill.

The two friends are giggling about something. I get the impression they are younger than Tharcia, or maybe less grown up. Twyla has flirty eyes tonight. What she's wearing also helps, short shorts and a light silk top with nip bumps.

They get into telling jokes, which go from bathroom to bedroom, doctor, parrot. Cute enough. She's looking in my eyes when we all laugh, that kind of thing. But she's getting kind of obvious and it pisses me off. Because I am figuring maybe Montana settles down, we get physical later. This Twyla chick is way out there tonight. She can't know I'm on pro, and even if she's not a minor it would be idiotic to mess with her.

This is when I inwardly lament for the millionth time the face I was born with. It was too pretty in grade school, at least until half the football team decided to adjust it my soph year of high school. But even after, some things have been too easy, the I-shouldn't-be-doing-this-with-you kind of too easy.

What's killer is psychological stuff, make 'em feel unattractive and therefore insecure. Doesn't work with the plain ones, they're already insecure. Looks have zippo to do with that. Wade was great at it, I learned it from him, and he is basically normal looking.

For example when I see a chica knows she's hot I won't give her the smallest notice. Because that's what beautiful women are used to. Conditioned to it. If they don't get it there is something wrong, the world is all of a sudden off its axis and they begin to tilt crazy. Women get insecure they hit on you. First they hate you, then they have something to prove. It's like an equation. Last few years I begin to feel it is not healthy. Like, where's the actual relationship? Lots of friends lots of action. But the way my life is planned out right now I can't afford anyone close.

Twyla pushes by getting to the fridge, grazes her hip against my leg, kind of falls against me with a laugh, doesn't pull away, quietly offers me something to get high. Shall we blast a stick, she whispers close, a couple blades, some dank, a roofie. A little Ecstasy? Pink or brown?

Her neck-tat friend has seen this behavior before and her eyes roll. We share a wink, she gets it. After a minute she walks off, into Tharcia's room. While I note mentally that I have a lesson tomorrow, and therefore cannot do any drugs tonight, that is no part of any calculation about partying with this little wet spot. And not to forget the fact that the police will surely be talking to me again and will do any manner of random drug tests on the slightest suspicion I'm using. Montana as well. She will throw me under the cement mixer if her professional cred comes in the crosshairs. Even though I have my shiny new probation officer, oops, Parole Agent, in a compromising position, namely Missionary, I know she'll turn on me in a second. Because she hates me. From somewhere deep down the years, she finds me lacking.

What is taking Tharcia and Montana so damn long? This Twyla chica will not take no. Jail bait for sure and all my red flags are up. She is totally blazed, oblivious, probably sampling everything she mentioned, but finally it soaks in that I am refusing her. She sighs, and says, "OK, want another beer?"

So I say sure and she says, "Thar and her mom are coming out. I'll bring it in to you."

"Whatever." I saunter off to the living room.

I'm flipping through an iPod plugged into the stereo looking for a tune I halfway recognize, finally find *Werewolves of London* and it starts playing. Twyla comes in with the beer takes a swig out of it says whoops thaz yerz and hands me the bottle with a smirk. Sheesh.

So the girls are not leaving, apparently they are having a sleepover, which harks back as very much like my life as a high school kid, laughing and telling dirty stories all night. My life, before Wade left and our dad got killed.

Finally Montana comes out with a couple shouted reminders over her shoulder, the girls all pile into Tharcia's room, door slams and we can hear the music from in there. Loud, but I figure I can sleep through it. Hidden advantage is, me and Montana won't have to be too quiet while enjoying ourselves later. That is if we are on any kind of speaking terms. I half expect her to tell me to take a hike, meaning take the couch or adios. But Montana has swung back into her this-is-ok mood and is sitting close on the sofa, kind of cuddly.

"You have a wonderful girl," I tell her.

For a second she smiles. "Thank you. And you need to stay away from her."

"How come?"

"You just do, that's all." Female logic, what did I tell you?

I try another tack. "I felt good yesterday when I saw you in your office. You've got it all."

"I really hate that job." Dismissive, like she doesn't want to talk, her mind seems far away. I kiss her, Soft kisses on her delicately open mouth. My head starts to explode. She pulls back, looking at me.

"I haven't forgotten how things were, Clay. It was nice. But."

But what is my unasked question. I want to ask her why she disappeared back then but at this moment I'm too stupefied to form the words. Now she's off on something else.

"Who was that guy? The one you found at your place?"

I shake my head. Question of the decade. She looks away.

"Too sad. He was only some nobody showed up somewhere he didn't belong."

"He was there for a reason. He tried to kill me," I suggest for maybe the hundredth time. "He was coming to make sure he finished the job."

"Do you have anything worth stealing?" Soon as she says that, her face gets this look of regret. "Oh Clay, I'm sorry, of course you do. I meant, are you in business with anyone?" The way her voice lilts over *biz-ness* clearly says, *What have you fucked up in your shady and nefarious little life that would make someone want to pop you?*

I'm not answering that. She is still my Parole Agent. Then out of nowhere she adds, "I felt bad about that guy."

"You felt bad."

"Oh, you know what I mean. He must have a family, a wife." Undertone in her voice is remorse, not pathos. Pathos for a stranger I almost get, but remorse? Definitely not.

"Ah." I am feeling all limp and ropy, wondering if I am catching something. I pull her in and she lets my hands wander to her heavy breasts. She kisses me, nice and slow, and says go on in. She has to feed the fish.

It takes her a while to come to bed. Feed the fish, yah right. I can hear her yakking on the phone out there, her soft laugh. Through the wall, from Tharcia's bedroom, a sharp yell of pain then laughter. What the bleep are those three doing in there? For a second I'm thinking I'll tell Montana she can see her friend if she wants, start to get up but can't control my muscles. Except for one, which is quite the opposite. If she talks to that guy as much as she seems to, why doesn't he come over? And, why would she want me here? That's all I can muster for logical thinking. I am getting delusional, as I do when I get real sick. Dozing off, drifting in and out of fevered dreams. It's been ten years since I've had the flu, so why now?

Montana finally comes in and by then I can't move. Or even talk all that well. I can grunt my likes and dislikes, which is okay with her. She slides into the sheets, gets us both naked and does the driving, seems to like it just fine. Apparently I'm OK as a fixture. Sometime before the end I lose track of events. We drift off, or at least I do.

Deep in the night Montana's phone goes. I am vaguely aware of her talking, business, work. After a while I'm thinking I hear a car start up outside. Montana's not in bed.

Room is dark. Then I vaguely recall her getting dressed a while ago. I zonk out. She'd whispered something about a parolee got arrested. So fine, it's her who's on call not me. I drift back into my delusions.

Sometime after that I feel a smooth bare rump pressed against my stomach. My limbs are too relaxed to respond to any conscious thought I might have. I am thinking in the back of my mind I have to cancel tomorrow's lesson. The regs say I can't fly when I'm sick. The womanly derriere pressing against me is moving though, and does so very nicely. Her hand takes mine and slides it up to her breasts. While part of me stays with the program in that hot insistent grip, my mind goes tripping, except for the bit at the end. When I wake again it's light, Montana is lying close with a leg thrown across my hip. Her face in sleep seems peaceful.

She gets out of bed, I hear the shower running. Then she is dressing in the room, fun to watch, and talking to me. She is all business though, no echo of the all nighttime fun and games. I am trying to follow her but it's tough going, my brain is not exactly tuned in.

Thrown in with her chitchat, which is mostly about how dumb Wolfe is, there's some advice about leaving as soon as I get up. She hurries out the door. I drag myself into a vertical posture.

I'm sitting on the edge of the bed rubbing my face, intending to get up. My phone on the bedside table goes. Wolfe. I struggle to listen.

"Mr. Clay, the police have finished searching your house."

I wait. I don't ask whether they found anything, what would be the point? If they had found something they wouldn't be calling, they would be banging on the door, handcuffs, perp walk to a car out front. I realize I am actually hung over, not sick, but on three beer?

"So I can go home." I'm staring absently at the bedside table. Montana's costume earrings there with the matching necklace of five pinkish stones.

"Yes, Mr. Clay you can go home. We would like it if you stay between your home and your work for the next week."

"Am I under suspicion for anything?"

Wolfe ignores this question and throws me a good one. "Why would Mr. Roswell want you dead?"

"I am fresh out of ideas on that one, detective."

"Indeed. We would be fascinated by any hints you may give us as to why anyone might be targeting you."

"You'll be first to know when I get a clue."

"Ah. I have something else of interest. We spoke to your neighbors."

"The Grant kids?"

"Actually no. Their house guest."

That, I think, is weird. The main house was dark both times I drove past it that night.

"Any help?"

"Perhaps. The guest said that three cars used your road before I arrived. One car drove in between 7:40 and 7:50 and left a few minutes later. Then twenty minutes after eight, two cars drove up and stayed. Then the police arrived."

I think about this a minute. "You are saying someone drove in and out before I got there with Agent Harrison." I have to be careful. I know that the first car was probably me, but don't want Wolfe to think that. The next two cars were me and Montana. This is getting dicey. But it also means that Roswell did not arrive by car. I'm sure Wolfe doesn't know this.

Wolfe is silent for a while. "Also, this witness thinks they heard someone hurrying down the road on foot around 6:20."

"Any abandoned cars, rental cars? The house guest see anyone?" I want to know who the heck that person is but don't want to ask.

Wolfe ignores my questions and goes on. "While I have you on the phone, I'd like to see you and Agent Harrison in my office Monday. We need to clarify your whereabouts on the night of the murder."

I say something like oh sure anything to oblige, and hang up. Damn! Just like Montana to push me deeper in the guano. Why did she have to lie? What's she covering by saying she was in San Jose? And this supposed witness Wolfe found, how accurate is that evidence? Did they see the cars, or just hear them pass the house? The Monday thing scares me spitless. I can get a violation for lying to the cops and right back in jail, no discussion.

I call the gliderport and cancel my lesson for that day. Turns out one of the other instructors can take it so no harm done there. I get a shower and check myself in the mirror. My eyes are red-rimmed, strange. My head feels thick, stupid. In the kitchen there is coffee on, I hope. I need to start thinking.

CHAPTER 5
TOTALLY IN CHARGE

THE SUN IS WARM on Montana's front porch so I'm sipping coffee and collecting my wits. And doing my daily gratitude meditation. Today that means going over how many times I could have perished in the last two days. I'm astonished to be here.

In the bathroom mirror a minute ago my eyes were pits. I feel stupefied. Glad no one at the gliderport gets to look at me today. Or worse, Probation. A urine test, gawd. What the bleep is wrong with me? It's not the flu.

I'm thinking everyone has left the house, but wait, noises in the kitchen and a minute later Montana's daughter steps out onto the porch. She smiles, holding an iPad and a coffee mug with a picture of Garfield on it. We do the usual, like good morning sleep okay, blah-blah.

She's not into conversation, doing things with her iPad. Playing or working, how can one know the diff anymore? She grins a time or two and I figure she's catching up with friends. Well, full disclosure, while enjoying the morning light I am going through my phone looking at email and texts. There is one I don't recognize, from someone calling themselves enforcer88, so that hits the trash.

Our eyes meet as we sip coffee so just for conversation I remark, "Guess we're both on pixel crack this morning."

"Busted," she laughs.

"I felt way strange last night," I tell her.

"Did you have anything... recreational?" she asks. The way her mouth turns up, just on one corner.

"Nope."

We're quiet a minute. "Not that I wasn't offered plenty of other, um, things," I add.

Tharcia's brow wrinkles for a sec and her eyes narrow. "Twy's a bit of a klepto. Also a snoop. Need to watch her. Her career goal is webcam ho."

I make a mental note to catch up on my street slang. I can see Twyla being a kleptomaniac by the way she copped a free feel.

"What was the screaming and giggling last night?"

She chuckles. "Waxing is such torture."

My instant vision of three coeds bikini-waxing together tells me to change the subject, fast. "What year are you at SJSU? Is it cool?" Hoping I don't come off like some out-of-it dad at the dinner table.

"Great, actually. Awesome." Her face is animated. "My profs and classes are good, better than first semester. It's interesting."

"You after a degree?"

Her laugh is musical on the morning air. "Well I am only a frosh, but if I keep feelin' it, I'll probably work in journalism. Do in-depth stories on interesting people. Political blogs, you know? I like to figure out how stuff happens."

"So, writing for newspapers?"

"Journalism is not only writing for print. It's video, photos, graphics, and audio. Social media like Twitter and Facebook, Reddit and Digg and so on. It covers a lot."

I am watching this chica. She either got over her resentment of me yesterday or Montana told her some half-truth. Ordered her to cut it out. I wonder how Tharcia goes along with Montana's 'orders.' She seems soft, easy-going, but I bet with her mother she can be steel against steel.

Warm day, she's wearing black shorts, long legs bare in the morning light, a man's blue work shirt that brings out her eyes, sleeves rolled to the elbow. She comes across as a fully formed human being, not self-conscious, serene as a mermaid.

Looking down at her iPad, tangled white-blonde hair hoods her face. And I suddenly get it I am jealous of this kid. Young, hellacious hot, mind of her own, gets to pursue her interests instead of being cast in the role of family breadwinner at 18. I have to give props to Montana for that, she's providing her girl's education. You bet I'm jealous. Me and my Grade 12 diploma don't know half what she's talking about.

"Nice. Be great if it stays interesting. Will you go somewhere for that?"

"Besides debtor's prison?"

"Ah, student loans."

"Actually Mom is all pay as you go. Also I got scholarships. It's like, when I grad, will I ever get a job in this busted economy?"

"How about other parts of the country?"

"I'd relish an adventure! Anywhere in the world will do. But this is my home, I was born in this area. Well L.A. really but we always lived in San Jose. Been in this house nine years."

"So call me a snoop, but was your mom ever married?"

She scowls, thinking. The look reminds me of Montana at that age. "Mom still has her maiden name. There was a guy lived with us when I was small. Called him daddy for years, then we left and Mom said no he's not." Tharcia makes a guarded face, as though recalling something unpleasant.

"Hey, it was so lame showing up at your house like that. The other morning."

She grins. "It's OK. Twy needed something for her Facebook page."

I feel my cheeks go warm. "I do hope you are joking. My agent will want an advance for that."

"Ah. So you are a paid professional?"

"I don't yet have my cabaret license, it's still an internship."

"Ah, building up your hours with private demos in suburban living rooms, I see." Her smile is unwavering so I soldier on.

"Truth is, there was a crime at my place night before. Cops told me I should stay away until they sort it out."

She looks at me with a penetrating gaze. Way she listens, the silence is deafening. "What kind of crime?"

"Someone tried to kill me."

"Kill you? Whoa cowboy, what's with that?"

So I spin her the yarn about Roswell jumping out of the glider. She's watching me, thoughtful.

"So the glider is spinning down and you are holding onto a strap?"

"Yeh. That's about it."

"Retarded! You barely made it."

"Most scared I've ever been. But there's more."

"OMG what?" She is sitting forward in her chair focused on me with those intense blues.

"When I got home there was someone dead on my porch. And get this. It was the guy who jumped."

She blinks. I watch her face as she sorts it out. What surprises me is her next question. It's not about what happened.

"So, how are you holding up after all that?"

I grin at her like I just found a friend. "Feeling flat-out grateful to be here."

"I guess," she says. "Is that why Mom brought you home?"

"Actually, it is. We'd just run into each other by chance that same day."

She sits back, looking at me thoughtfully. "Nothing personal, but I'd like to know less about my mom's social life."

"I get that." Tell your mom to keep her moans down is what I'm thinking.

"A lot less."

I nod. "Have you guys lived in San Jose all your life?"

"Mom and I lived with my aunt in L.A. for a year after I was hatched. Mom got her GED and started community college in law enforcement there. We moved back up here and she took a four-year degree program at State, while working as a clerk for the probation department. They liked her so she stayed."

"She's done well." Back of my mind is wondering how Montana could afford four years of college while toting a kid around. Her folks didn't have money and besides they split up. She has two cars and a mortgage, plus Tharcia's tuition, which in California goes up 15% every year.

I shake my head to clear it. I still feel poleaxed from the night before. "Not to pry, but were your friends jacked last night?"

She thinks a second. "Weed I think. Course you never know about Twy. She is such a doper. She's going through a rough patch."

"How come?"

Now it's her turn to look uncomfortable. "We broke up."

Comes the dawn. Montana's little girl is lez. Wonder if that's the reason for all the back room lectures.

I nod in sympathy. "Love pangs are hell at that age. You okay?"

Her head tilts to one side looking at me. She's just revealed her sexual identity to a complete stranger. She smiles with her lights on. "I'm okay. Thank you for asking."

"You were ready to move on?"

"Huh? Oh. Learned not to trust her."

"That's harsh."

Tharcia shakes her head ruefully. "Twy wants to be just like Mom. In every way."

I nod. Teen angst. "If I didn't know better, I'd almost say someone gave me something."

Her look tells me nothing. Guilt free, she only shrugs. Then she says, with an easy laugh, "Oh you mean like... lemmee see your eyes."

I lean forward and so does she. I watch her face as she gets close. Perfect skin, shining eyes. She sits back.

"You do look a little tweaked. What did you take?"

"Nothing, s'far as I know. Beer."

Fooling with her iPad again. After a bit she looks up. "How well ya know my mom?" She says it soft and casual but I see there's some heat on it.

"Okay. We were at the same middle school then high school. Senior year we hung out a lot. Her mom was pretty liberal."

"Grandma Marcia. She's cool."

I nod. "We played Truth or Dare all the time." I smile, thinking back. "Nobody could keep up. Friends thought we were over the top."

She thinks a minute. Face lights up like she discovered a new planet. "You're Stuka!"

Holy hell, the last person said that name around me was Montana. I was interested in World War II warbirds, still am. The Stuka's a German dive bomber.

"Wow," I grin. "What a shock to hear anyone call me that."

"She told me stories about Stuka, but never about Clay. What else did people call you?"

"The mechanic."

"You fix things?"

"Mostly I used to build model cars."

"So how did you run into my mom?"

Now here's a question I am uncomfortable with. Nothing to lose, I suppose. And hey, she was up front about who she is. "Truth is, your mom is my Parole Agent." I wait to let that sink in. "I'm on pro."

Tharcia tilts her head to one side, tasting the idea. "Okay, so what did you do?"

"There was a little dope deal. I was the driver. Purely. Transporting the cash."

"And you got caught."

"Not really, no. I got away."

"So. You confessed out of remorse?" She's got this infectious little grin. Chica is being light about it.

"Oh yes I felt just terrible. Heartsick really, wanted to come clean. Actually, someone helped with that."

"Turned you in?"

I nod, feeling the anger surface again. My plan was so tight!

"You got away and somebody ratted you out?"

"That's about it. The charges they brought weren't true."

"Harsh. Well, my mom will take care of you if she thinks you're for real."

"I think she transferred my case when she saw my name on a list."

She just nods. My coffee is gone, I'm getting antsy, thinking about getting home to see what hell the cops left behind. Need to check out the swimming pool and talk to the twins. I tell Tharcia I'm heading out. She asks will I be back, I say no, and thanks for the hospitality.

She surprises me by holding out her phone. "Dial your number?"

I do what she asks, thinking why does this babe want my number? Not that I mind her knowing how to reach me. I hand her phone back.

"See ya," she says, looking down at her iPad.

I get out of there without seeing any of the friends, klepto or regular. Stop at the market in Felton and pick up some basics, drive to my place and park. Lots of tire tracks in the dirt around my porch. Steps where I found Roswell have been cleaned professionally, but my mind still conjures images of dark blood soaking into the wood. It is either wet there now, or permanently stained. I don't touch it.

I'm all prepared to fix the mess the cops left, but once I get inside it's not too bad. They put stuff back in drawers, but not the way I had it, just piled in. Kitchen cupboards are open and empty, dishes stacked on the counter top. I go upstairs for the first time in months. Cops were up here too, most of this isn't my stuff, old furniture and boxes of curtains, dishes, things piled all over, I don't pay much attention. The bathroom up here is practically empty.

Telltale lights in the holiday decor tell me the twins are working in the pool. Need to talk to them. So I'm putting things back in their rightful order and starting to miss a few items but nothing important yet, maybe misplaced. I start a list to ask Wolfe about. My phone whistles, new text.

From someone named 269Twy. The avatar pic, close-up of a laughing face, has to be Tharcia's friend. What the hell? Message says, *Bummed you left call me stud muffin*, a phone number. Like hell chica I am thinking, you are dangerous. Flip her to blacklist and delete delete.

I don't need to go back there anymore. I mean seeing Montana was great and her daughter is a sweetheart, but girls like that Twyla I can definitely lose.

Then I am asking myself hey wait how did Twyla get my number? Tharcia wouldn't have given it to her. She called Twyla a klepto, I say she's mental. Did Twyla peek my phone? Two to one she laced my beer.

So I'm throwing out all the stuff that's questionable in the fridge because cops unplugged it half way across the kitchen. Least they could have done is sweep back there. Making a grocery list for a trip down the hill later.

Chimes from the decorations, *We wish you a merry Christmas*. The orange light among the others is now green. Car-Dar have closed up the pool, and are heading for their pickup, where they'll wait a bit in case I want to talk. And I do. A conversation with actual friends about ordinary stuff will be a relief after this wretched week. I text Carla saying come for a beer, get a smiley face back.

All this extra scrutiny thanks to Roswell is whirling around my brain, telling me I am more than ready to leave right now. I have all my new-life ID. Even though it cost a ton, I'll be scared spitless using it. But since Wade went stealth ten years back, the idea has gone from curiosity to hobby, headed for obsession. In prison it became my focus, to drop the damaged life I made and become nobody. No past. Start over new. Wade will help, wants me to. When I cross over, we'll be brothers again.

Mentally I savor a victory I'll never actually see: all the cops, hacks, jailers, parole agents, cons and gangstas who think I am all predictable and known, suddenly getting it that I can't be found. I proved it that time on Mt. Baldy. It's only because of Mick I was caught. I am sure he's behind the pack of blow that showed up in my evidence file. I need to work out a payment plan for him.

There is one solitary *if*. If I had the cash, I'd hire a cutthroat lawyer and fight to get my case reopened, clean it up. And with luck, take Mick down in the process. If I could do that, I'd clean up the grow operation and become a law-abiding citizen again. Until then, my life will be a child of necessity.

Outside, tires crunch on gravel. Stepping out onto the porch, I sniff the forest air, the fresh earth scents. Doors slam and here they come, Carla, dragging on her cigarette, Darla, a nonsmoker, walking upwind of her, both wearing wide smiles. Don't twins do everything the same? Well, they are fraternal but that is only part of their captivating story. We three were big friends in school, I was in love with Darla for a time. I blow across the beer bottle mouth, a resonant note that floats through the redwoods.

"Fleet's in," Carla cracks. "Hey, Farmer Clay."

I get a hug from each of them, smell their damp hair. The swimming pool routine includes a hot shower-shampoo at the exit. We always wear one-piece disposable paper coveralls in there. It's hot under the lights so we leave our shoes and clothes outside the grow room. Once out the door, there are no traces of budding hemp to follow anyone through life.

"Want a beer, something stronger? How was today?"

"Short," Carla replies, nodding yes to anything alcoholic. "Tending the nursery, took clones off mom.

Thinning the bottom leaves like we did two cycles ago. Checking for mold. Spider mites. Typical drill. It's in good shape. We made a nursery supply list for you."

"Yah," adds Darla, popping her chewing gum. "Five more days we change the light timer to start the buds. This one's going to be good. How's by you?"

"I got your last blast. You took care of yourselves, right?"

While Darla nods yes, Carla says OMG we forgot we'll take that now. We laugh. Carla's the trickster.

I give them an abbreviated account of the last two days, a new glider student who jumps to his fake death. The cops. I don't mention the DEA talking to me. Too damn close to home.

"Did he suicide?" Carla asks.

Darla gets it, "Clay, he could have killed you!"

"That's what it felt like."

"Why?" In unison.

"Then that night I come home and guess who is lying on my steps sporting a hole in the noggin?"

"Was that all the flashlights and cars down here? Who was it?"

"The same guy."

"You're shitting me. Is that the stain out there?"

I'm nodding. "Unbefuckinglievable, right? Meanwhile I totally get involved with this old friend, you're not gonna guess what her job is."

"Umm, I say dwarf hooker," Carla suggests.

"My shiny new Parole Agent," I say solemnly.

They do this Val-Gal gape at each other.

"This is seriously twisted," Darla informs me. To her sister she says, "Do we need this bumpkin? He's creeping me right out."

Carla scowls. "You are friends with your probation person. And it's a she? Ewwww."

"Did you bang her?" Darla wants to know with an expectant leer.

Carla interrupts, both hands over her ears. "No no no, too much information. La-la-la-la-la."

"Yah right, it's sticky weird. You'll choke when I tell you who it is."

"OMG," Carla says, "who?"

"Montana."

They shriek with surprised laughter.

"Didn't she totally break your heart?"

"I heard some old troll carried her off to his lair."

I'm grinning. "I don't believe me either."

"She is your new owner?" Carla says. "Where is she living?"

"We saw her at the fifteen year reunion," Darla puts in.

That missed reunion is a sore spot with me. I was awaiting trial then.

"But hey look, I might be having more visitors. It might be better to coast a bit. Will the pool hold up for a few days without you guys?"

"Yeah," Darla said. "It's so on autopilot anyway. You check it."

"Sunday, then," I tell them. "I'll text. Hey we might play some music Saturday night. Come if you can. See if you can find us a bass player."

"Sunday."

"Saturday."

They finish their beer then hugs and they are off. They look closely at the steps. Professionally cleaned or not, that dark stain is still noticeable. They give it a wide circuit.

"See you in jail don't call for bail," Carla cracks as they walk to their truck. Darla playfully slugs her sis in the shoulder.

"Yeah," I call after them, "I'm sure the dollhouse biz will take care of you just fine."

"Warden," one of them shouts.

They'll be back. We've had tricky moments over the last year, setting up the swimming pool grow operation and making sure it's isolated. But everything spewing off this Roswell biz is weird and dangerous and I have to watch my back. Their pickup eases toward the main road.

Alone again. But something comes to me. Surprised at my own move, I'm finding Wolfe in my call history, then waiting for him to pick up. I get his voicemail and hang up. Then I decide okay, I will leave a message, and call back.

"Detective? Clay here. Why did I get assigned to Agent Harrison the same day Roswell attacked me? Everything was fine with my regular parole officer. Yamamoto. It seems more than coincidental. What do you make of it? Didn't that happen kind of fast?"

I hang up. I get into a jag of house cleaning. Don't you make fun of me, I like things tidy. Gives me the willies cops have been through my stuff. I'm pissed at them, at Roswell, Montana, the whole cast of characters. Feels like the gods are taking a dump on me for sport.

While I'm getting things back in order I'm calling people randomly for a Saturday jam. Lots of folks are busy gigging down in Santa Cruz and Pebble but some of the regulars are around and I have a good place to jam, wood floors, the noise doesn't bother anyone here in the redwoods and there's lots of parking.

But then I have this thought. Wednesday evening I left Montana's office and Highway 17 was a parking lot. So I stopped for a beer, something I seldom do since I'm on pro. That brew pub could have saved my life! The Santa Clara County medical examiner put Roswell's time of death at 6:30. I got here an hour later. No wait it was Roswell saved my life! The shooter popped him thinking it was me, then left. So now I'm not quite so mad at Roswell, but would still gleefully strangle the bastard if he wasn't already extinct.

So the day becomes a peaceful one here in the redwoods, more like normal life, and for a time I can forget about things, working on my shopping list.

I haven't had a decent workout for three days, so I get out with my KHS Tucson twenty-niner, my good trail bike, not the one that bangs around in the El Camino, and hit the trails for a couple hours. Of course in the forest quiet I glide by the swimming pool, check the hidden telltale panel, then accelerate away. Feels good to be out on the hilly twisty trails and not thinking about my life, the instant shit storm.

As my mind slows down I remember something from the day Roswell jumped. That P-51 Mustang fighter I saw in the pattern while limping home in the K-21 from Roswell's murder attempt. A few phone calls to the gliderport to track down the pilot, and I've arranged a demo flight for Sunday afternoon. I have a flight simulator on my computer with a P-51 in it and have spent a lot of time with that, but flying in the real thing will be over the top. Never flown a power plane, but maybe the guy will let me feel the controls.

Checking my phone messages later I get this frantic one from Montana asking did I see her earrings and necklace in her bedroom. She sounds anxious but I have no idea.

Come Saturday, haven't heard from Montana or Wolfe again, starting to feel things might return to normal. Spending time with my parts business. UPS had delivered several boxes of items, which the cops helpfully opened for me. No thrill there guys, vintage airplane parts that I resell, I can show you my bookkeeping. So my usual drill as a middleman is this: unpack them, repack them in my boxes with my labels, make up invoices on my company forms, stick UPS labels on them, flag UPS for pickup via my online account, and set the stack out on the porch.

Feeling good, the house is ready, people are coming later on, I'll be picking up a keg and some ribs for the BBQ. It's totally pot luck, good live music jam and lots of greasy food and beer.

So chores all done work's done swimming pool is OK till at least tomorrow. I'm sitting on the porch with a beer and my phone goes. Dayum! Spoke too soon.

It's Wolfe working the weekend shift. My bubble of serenity pops like a teenie's cherry but I did want to talk to him.

"Hey, Detective. Get my message?"

"Yes, Mr. Clay, we did. It is rather peculiar."

"Peculiar how?"

"The probation department has clammed up about that change, moving your case from Officer Yamamoto to Agent Harrison." He sounds a little peeved. I am thinking wait a minute, this guy's a seasoned detective, practically FBI level, and the Parole Division under the same County director stonewalls him?

"How does that work exactly?"

"The technical term for it Mr. Clay is Red Tape."

I think a minute. "Well there's another layer to this, you prolly don't know about."

"Yes, I'm listening."

"Montana, Agent Harrison, is a friend from school."

"You mentioned that, Mr. Clay. And which university was that?"

I twitch slightly at the fact I never attended any classes after high school, unless you count three years of legal studies and online courses at the Country Club.

"San Jose High School to be perfectly accurate." I tell him the year we graduated. "Montana, Agent Harrison, left town for a couple years and came back with her baby daughter. Up until yesterday I hadn't seen her since before grad."

While Wolfe is mentally chewing over that, out of the woods comes Bomber, my Maine Coon, sauntering across the clearing. Sniffs at the El Camino's tire. Walks up to me and butts his head against my hand a few times, then wanders inside to check what's in his dish. Hope ya like crunchies, Bomber. Easiest cat I ever had, feeds himself mostly. Probably takes himself to the vet too, except for that raccoon bite last year.

Wolfe's voice brings me back to reality. "So there is something between the two of you?"

"Not the point. What could be of interest is, she lived with a fellow named Mick McIntyre, who is now housed at Lancaster."

"We are aware of that, Mr. Clay. All that information came up in Agent Harrison's hiring process. He was clean when the two of them separated years ago. Is there some other reason you might be telling me this?"

As in revenge, is the question in his voice. Well damn, his senses are on target but Mick's in the slam and I am trying to keep myself out of it so hate me if you have to. But his insinuation pisses me off.

"Listen Wolfe," I tell him angrily, "I was not followed from the delivery chase. I was ratted out by the guy hired me, who happens to be McIntyre. So I'm in holding for three weeks on no charges and suddenly there's a charge of possession with intent against me. Something was not right about that. I think those two are still connected."

"Those two?"

"Mick and Montana. My prison record is spotless, my pro has been squeaky clean. Montana knows it. Yamamoto does. That's why this whole thing of switching me to a new agent is spooky. And besides that I was innocent. Framed. I didn't do what I was charged with."

I did do some not-so-nice things I have never been charged with and you just keep quiet about that.

"Okay, so you have an axe to grind against the system. At least, Mr. Clay, I believe you are trying to resolve it in the proper way. However let me point out, I do know that you and Agent Harrison were not together that night until you met in Felton. You were not sitting in your cars in San Jose for 90 minutes before you found Roswell's body. Would you like to tell me what really happened?"

I take a deep breath and let it out slow. "The simple truth is, I found Roswell first. I was alone. That was about an hour before Montana called you."

"You found Mr. Roswell first."

"You can quote me. If the rest of the day hadn't happened, no problem, I would have called 911. But this was just over the top. Wanted to have someone else there when the cops showed up. But what's worse is the fact it turned out to be my acro student, whatever his name is, which I didn't know at first. So you're saying Montana lied to me about where she was. I asked her to come because I trusted her. I only repeated what she told me. If I had known it was him... shit I don't know what I would have done then. But either way it looks bad."

"So that is your story now?"

"Story my ass, Wolfe! That is the gospel. You find a corpse on your doorstep sometime, tell me how you handle it." I punch off the call. I pace my porch a couple times, swearing. I blew it. Always hate when I lose it like that. But the walls are closing in. Now I need to stay away from

Montana too. Her story was paper-thin with Wolfe before I punched big holes in it just now. She will be beyond steamed at me. Homicidal, that's how I'd rate it.

Anyway I can forget all that for the evening. Friends arrive later on and after dark the party is cooking along the way good parties do, people showing up in twos and threes unloading instruments, blowing joints before they come in the house cuz they know I must not be caught with it in my bloodstream. Everybody knows I'm on pro and can't be one inch off the yellow line, and they respect my wishes. No weed, no nic in the house either can't stand the cigarette smell. Got the Bar-B-Q going on the kitchen porch, good load of ribs cooking there.

It's all self-propelled now, couple guys volunteer to watch the keg and mind the grill. Perfect, I can mill around, check out who's playing. Which changes about every 20 minutes. Now there's a guy pulling out a banjo and as he starts tuning up the mood shifts over from blues to bluegrass. Some young guy there, dude I've never seen, is an absolute wizard with electric bass. He knows his way around anything.

Lots of nice ladies here too. Darla and Carla come in, Carla shrieking at the punch line of some joke Darla told, handing out hugs to all the guys young and old. Special ones for me when they come around, Carla says oh baby I need you so, whiskey and weed on her breath, the three of us laugh and they wander off in search of the keg or anything stronger.

I hang with a few guys talking about finger-picking styles, walk outside where there's always two or three people dragging on a joint or a bong, stand upwind from them while we chat. Checking out the *chicas* here tonight gets me thinking of one in particular I wish would come around. Stacy, for sure. Then I stop myself. She could be a permanent attachment if I weren't going bye-bye, but as things stand it wouldn't be fair to her. Gets me down to the fact that what's missing in my life is letting anyone close.

I've cut away almost every kind of contact except large groups where everybody's interchangeable, everyone's drunk enough I can get out my own guitar and play a little, and don't have to finish a conversation. Looks normal from outside, but my life is entirely focused on the day I can vanish.

Phone goes off in my pocket. It's Montana. Oh, what a treat.

"Hey."

"Hey yourself. What's all the noise?"

"Little kegger up here in the woods. Me and the mountain folk."

"Sounds like fun. Maybe I'll come by later."

"Mm."

"Hey did you do anything with my earrings and necklace the other day? Did you see them in the bedroom?"

I'd thought about it since her message and recall I saw them on the bedside stand after she left in the morning. "Well yah, they were there when I rolled out."

"Did you do anything with them?"

"Jewelry? I'm not wearing any these days."

"It's not a joking matter you blockhead. My stuff is precious. Anyway I talked to Wolfe. We have to meet him at his office tomorrow."

"Tomorrow is Sunday."

"Oops yah haha having a lil drink here, I mean Monday. We should have coffee." This is Montana-speak for *we better get our stories straight*. She turns away from the phone, her hiss-whisper. "No you can't go out do your homework."

Then to me she says, "What are you doing?"

"Local jam session."

"Sounds like live music. Maybe I should come later."

I think of inviting her. The part about hitting the sack with her would be great. Then thinking it's better she doesn't get into my life. There's weed here. She could turn all official. Besides, there's the off chance Stacy might come around.

"Sorry Montana, tonight's not a good idea."

"So! You've had all you want of me already? Now you have some new little bimbo over there. Well fuck you Stuka. Monday three o'clock. Asshole."

Jeez Montana, you are so smooth. I listen to the dead air as she punches off and remind myself that Montana could never contain her temper. Even when the chips are down she's impulsive and jumps ahead without thinking. Damn near got me into a lot of trouble couple of times. I don't have to think very far back. She already has, with Wolfe.

I'm leaning in the open doorway watching the scene in the living room. Seated on folding chairs in front of the woodstove is a cluster of five or six guys with guitars, conga drums, one gal named Bonnie who always brings hi-hat and brushes, and the kid with electric bass. Age range in this room is probably 13 to 75. The best fiddle player is the oldest graybeard here.

Then I notice sitting in my easy chair some dude with dark glasses lighting up a joint. Who is this guy with? He doesn't know the score. I walk over.

"Hey friend, house rules say we smoke outside, okay?"

Guy ignores me. Takes a drag on his roofer and blows it at me. I bend down right in his face.

"Take it outside now."

"Blow me." Cocky behind his dark glasses.

Guy's about my size wearing a leather jacket jeans and boots. Rule I learned in prison is simple: respond to any shit with instant aggression. I grab him by the lapels and jerk him to his feet, spin him around fast like a Tango and back him up through the door. I bounce his head off the door jamb, get him going again and toss him down the steps. At least that was my plan. Way he rewrites things is to grab my shirt so we tumble down together. We're at the bottom I'm on one knee with a fist cocked back to cool the dude and I notice he's got a wicked pistol pressed to my cheek.

"Got a message for you asshole. Next time you get a text from enforcer88 you call. You call or you get dusted."

"What the hell you want?"

"Message from management."

I'm quickly adding up two and two. For some reason it comes out Mr. Mick McIntyre.

"You pee wee. I can talk to Mick whenever I want to. I don't need any chain of command."

Which is a lie. I have no idea how to reach Mick. Except Montana would know. For all I know that's who she talks to every night. We're slowly standing up, but he still has the heat pressed against my forehead. I notice the music has stopped, there is not a sound from the 30 people in the house.

"The message is you need to call him."

"I might do that," I say. "Now put down your squirt gun, and leave."

Now this enforcer nitwit is looking over my shoulder up the stairs. The pistol lowers. I follow his gaze. Somebody up there is holding a .12 gauge pointing right at us. Who the hell brought the sprayer? Right now I don't actually care because I think it got this fucked-up dude out of my face. He flicks a card in the dirt. Mick's current burner is my guess. He walks down the driveway, sticking the gun in the back of his belt.

Then everybody's talking at once, lots of questions, lots of who was that guy, lots of are you okay, and so forth. Ladies coming around for hugs, guys come shake my hand, same questions. Same answer.

"I don't know. I do not know." However I have a couple of guesses. Mick. And 25 centavos says Montana's mixed in it ass deep. Guy with the shotgun shaking my hand.

"I'm not really a gun person," I tell him. "Why is that here?"

"Brought this to show Michael. Sellin' it. Tain't loaded. "Scared the bejeezus out of me. Hadda do something. Mexican standoff."

"Well, I'm damn glad you did."

I hear a V8 fire up near the road, funny whistling sound to that engine. It rushes off with a squall of tires. I wander around the back porch, pump up the keg, trembling now. Glad for the jostling group of folks around me, but really distracted inside myself. Draw off a cup, take a big draft. This week is about the weirdest my life has ever ever ever been. And I know the fates are sitting up there chuckling to each other saying, hold on little man, we got more for you.

My phone chimes, I'm getting a text. Somebody calling themselves nrrdgrrl. What nerd girl writes damn near blows me over.

nrrdgrrl: *Stuka, where UR? wanna talk - Thar*

Thinking to myself, now on top of everything else I'm having major temptation thrown at me. Is she legal? I text her back.

Stuka109: *UR mom doesn't want me talking 2U*

nrrdgrrl: *Need 2 tel U sth*

Stuka109: *ask me here*

nrrdgrrl: *negatory what's your 20?*

Stuka109: *jam nite my place*

nrrdgrrl: *where?????*

Stuka109: *GPS coming*

I send her the coordinates of my house. Does that make me an idiot?

nrrdgrrl: *CU thx I am out.*

I read back over the convo, the text interchange that took less than a minute from start to finish. And which could kick me down a road of no return. What the hell does she have in mind? There are probably two or three people would either kill me or throw me in jail for what I just did. Or possibly am about to do. Hormones, shut up. But then I remind myself, she's not into men and seems sane. Whew.

The party tries to get going again but it's running on three wheels, energy's out of it, everybody wants to tell their view of the takedown and standoff, people who haven't left are into talking, not playing. After midnight. Most folks in the house are sitting down, not jumping around and hollering, just a couple dudes picking at six-strings now. I'm on the back porch starting to clean up the barbecue when tires crunch up the dirt drive. Slim woman in black jeans and a leather jacket gets out of a little gold Mazda, starts for the front porch.

"Tharcia? Back here."

She adjusts her aim and heads for me, walking quickly, black boots with pointy toes, but her posture tells me she's carrying some weight. She stops just outside the circle of light from the porch. Her hair is down and she's wearing shades. Shades at midnight, too cool, I first think, then I second think she's not the type to act cool.

"Find it okay?" I ask.

"No prob."

"Care for a beer?" She nods yes and I draw off a cup. When she takes a sip I see that there's some discoloration on the side of her face.

"You hurt yourself?"

She takes a deep breath, looking down. After a second she pulls off the dark glasses takes a step closer and raises her face to the light. I see she's got a mean shiner going, her eye's swollen half-shut.

I am instantly ready for war. That little go-round with enforcer88 was nothing compared to what I'm up for now. I'm right in her face holding her elbows. She looks straight back at me. She's not afraid.

"This is what your girlfriend is really like," she says, meeting my eyes. A tear lashes down one cheek.

"Montana?" I am incredulous. "You call the cops?"

She makes a disgusted face. "Big N-O to that."

"What are you going to do?"

"Doing it now. Got away from her is what."

I think a minute looking into her face. Her expression so untroubled, given what's just happened to her.

"Who have you told?"

"Nobody yet. Twyla. You. Rayne. Mom's getting way weird lately. I hurt for her, something's going on and she's not talking."

Knowing Montana as I do, or at least the way I did, I can well understand that she gets terribly caught up in herself sometimes.

"She ever hit you before?"

Tharcia laughs. "On my butt, when I was a little kid. Not for years now. But she has never been like this before. Ever. She is deep different."

"Get you something to put on that," I tell her. "Come inside."

She follows in the back door. Lots of curious looks as we push through, the guys at her style, the ladies at her shiner. In the kitchen I grab a bowl of ice from the cooler, clean dishcloth, she follows up the stairs. Someone calls out, Clay you go bro. I ignore it. The bathroom up here I never use, bigger than the one downstairs and usually clean. I look at her face closely, touching gently around the bruise. She winces. I pack the cloth with ice and hold it to her eye, lift her hand so she holds it in place.

"So why'd you come here?" I ask, leaning against the counter.

"Something she won't expect."

"Any other reason?"

She shakes her head. Black eye and all, I'm taking in how she's like Montana at that age, but with a different quality. She maintains her calm, no matter what.

"Funny," she says out of nowhere, "at our place the other night I said to myself, you were the only person there who's not broken."

I look at her surprised. "No. You were."

"I'm a mess," she says. "You were the one."

I'm grinning now. "You're the healthy one. Want to fight about it?"

This gets half a smile. She takes a swig of her beer, holding the icepack to her face. Footsteps on the stairs. Dan, the kid with the bass is at the door.

"Clay we're taking off. Thanks man." He catches sight of Tharcia, looking at her face in the mirror. "Whoa, what happened here?"

Tharcia keeps her back turned, glances at him in the mirror. "Little family riff, no big."

"They have 911 for that ya know."

"Dude, I'll make a note of that," she says.

"Hey Clay," Dan goes on, "Rodrigo is passed out on your sofa."

I lift my glass. "All hail Rodrigo. His lady split?"

Dan shrugs, no idea, heads back down the stairs.

"It was a bad idea for me to come here," Tharcia says when Dan is out of earshot. "I've got to fix it up with Mom. But not until she's cooled off. She gets enraged, she turns into someone strange. All I can do is wait. She didn't mean it."

Downstairs there is the racket of goodbyes, instrument cases bumping out the door, dishes clattering in the sink. One loud crash.

"Take your time," I tell her. "I've got guests leaving. You need to be going yourself." I head down the stairs to wrap up the night.

"I'm staying," says a soft voice behind me.

"Leaving."

"Staying."

Women. She doesn't know it yet, but I am in charge here. Totally. She's leaving.

CHAPTER 6
RIDE THE STORM

I'M HUNG OVER this morning. So sue me. An occasional loud party is good for the soul. I'm sitting on the edge of the bed rubbing my face and trying to figure out where that funny sound is coming from. Somewhere inside the twisted up sheets and pillows must be my phone. Oh great. Montana.

"Gronk."

"You sound hung over. You shouldn't be drinking so much at your age."

"Hey look who's all full of sage advice. Gin girl."

"You should be grateful, it makes me horny."

"Sharpening a pencil makes you horny."

"Ah shove it. Did my daughter call you last night?"

What to say what to say? Truth, I decide, is easier to keep track of than Dare.

"Yes. Actually she was here for a while. Had a major shiner. What exactly happened?"

"None a yer biz Bozo. What happens in my house stays in my house."

Meanwhile I'm thinking I've got to warn her that Wolfe is wise to her lies. But then, she is not being that civil lately. Pluswhich, the way I'm being watched, the phone is not the place.

"A nurse friend of mine here looked her over. She wanted to file a report. Tharcia said no. You have one hell of a loyal girl there, you know that? She deserves better."

"Stuff it Stuka. Don't you lecture me on parenting. What I do with my daughter is none of your business."

"Doesn't seem like you, Montana. I never figured you for the battery type."

"It wasn't battery you moron I was trying to grab her keys and I slipped."

"Sure Montana, whatever. But you'll be talking out the other side of your face if she decides to file a complaint on you. Child abuse is serious."

"My Tharcia would never do that to me."

"Funny how kids wake up as they mature. Later."

I punch out asking myself, why would Montana call me, looking for her daughter? Unless she's calling everybody in her phone. Serve her right, sweat the bitch a little. Then I discover I'm a bit worried. Wondering where Tharcia went when she left here last night.

So I'm finally into jeans and a sweatshirt and the big room smells kinda funky. I open the door wide and Bomber steps in past me like I'm the butler. Cat cracks me up. Absolutely no expression on a cat's face, they say it all with body language. Couple cars still out there, which is typical. Now I see why the living room smells like something died. There's a dude's lying on the sofa. Fully dressed, leather jacket, boots and all. Gray beard sticking out. Two to one it's Rodrigo.

Finally I get coffee made and I'm playing the Warbirds game on my PC. Going over and over the startup sequence for a V-12 Merlin aircraft engine. Memorizing it. Hark, the toilet just flushed upstairs, so I have two sleepovers. Who did I miss? Well there's enough coffee.

I finally get this fighter plane off the runway, too sideways to survive in real life, and guess who wanders in?

The party I was just speaking about with Montana. I put the game on pause.

"I thought you left."

"I came back. Talked to your friend for a while. He's interesting. Seems lonely but he's used to it."

"Lots of folks like that in these hills. It's why they're here. Coffee?"

She follows my head tilt to the pot on the counter. Pours herself a cup. Same clothes she had on last night but she's done some makeup work. Her face looks a little powdery but it covers the bruise alright.

"We had agreed you were leaving, I know you remember."

She smirks at me over her cup. "Yes Stuka, we did. And I followed that agreement to the last letter."

It's my turn to grin. "Crafty. You only *think* you know what's up. And by the way mommie dearest is looking for you."

"Took the batts out of my phone. She'll be looking for a while."

"So you're a geek, too."

"I do all right."

I get up to refill my coffee, when I turn around, Bomber is in her lap.

"Maine Coon never does that," I say.

"You're joking, he slept with me."

"Hasn't slept with me for a while. Sometimes when it's cold out."

"Maybe you lost your aura."

I look at her. Smart. Beautiful. Screwed up mom. Wonder how much of it did and didn't rub off.

"Tell me something interesting," she says, getting comfortable on the chair.

"About what?"

"Stuka's undoubtedly sordid past."

I squint one eye to look at her. "On an interest scale of 1 to 10, would you like a two, or maybe a nice six?"

"Give me the nines and tens."

I think for a second about what I have to do that day. No lessons, no students, no need to drive till maybe later. Plus which I could use a little hair of the dog. From a top shelf I pull out a bottle of Glenmorangie single malt. Yah, purists, flame me, but I pour a generous glub-glub into my coffee. Usually better straight, for rolling over the tongue. I gesture with the bottle but she shakes her head no.

"Wait. I know," she laughs, "when you got busted."

I remember I had semi-foolishly been candid with her last time we had morning coffee. My life is noted for bragging stupidly to lovely women then paying big time.

"Okay, your call. That's at least a niner on the famous Clay Disaster scale." I take a sip of my laced coffee, lean back in my chair and think a sec.

"Okay this is going to bring you right up to date on little me and who the world thinks I am. For the moment."

She nods with a bemused expression. Thinking about it takes me back, I can see the streets, the kind of Southern California morning it was. She's sitting there with her coffee all calm with this expectant little grin.

"I hadn't liked the idea, not at first. But I'd scouted the route, a ten-mile run through Claremont neighborhoods and up Mt. Baldy, lightly-traveled twisty stuff with a couple of long tunnels. All I had to do was make a 30-second lead on any cops, then pull a magic trick. I doubted any cops would be behind me though.

"Just as with piloting gliders, I assumed everything could go wrong, and thought carefully through each step. Assume cops are there. Assume there are cop choppers too. I'd have the advantage of driving the route many times, of taking in-car videos and studying them over and over. The advantage of being ready. Thanks to the tunnels, those cars and helicopters wouldn't be a factor."

Looking at Tharcia's face it hits me. Last time I bragged to a woman like this it was her mom, who barged into the action and got me near arrested. Questioned for attempted murder. But what the bleep is wrong with me? Here, I'm showing off for this teener who is way too hot. Need to get her out of here.

"Anyway, getting a lead on the cars was easy, handling the choppers was easy. My car drives into the tunnel. My car drives out of the tunnel. My car crashes in spectacular fashion. The choppers miss a minor detail, don't see I'd stopped in the tunnel for about four seconds. Long enough to pull a mountain bike from the trunk, yank off my mechanic's coveralls and plop a cycling helmet on my head."

"What're y'all wearing?" Tharcia's eyes all full of mischief as she pops my reverie.

I grin back at her. "Oh, a way cute thong, says *Rupert the Friendly Lion* on it. Nah, I had bike racer gear. Popular cycling area, bikes are always coming down that hill. Anyway the car takes off empty, veers over the side and crashes all fiery into a ravine. Simple matter of a handheld radio controller. I headed downhill on the bike, looking totally credible in shocking pink spandex, stupid helmet, swigging from a water bottle. The money's in my fanny pack.

"So the police copter was totally focused on the car bouncing down the hill. Cops screaming up the road had no interest in me on the bike, they hurried up to the wreck. It was ninety minutes before they found the car had no driver."

She's leaning back grinning, makes a head gesture toward the bottle. I push it toward her and she helps herself. She's no piker I'll tell you that.

She takes a swallow of her laced coffee. "Single malt is more than just a breakfast drink, don't you think?"

I grin back at her. "Oh it does wonders as a hand sanitizer. Great for that pesky sore throat too."

"So you got away from the cops," she prompts.

"Clean. And by the time the cop cars all stop at the wreck, I'm over the side and down a steep canyon, several miles away under trees. Stash of hiking clothes there. A small dry bag slung from bungee cord, attached high in a tree. The fanny pack goes in the bag, I cut it loose, and the lot shoots out of sight into branches 60 feet up."

"What's in the bag? Did you know how much you were carrying?"

I shrug. "Wasn't very big. Fanny pack with the cash, probably a few hundred thousand. Someone else was supposed to pick it up later. I rode the bike farther down the riverbed, wiped it down and dismantled it, and walked out to a small restaurant, looking like any day hiker. Three dudes were supposed to come in, sit separately, and order Tsing Tao beer. It was our way of finding out who made it."

"But what were you guys doing, was it a robbery?"

"Dope deal. But some complication made the handoff late. My job was to collect a small package. Something unexpected though. There was a gunfight."

Now she looks serious. "You shoot anybody? You get shot at?"

"Well, I got away from the gunfight because of my research."

"Research?" She smiles hearing 'gunfight' and 'research' go together.

"Yah, it was near a busy mall in Claremont. I had looked the neighborhood over and decided to pick up the drop on a bike, not the car, because a car could get hemmed in too easy. There was a narrow fenced bridge leading into the mall garage, lots of people walking to their cars, cops couldn't shoot in there. I rode through the mall and three blocks to my car.

"I was in the car, leisurely heading up Mountain Avenue. My tail was clean, no one should have made me. But then magically there were three cop cars and two choppers on me. Something fishy about that too. Like there was a tracker on the car. But my escape was not based on getting away, it was based on deception. In the end I got away by bicycle."

"Lucky."

"Luck has nothing to do with it, schweetheart."

Tharcia's smiling, eyes sparkling. Eyes so easy to fall into. I've seen it before, awakening someone's attraction to a life of crime. It's the power. Always, it's the power to fool other people. The power to do and take what you want.

"I made it home anyway, back to my normal life. It was normal for exactly 41 hours, until the Hollister police came to take me away."

My coffee is cold, empty. She'd finished hers and set the cup down. Bomber had wandered off. She lets out her breath with a kind of relieved sigh. "You got caught?" She sounds incredulous.

"That's exactly the way I felt about it. I couldn't have been traced, no bleeding way. Somebody tipped 'em. And I know who."

There's a feeble groan from the sofa. I go to the pot and start more coffee. By the time Rodrigo gets approximately vertical, we're at the kitchen table pushing eggs around our plates with sprouted wheat toast. Say one thing for her, she may be slim but an appetite she's definitely got.

Rodrigo sits, scratching his beard, smiling and looking stupefied. She says good morning with a smile. "Me and Rodrigo are old buds, we talked about banjo picking last night."

"Lunatic."

Rodrigo, leaning over his coffee cup at the table, is taking small fast slips as if looking for the one that'll save his life.

"So any theories on who bummed your trip?"

"Had to be Mick, one of the guys involved."

"Who is Mick? Is that the McIntyre in your story?"

"Mmhmm. He got 8 to 12 in Lancaster. They can keep him there long's they want."

Tharcia's face goes white around the bruise. "OMG, do you think this Mick knows my mom?"

I nod. That right there is an entire saga of deception, duplicity and betrayal. I'll tell her sometime maybe but not today.

"Mick. Mick. McIntyre." She's saying the name over and over like she's tasting it. Her head comes up. "Micmac!"

The picture clicks into focus. A child's name for her daddy, before she could spell or pronounce McIntyre. Of course. It was Mick who lived with Montana those years after she returned to San Jose. It was Mick who Tharcia thought was her dad. And could in fact be. No telling what Montana has been up to, ever.

"When was the last time you saw Micmac?"

Her face has clouded over, unhappy memories shoving through. "When we moved out of his house to the one we have now. Nine years. Mom never mentions him."

"Well, the Mick I know is in prison."

"You said."

Rodrigo rouses, heaves to his feet, tucking his blue plaid shirt into jeans which have the most tentative hold on his narrow hips. "I'll just leave you two kids in peace. Nice ta meet ya, Farsical." He stumbles out the door headed toward the road.

Tharcia is chuckling into her hand like she'll pop a gasket. I get up and stretch. This is way too much for my morning brain.

"Well now I can put it together," she says, "why he never visits. Why Mom doesn't really see many people, except for the one-nighters. Oop, sorry, no offense Stuka."

"None taken. Seems we both understand Montana." I give her a wink.

She nods. "He's in prison, she's waiting for him." That look on her face is completely without judgment, rancor, accusation, any of the dozen other emotions a kid could have about her mother's tweaked-out love life. Or missing out on her own personal needs.

I look at her. Thinking I could lecture Montana just fine on parenthood. "She ever go to Lancaster for a visit?"

"No idea. She goes everywhere for work though, I could totally miss it."

"You ever visit him yourself?"

Shakes her head emphatically. I see the time is pushing on for ten. "Ya know, I have a date with an airplane. Gotta motate."

"Oh, you're dating airplanes now? I have heard of people dating rocks."

"It's slightly easier than dating a rock climber."

"Hey! I am a rock climber."

"Well then how 'bout a week from Saturday?"

She cocks her head at me with a *watch it dude* expression. "Aren't you hanging with my mom?"

"Sunday, then?" I sigh. Fun is fun. But. "Tharcia, I think your mom and me were just tripping on memory lane."

She looks at me, serious. "Like her don't ya?"

"Busted," I nod. "I did once. Too many complications and other boyfriends."

"Yah. You'll find the right one."

I say nothing, reminded of my laser focus on simply vanishing. But the mention of airplanes starts her asking about my flying, teaching, how I got started, what it means to me, and so on. Interesting kid. She has a lot on her mind and seems genuinely interested in people. So we chat through another round of coffee, minus the Scotch. I won't be piloting today but I want my senses intact for what I'm about to do.

"Can I talk to you, Clay?"

"What we've been doing."

"No, Stuka." She leans forward in her chair. "I feel I can talk to you. I need to say something."

"Sure, OK."

She takes a deep breath, then goes right to the heart of it. "My mom hitting me the other night spilled this out. I cried last night. It was hard."

"I didn't hear you."

"I sat in my car. Until it was over. Then I came in and fell asleep upstairs."

I lean forward. "Tharcia, what is it?"

Another deep breath, uncertain. "I was abused by one of Mom's boyfriends." She stops. She's looking hard at me like she just succeeded at a difficult task. I nod slowly and wait, jaw clenching. This is the worst. There is nothing I can say. All I can do is look at her, the sadness of her bruised face.

"I'm glad you stayed," I say quietly. "You getting any help with this?"

She nods. "I have a dear friend, a psychologist and child counselor. She's helped me through a lot."

"Is it possible to make any headway? Can you feel better?"

"Some. It's better every year. Sometimes things just go black, to feel so worthless like this."

Sitting closer to her, I put my hand on hers. Practically whispering I say, "You, worthless? You're courageous."

She shakes her head. "I'm like a scared rabbit sometimes."

"You realize how important it is? Telling someone it happened?"

"It's what my therapist always says." Abruptly she slams the table with her palm. "I am worthwhile. Nothing was wrong with me. My mother made me shut up about it!"

To me this is ten times worse than Montana hitting her. "She made you shut up? Did you tell anyone?"

Tharcia looks down, face hidden behind her falling hair. "Only my mom. She said we don't talk about things like that."

"But when? How long did you have to wait to talk about it?"

"When I was a senior."

"High school."

"Mm."

"So your treatment is what, couple years on?"

She nods yes. Now it's my turn to get furious. I walk a couple fast laps to the living room window and back. I yell.

"Arrrgh! That stupid little twit left you to suffer! How dare she! How fucking dare she!"

Tharcia gives me a minute to wind down.

"This happened when?"

"I was nine."

"For a long time, or only once?"

"Couple months. Weird punishments, spankings when Mom was at work."

"Did you tell your mom?"

"She saw bruises."

"What happened then?"

"She screamed at him. He left. Next day we went to a motel."

Again I am furious with Montana, and whichever of her lunatic boyfriends is responsible. "Why did you tell me? I am glad you did, but why me?"

"It's part of my therapy to stop hiding it. I felt I could trust you."

"Ah. Could you share with me who this person is?"

"We already mentioned him."

Even before she says the name, I know. Before she comes out with it I have already consigned that person to the blackest depths of hell. Forever.

"You said..."

"Micmac," Tharcia says. Tears shimmer. "Mom's old boyfriend, Mick McIntyre."

CHAPTER 7
INTERVIEW WITH A MONSTER

I'M EMOTIONALLY WRUNG OUT as I point my El Camino down Highway 1 to 129 and out 25 for Hollister airport. But I'm not headed for the gliderport. Today I drive around to the other side where the big hangars are, and the power planes. After the convo with Tharcia about her childhood abuse, I need a lot of cheering up. I can't imagine what it will take for her. Something inside me aches, and I can't find it.

So here I am staring up at a working example of the best American prop fighter of World War II, the North American P-51 Mustang. It was the first long-range bomber escort, used by the Tuskegee Airmen and several thousand other brave pilots. The P-51, flown by the Army Air Force before the Air Force became a separate branch of the military. I have an original maintenance manual on DVD, and believe me I've been through it a few times. About half the aircraft parts I ship are P-51 parts. There are fewer than 200 of these aircraft still flying, and I'm about to go for a ride in one.

With slender wings and sleek fuselage wrapped around a powerful Rolls-Royce Merlin V-12, the Mustang fighter is fast and agile, and a royal handful for the unwary pilot. I've done my share of reading on this aircraft, plus flying the sims on my computer. Every time, I learn something. For example, when both internal and external tanks are loaded, such as to fly from England to Berlin and back, the P-51 could be downright treacherous on takeoff. Especially if the fuselage tank behind the pilot is full. That balance thing again.

Come to find out when I looked this owner up, he's a customer of my parts business! I can practically recite the various components he's bought from me, because this version is rare. Sean is telling me about his ship.

"It's a rare Mustang, the TRF-51D two-seat trainer conversion of an F-6D, which is the armed photo recon version. It's a very down to earth airplane, not difficult to fly or hard to handle. But it will bite hard if you're clueless."

I am dying to know exactly how he defines *clueless* and am semi-hearing him as we walk around her. Lots larger than they look on video, or my PC simulator games, damn thing is 37 feet across the wingtips. Prop is 11 feet in diameter, four massive blades with squared-off tips.

"Two thousand horse the way I have this one tricked out. Thanks to the supercharger parts and pistons you found for me." Sean says this with an appreciative grin.

At last the gab is over and I'm settling down in the front cockpit. First thing I notice is the nose. It sticks out there a long way. I'm 5 feet 11 and although I'm in the front seat I am not going to see over that nose. From the front seat of a glider you can see the ground a few feet ahead. This bird sits back on its tail wheel so the nose is already pointing at the sky. Sean, getting set in the aft cockpit, tells me you have to use the rudder and make S-turns to see where you are going during taxi.

He's clicking and punching things back there. Levers and knobs move in my cockpit, showing me what he does, after all it's a trainer. I point my small vidcam at everything. Sean sets primer, the automatic mixture, and engages the starter. The whole plane jumps as the prop starts to turn. He counts to six out loud as the squared-off blades pass, then he throws the magnetos to the BOTH marker. Like playing a complicated instrument, he hits the fuel boost pump switch to the left of the starter, then the electric primer to the right with another finger switch. The mixture lever in my cockpit moves up into the NORMAL position.

The whole plane shudders, then there's this ferocious dragon roar and the blades become a blur. All kinds of black smoke belching out both sides of the nose, blowing by the cockpit. My insides are vibrating, the sound goes right through me.

Sean taxis us out to the run-up area of runway 3-1 and does his engine checks at 2300 RPM. Magnetos, prop, Simmonds regulator, supercharger, carb air, radiator air, a dozen switches to set. I won't remember them, they are on the checklist, and now on my video. The thought of starting one of these on my own is sobering. How would it be if I were sitting here alone right now, behind this huge engine bellowing a challenge at the sky?

I hear Sean through my headset, making his radio call to take the active runway. He puts us on the centerline, sets rudder trim. He pulls the stick aft of neutral to lock the tail wheel, pushes in on the throttle quadrant and the manifold pressure comes up to about 40 inches. Brakes off, we start to accelerate, Sean adds boost up to 55 inches and we're pushed into our seats hard.

At this point the world's only sound is that V-12 up front. The six exhaust stacks each side of the nose are lined up with my head and it is deafening. I see how Sean anticipates the nose wanting to swing left by easing in right rudder. That's the propeller torque. I'm lightly following through on stick and pedals, to feel what a real warbird pilot feels. We're heading down the runway much faster than I ever do in a glider, and about eight feet farther off the runway, the landing gear is so tall. Sean eases the stick forward when we hit about 100 MPH. The fuselage comes level, I can see ahead.

It gets quieter as we lift away, but not that quiet. We're flying now. Sean starts cleaning up the ship: gear up, flaps retracted, power back to 46 inches boost and the engine note drops to 2700 RPM. We're doing about 190 MPH in a steady climb and it feels like she can keep it up all day. We're at 3000 feet already. On tow in a glider at this point I'd just be clearing the hills at the end of the runway.

What a feeling! A light airframe, enormous torque and combat-grade aerobatic capability. And, I remind myself, a potentially treacherous aircraft in the hands of an amateur. That's a humbling thought, and the rest of the ride, great as it is, takes on a threatening cast.

Amateur = me.

But unbelievably, Sean lets me take the controls. I do some turns, some climbs, a couple dives, not very steep. This aircraft is your literal Bat out of Hell, but smooth and predictable, I am loving it! Visibility from the cockpit is good, I get over looking at every dial knob and switch and just fly her by feel and she's beyond sensational. I can do it, I can fly this aircraft. I put us in a 70-degree bank and we pull about five gees and the feeling is incredible. Can't wait to tell Wade about this! And we can't wait forever for his nutter pilot friend to show up. Something says it might be up to me, and an inner voice, a very brave one, says bring it on!

We make a pass over runway 3-1, and Sean says something unexpected through the phones. "You have this pretty solid. Want to land it?"

"Oh hell yes," is my instant reply. That's when the sweat starts to roll.

"Fine. I'll follow through and take care of airspeed, flaps, gear and such. You just set us down, three wheels. Stall her in from a couple feet at about 100."

I fly a normal pattern from 1200 feet, turn base very late to give me a longish final leg so I'll have plenty of time to line her up. Sean handles the countless other tasks. I am glad my video camera is on! Every throttle adjustment I make requires a change in rudder trim, and although I see it happen, I am damn glad Sean is on it.

I can't tell if it was a classic three-point landing, but Sean is pleased with the result. At least we don't bounce. Climbing down from the high cockpit, I shake hands energetically. What he says next blows me away.

"What planes do you fly, Clay?"

"Gliders. Tandem and singles."

"Single engine?"

"Gliders, purely. No power."

Sean gives me an appraising look. "You got a good touch, Clay."

So, go ahead and make my decade. Later, after my exhilarating kilobuck joyride, I'm sitting in my El Camino looking over the video I just took. Even on the small screen I can tell there's a ton of training in that 35 minutes and I'll go over it time and time again.

I drive around to the gliderport office, not because I have a schedule today, but because I like to say hello to folks. Nice group of people out here, lived their lives around aviation, very solid and dependable. And there's one in particular I always like to see.

Late on a calm Sunday morning, the rich folks are just starting to stir. In the office Julie looks up from the counter with a smile. She's talking to a new student about the books, manuals and charts he needs to begin training in gliders. Place the school uses for an office is a relic of the 1940s when it was part of an Army training compound during WWII. I can see past Julie into Stacy's office, peek in and Stacy is there. I tap lightly. She looks up and her face changes, but not in the way it's supposed to when she first sees me. She looks at me for a long moment, leans back, finally summons a kinda-sorta smile.

"Clay. How's it going?"

I grin at her. "Can't complain, how's by you?"

Stacy now looks more than merely uncomfortable. "Would you get that door? Thanks."

In spite of the gloomy overtones, I don't mind closing the door and being in private with her. We've had some times together, great ones. When I get a better look at her face, seems like she's genuinely upset.

"Hey girl, what's up?"

"Clay this is very difficult. The school has to let you go." She delivers this straight, rehearsed, not cold but not too warm either.

"Stace, what?"

"There have been questions, Clay. Too many questions. The NTSB has been around, Hollister police have been around, San Jose detectives, your parole person..."

"Montana? Agent Harrison?"

Stacy nods. Ice of jealousy tugs at her lips. "The DEA has been around talking to us. Agents were here again just this morning. They are all groping for something, Clay. You are a fine pilot and a super trainer. We've really depended on your expertise the last ten years." She doesn't mention the three-year gap when I was locked up. "I hope that sometime in the future..." Her voice trails off. "Clay right now we have to take a break. I'll send your final check."

At this point she looks down and brings a hand to her forehead. I know what she's thinking. Not only the job here, the great relationships with the school personnel, but all the promise several years back when she and I were talking. But that was before prison. Thanks again, Mick.

Should have been easy, after three years behind bars, to come out into society and not form any attachments. But Stacy gave me my old job back. And just being around her, well, she's so damn easy to be with.

"So I'm off the schedule as of now?"

Still looking down, she barely nods. I think for a second. There's nothing here at the school that's mine, no desk to clear out, everything comes and goes in my flight bag. I take a deep breath.

"Stacy. I get it. You need to protect your business. I'm down with that. I wish things could be different too. I'll miss you. We'll talk sometime."

She nods. The scrape of my chair on bare wood puts a ragged end to the conversation. On a whole nice chunk of my messed-up little life. She's not looking up. Silently, I leave the office.

Walking out into the sunlight, I barely have time to draw a deep breath when I take in this scene at the curb. Parked behind my El Camino is a dark DEA car like the one visited me after my flight with Roswell. Man in a dark suit, leaning against the car, looking down as he flips through his phone.

Second man, the driver, jumps out as he sees me, walks toward me with aggressive purpose. I've got one on each side of me now, hands poised to take my elbows if I don't walk directly to their car. All right, I'm thinking to myself, play this out.

All three of us get in the back. Sandwich-style and I'm the filling. I wonder if Stacy sees from inside. It will only make her more settled in her decision.

"You got a hard head," one of them is saying. Deep bass voice, growly. I have seen this dude at the probation department, what's his name? These are not DEA. They are from Mick.

The other one speaks with more of a Boston accent, more direct.

"CEO doesn't like it when people don't return his calls." Without elaborating, this burly fellow pulls out a phone, dials, listens.

"Yo, M, we got your dude right here." He hands the phone to me with a menacing expression. I look at it for a second. Burner phone, untraceable. I raise it to my ear.

"Somebody wanna tell me why these fake DEA suits have me in the back of a car?"

The laugh on the other end I last heard four years ago, no mistake. Mick McIntyre. If the world is not totally out of shape, Mick is somewhere inside the concrete walls, chain-link, bars and barbwire of Lancaster prison, doing Fed time for major drug distribution.

"Only one person can really take care of you Sonny, and that's me."

"Like the way you took care by giving me up. Asshole."

The suits on either side of me cringe then start sending out aggressive male vibes but don't really know what to do. They do know nobody talks to Mick like this. Ever.

"Sonny, Sonny, you are too mean. You don't know what's good for ya. You know the best thing was for both of us to be inside. That's where we could keep on building our team. I've had to do it without you, but I must say it's worked out okay. There is still a place in the organization for you Sonny, we just have to work it out."

Super charming dude, real charisma, voice full of warmth and confidence, covering raspy-edged steel that will show when you cross him. It's been two decades since me and McIntyre first met, at a gas station in Hollister. I was filling my Yamaha trail bike, Montana on the back showing off her ass in tight black leather.

We'd talked bikes, hot cars, racing. McIntyre had wanted to buy my Yamaha, or so he said. Hot eyes for Montana's bootie. But the man had kept in touch. We got to know each other, McIntyre became interested in my ability with electronics, in the oddball gadgets and model race cars I built. Few months later he'd mentioned a "little job." Just pop some idiot, he said, and make twenty large. I'm a high school kid who had recently lost his dad, totally susceptible to the charm of a powerful older male and thinking I'm immortal, as teenagers do. I come back to the present.

"Yah we'll work it out soon's I get my hands on your throat."

Mick laughs, this time sounding more dangerous. "Listen to you. You fucked up big time. You were s'pose to give me the location of your drop when we were at the restaurant."

Oh I get it, this goes back to the drug run. "Like hell, Mick. I was there. You were there looking right at me. You walked away. That wasn't even the plan."

"No it was you that screwed up. That's why I wanted you inside so the hiding place would be our little secret. Now you are out and my guy already located your little stash."

"Okay then where was it?"

Mick stalls, I am sure he is bluffing. The way I hid the stash made it damned hard to locate. He goes on.

"You don't improvise on my jobs, see? You were supposed to pick up your package in the car. You rode up on a bike. Amazing they didn't pop you. They handed you the wrong one."

"Mick you been around too many hacks, you're thinking like one. I did what we agreed." He's trying to make it okay that he fingered me.

Mick only laughs, more menacing than before. "Something you gotta do to get back on the team Sonny boy. Ask Esteban for the envelope."

This can't be good. I look at the guys sitting on both sides of me. "The envelope." One of the suits reaches into the front, comes back with a bulging manila package. It drops heavy in my lap.

"And just what's this?" I say to Mick.

"Your dues brah, your assignment. Just like the old days. Check it out."

Juggling the phone I rip open the envelope. Inside are three photographs and a vicious-looking pistol and loaded clip in a clear Ziploc bag. I look at the photos. First one's a suit, pasty looking face, nothing exciting. No idea who. I look at the second one. I get the drift right away and I'm furious. Seeing this photo, my instant desire is taking a baseball bat to Mick's head.

It's Montana. Shot from across the street near the Adult Services Division on North First. She's on her phone looking hot in slacks and a thin sweater, unaware she is being watched. I look at the third photo. Just like 20 years ago, Mick's usual *modus operandi*, a clean gun, photo of the hit, photos of all the people he will hurt if I don't follow through. Then, it was my mom. Now...

It's Tharcia. Picture taken on her own front porch, holding a coffee cup. I remember that cup, the way she had her hair, the shirt she had on. I was there. They were watching us! I'm instantly yelling salty profanity into the phone.

"You insane moron, whaddya wanta do this for?"

"It's just business brah. You scratch my back I scratch yours."

I grab a minute to think before I answer. "You might be done with Montana, I get that. Maybe after all this time you figure she's in your way. But I know the deal between you and Tharcia. She's your kid. If anybody is in a position to hurt her it's not you. She's with me, Micmac." I sneer out the name.

Now it's Mick's turn to yell at a phone. I'd guessed right. Tharcia's childhood name for him gets his attention big city. I have a quick impression of the guys on either side of me squirming uncomfortable, seeing some nobody face down their big boss. Thinking maybe, can we get in trouble for this?

On the other end he's screaming loud profanity, I hear crashes in the background like he's wrecking shit. Let him destroy his cell. He can think about me later while he's picking up the pieces. I already played my Ace in this convo and I'm hoping we're done. It was one thing to get me as an 18-year-old kid to take a silencer pistol and pop somebody for what seemed all the money in the world. A kid who was arrogant and stupid enough to take his low-impulse-control girlfriend along for a high. She is the damn reason I missed, not that I'm unhappy about that. But it's a different story now, I'm on probation, ready to trade my life for a fresh one if I can't legally prove I'm innocent. And here's this career smuggler wants to suck me back into my sordid past. Not going to happen.

And I'm furious as never before at anyone, the fresh memory of Tharcia's sorrowful and angry words about what this abuser did to her as a child. I come close to going off on Mick with what I know, but then I think, wait. Just you wait.

We're on the phone like that for another few minutes, mostly swearing back and forth at each other while the fake DEA suits inch away from me. Finally Mick pulls out his hole card. He summons an evil laugh, smoothing over the fact that I made him lose control.

"We know where your brother is, asshole. So if you know what's good for you you'll take that package and you'll deliver. The schedule is there."

"Which brother you talking about? Is it Wade, or is Cassius?"

Mick is silent. Finally he snarls out a name, just before he clicks off.

Furious, I sling the phone at the windshield. Before it stops bouncing around inside the car I'm giving one of the suits an elbow, hard. He's moving, jumping out, letting me past. The interview is over. There are wins and losses, neither of us has a clear victory. We all notice though, as

I'm stomping back to my El Camino, I do have the envelope with the gun and photos.

But as I exit the scene leaving two dark patches and a cloud of tire smoke, I'm the only one knows there's no brother named Cassius. It's my own middle name. I have only one brother. And these days, his name isn't Wade.

CHAPTER 8
THE GAME'S AFOOT

AFTER TODAY'S MENTAL BEATINGS, fired by my friend Stacy then hired for a 'job' by my enemy Mick, I'm relieved to get home. Thinking what I'll tell them at unemployment. *Oh, the flying school let me go after my student killed himself.*

Great.

I see by the lights that the twins are in the swimming pool, taking care of biz. I'd like to sit with them and trim for a mindless chore, but working in there is too dangerous for me. The amount of THC I'd take in from breathing and touching plants would show in a piss test, which for a parolee can be any random time.

The wind is coming up, maybe a blow tonight, weather's finally acting like November. I'm so juiced, not into sitting around the house trying to figure out why this blew into my life, so I tog up and get out my trusty KHS Tucson twenty-niner. A ride I like follows shady roads uphill from Felton to the redwood forests of the Santa Cruz mountains. Most of the time there's scant car traffic, except for Highway 9 from Boulder Creek back to Felton. Since that part is mostly downhill it's easy to stay ahead of cars. There is one steep section, a long climb along Felton Empire Road and then continuing along Empire Grade. It's about 30 miles, elevation change over 2500 feet, I expect it to take maybe two hours.

Everything is fine I'm zooming along the dirt trails, the 29 inch wheels are soaking up the bigger bumps with ease. I see a couple riders ahead of me and I'm catching them so I push a little harder. After a while I'm close, the trailing guy is glancing sideways whenever he gets a chance to see who's back there.

I call out I want to come through. Next switchback the guy slows on the outside, lets me by. Calls out a name, telling the guy ahead someone's coming up behind. Someone is me. Other guy doesn't slow down, not letting me pass. There's a place down lower, where knowing how to use the brakes hard is a real advantage. The KHC brakes let me wait really late coming to that switch back, I get next to the guy, scoot down the inside of the curve and take him. Rear tire scuffs sideways a little as I power out.

Now it's the red mist before my eyes. Didn't think I'd go flat-out this ride but all the frustration fear and anxiety I felt since Roswell's glider stunt, him showing up dead, Montana, Wolfe, Tharcia, Stacy, Mick and all the rest of it being swallowed by my speed down these twisty trails.

Guys behind can't see me anymore. I push harder anyway. On pavement again, the downgrade from Boulder Creek back toward Felton, my legs are starting to tire, but my lungs feel great. Coming across a little bridge, easily staying ahead of some folks back there in a station wagon, I encounter my first difficulty of the ride. A thin stream of water coats the road for a few feet, hard to see in the waning daylight. All at once the rear wheel says bye-bye, sliding out to the side. Nothing to do but correct and let the front end follow where the back is headed. Which happens to be a muddy ditch at the foot of a dirt embankment.

I lunge for a couple small trees on the loose slope. The bike disappears somewhere while I get the shit slapped out of me by rocks and branches, finally I roll over backwards a couple of times and slam into a fat boulder. Knocks the breeze out of me that's for sure. My head is ringing like a gong.

I get up, trying to find the bike. I can't it's too dark here under the trees, which by now are swaying in rising wind. Long story short I hobble back up to the road and wait for a bike to come by. Guy and a gal stop, with their lights help me find my Tucson. The back wheel is toast, tire's off the rim, which is bent, broken spokes. And here I am six miles from home. I cross the road and start walking the bike downhill. Wobble wobble. Something's dripping down my leg. I dig a light out of my saddle pack and sure enough it's blood. I wrap a spare sock around the cut on my calf and keep going, but walking my bent bike along this road is stupid. At a wide spot I flip through my phone trying to figure how I can get some help here. Lo and behold there's a text from nrrdgrrl, three hours ago.

My reply is simple and to the point.

Stuka109: *You there?*

nrrdgrrl: *hey (smiley)*

Stuka109: *just had a major crash in my bike. Where you guys at?*

nrrdgrrl: *my fave thai place los gatos - you hurt?*

Stuka109: *feel like taking a ride to Felton?*

nrrdgrrl: *ok sure what's your 20?*

I send her my GPS coordinates.

I continue walking the bike, but thankfully she makes great time, pulls up in a steel gray Dodge crew cab 15 minutes later. She's the passenger, I can't see who's driving. Throw my bike in the back, pile in next to her.

"Stuka, this is Rayne."

"Hey Stuka. Don't bleed all over my floor mat. LOL." Tharcia's friend is dark-haired, athletic like she is.

Soon enough we're pulling up at my place. House is dark, wind is howling through the trees. We get out, the truck lights go off, it's pitch black. I look up.

The sky is clear and what I see overhead are sprinkled suns amid dark shapes of thrashing trees. For a minute I can't move, just stand there staring. Tharcia is next to me, she looks up too. Rayne walks over and the three of us gaze up at the sky. No matter how many times I see this it's magic. And this idiotic nonsense I'm doing isn't that important. Except to me.

We get ourselves in the house, I'm sitting on the edge of the bathtub. Pink blood rinsing down the drain. Turns out I'm also filthy in my riding tights, mud guck up one side and down the other. Rayne gets a good look at me, curses, grabs a towel and runs outside to her truck.

"Dayum," I say to Tharcia, "I hope she's not mad." Her bruise is looking better today, the eye not so swollen.

"She'll get over it."

"Thanks a ton for coming out. Hope I didn't interrupt anything."

"We were just about to stop at a restaurant."

"Hey, you guys meat eaters? I've got a bunch of leftover ribs and corn. We could make a salad. Scotch and beer."

She puts her hand on my shoulder looking down at the cut on my calf. Her touch is electric, like Montana's, but in a calming way.

"We're on it." she says. "I'm starved."

"Tell you what, you guys get that together. I'll be along after a shower."

Later were sitting around the kitchen table picking at the last of the ribs. I'm sipping on a little Scotch, Rayne and Tharcia are working on some Merlot I dug out. Tharcia asks what it was like to know her mother in her teens. I tell them a little about the love-hate-sex addiction we had, and Rayne starts describing a paper for one of her classes, about the basis of physical attraction. She's also enrolled at San Jose State, about to grad in biology, but they know each other from much farther back. I find it interesting that Rayne's coloring so resembles Montana's. Dark hair, pearl skin.

"It's not only facial features that determine attractiveness," Rayne begins. "Sure, distinctive features like eyes, nose, mouth, smooth skin are all important. One of the biggest factors is facial symmetry. But there are other things, such as the walk, the way shoulders and hips move together. One of the things we try to figure out when picking sex partners and mates is, will this person live long enough to raise young ones, are their genes good enough to mix with mine?"

"Which of course are superior," Tharcia puts in. They share a laugh looking into each other's faces. The voltage is there.

"Then there's scent, or in the case of men, male odor," Rayne says wryly, eyes flashing. Tharcia cracks up. I can't help but grin.

"When it comes to smell, a lot of the information about genetic compatibility is in the histamine system. There is a complex of 100 genes that tell us about the other person's immunities, all communicated through body odor. It's because those genes determine which bacteria can live on our skin, and therefore what diseases we'll be immune to.

"All of this processing, not just through smell but through vision hearing and touch, is related to the overall emotion we feel around someone. Biological basis of sex appeal."

"Ta-Da!" Says Tharcia, I give you Dr. Rayne Chuley, Ph.D."

I say musingly, "I'm descended from a long line my mother should never have listened to."

"Totally believable," Rayne laughs. She's taking little jabs at me, or at men in general. She fastens onto the point. "Persuasion works too, but not so much from a distance.

It's why some people are born sales types, the gift of gab fills the gap when natural attraction is less."

"I saw a documentary where women smelled T-shirts collected from men after working out," I say. "The adjectives they used were telling."

"Telling or smelling?" Rayne jibes.

"Tell you guys what stinks," I'm coming back to my own private hell. "Got fired today at the gliderport."

Rayne looks like she wants to keep going on her topic, but says, "Harsh, dude."

Tharcia rests a hand on my arm. "Stuka, I am so so sorry. What happened?"

"Stacy feels there's too much attention around the suicide jumper. I totally see her point, bad for the school. Problem for me, because I'm on probation, is now your mom's going to be trying to get me a job, which will probably be a stupid job, take up a lot of my time looking for a stupid job, and I'll probably have to go for more interviews with my dear case officer. Not the picture I was hoping for. I'm going to keep this from your mom as long as I can."

Rayne has been listening in silence for quite a while, head going back and forth from me to Tharcia like at a tennis match.

"You are on probation?" Rayne asks evenly. Her suspicious look could have been copied from Montana. I just nod. Tharcia nods too, looking at Rayne with a glum expression. For a moment it is silent in the kitchen.

"Wild Thing," Rayne says. "Can I see you a minute?"

Tharcia says sure, excuse us, they go out on the porch. Blustery wind blows through the door. I throw more wood in the woodstove, begin clearing the plates. I can hear them talking some, mostly swallowed up by the wind. They come back in and sit. I glance over from where I'm rinsing a dish in the sink.

"We all cool?"

Rayne looks at me. "No were not all cool. I want to know what's going on. Ever since Thursday I see Tharcia, all she can talk about is Clay this Clay that. Then Friday I see her, all she can talk about is Stuka, Stuka, Stuka. Who are you and where you coming from? You're on probation? What did you do? Who the hell are you?"

She says this last part all desperate, like she's ready to cry. I turn around and look at the two of them. I am strangely gratified that Montana's daughter mentioned me to her friend. Tharcia is somber, worried, looking at Rayne.

Ah-hah. Something here I didn't see before, the picture about them.

"I get it. You guys are together."

Both of them nod, looking from me to each other. Tharcia gives me a grateful smile, looks over at Rayne, reaches for her hand. "We are," she says. "Aren't we?"

"You fucking well better believe it," Rayne says hotly, tossing a challenging look my way. Another tumbler ticks into place. She's jealous.

"And you, Tharcia, you. Now I find out you slept here last night. And the way you touch him." She shoots Tharcia an angry glance, doubting, uncertain.

"Rayne, it's okay." I sit down at the table, smiling at them. "You guys are flat out in love with each other. How long since you had the talk?" I place a certain emphasis on the words, *the talk*. Every couple has one, when they get it they're gonna be together.

"Two months."

I see it. A new relationship, confidence not yet strong, inclined to be private and protective. They'd had plans for the two of them this evening, I'm an intruder and messed that up and Rayne's alarms are all going off.

"First of all, both of you are always welcome here." For Rayne's benefit, I fill in a few high points of my incarceration, my parole, again asserting my innocence.

"But what are you doing hanging out with Tharcia's mom?"

"Me and Montana were friends in school years ago."

"You call her Montana?"

"And other unprintable stuff. But Rayne, you don't need to be jealous of me."

"I'm not," she says defiantly.

"You said you are, in so many words."

"Oh, well, Tharcia's mom keeps wanting to bust us up. What the fuck do you want with her?" She's looking hot daggers my way.

I look at Tharcia, shaking my head slowly. "I just don't know." There's a connection neither of us can name.

Tharcia grins. "He listens to me." Then she says, apropos of nothing, "do you have a high school yearbook?"

Makes me think. I have been getting rid of stuff lately. "Somewhere upstairs there are some boxes. Might be around."

Tharcia looks at me appraisingly, her eyes down to slits. In the other room, my phone is chirping. When I pick it up, I am so delighted. Montana.

"What are you doing?" she demands without preamble.

"Washing my dishes. Want to dry?"

"You know we're seeing Wolfe tomorrow, three o'clock."

"How could I forget? You want to have coffee before that."

"You got it."

There's a silence. Then, cautiously, "Hear from my daughter today?"

"Your daughter is sitting right here with her friend. We're having a beer."

"She's there? With who? Who with?"

"Rayne."

Montana curses under her breath. "I have told her they're not to hang together. I want you to send her home right away."

"Jeez Mon, grab a brain. She's eighteen not eight."

"Nineteen," yells Tharcia from the kitchen. Rayne laughs and whispers something.

"You stay out of it Stuka. That girl is a bad influence on her. So are you."

"Hey look. I'm not messing in your family crappola. You guys work it out. Later."

"I want to know where my jewelry is," Montana gets out as I hit the bye-bye button.

Walk back in the kitchen, Tharcia's sitting on Rayne's lap, looking into her eyes and winding a strand of dark hair around one finger. They've been whispering quietly together while I was talking to Montana. Tharcia kisses Rayne soft on the lips, then moves back to her chair. I have a momentary image of how sweet they must be together. And jealousy? It's me that's jealous of Rayne, not the other way round. *Wild Thing.*

"Nineteen, eh? Thought you were eighteen."

"My birthday was yesterday, you had a big party to celebrate." Tharcia smiles.

"Hey, you didn't play the birthday card. But I'm in the double doghouse with your mom. Not only are you here at my place but your banned girlfriend is with you. What's up with that?"

"My mom," Tharcia says, "is less than open-minded."

"To put it mildly," Rayne adds.

"That bites. And her birthday gift to you was a shiner."

Tharcia finds this funny. "Stuka, it feels so normal," she says, "hanging here with you."

"Way different from my folks too," Rayne adds. They are nodding agreement at each other. I get that Rayne is a few years older. I'm sure she sees Tharcia as a gift from the mystic universe, one she's waited a lifetime for. No wonder she's edgy.

My phone goes again. I can't believe my luck. Wolfe. Who next, Mick?

"What?"

"Good evening Mr. Clay, so sorry to disturb you. So happens I have an urgent matter to attend to. In your neighborhood, as it works out. Will it be convenient for me to drop by in a short while?"

"I'm actually having a quiet social evening, detective. If you don't mind. Private. We are meeting tomorrow afternoon, correct?"

"Mr. Clay I do hope you understand, a matter of some delicacy has come up. I need to speak to you directly."

I sigh. "Knock yourself out. I'll be here."

Looking up from the phone, I see headlights cutting through the trees outside. Wolfe already? I walk out on the porch waiting for him to park. Stiff wind blowing now, small branches and other debris fill the air. Car parks, someone gets out, definitely not Wolfe, his jeans aren't that tight. Dayum, Montana made good time. Or is it because, like the night Roswell got shot, she was magically just around the corner? And recalling my convo with Tharcia the night before, I am so pissed at Montana I can't think straight. She's become a major lowlife in my view and I am completely unsympathetic to anything she might want.

"Drop in any time. Were you down at the pizza joint?"

"Where's Tharcia?"

"Inside talking to Rayne."

"That little twat." No idea which one she means.

"Verbal abuse is abuse, dim bulb. You had better start thinking straight about your daughter."

"What the fuck you talking about Cicero?"

"I need to know something," I tell her. "What were you doing in Santa Cruz the night Roswell was shot?"

"Screw you bozo, last thing I need is you asking me questions."

"I'll ask all the questions I want, Montana. How did my case get switched to you in the first place? I was doing fine with Yamamoto, we understood each other. And why did that happen exactly on the day Roswell jumped out of my glider?"

"It was a procedural thing, merely routine. I'm getting cold let's go in."

"In a minute. Also the second night I stayed at your house, you got up and went out, late, maybe 2 am. Where did you go?"

"Happens a few times a month. Parolee gets busted, or some domestic situation. Smooths things over if I can be there. Only gone three hours. Plays hell with my Z-time."

Meanwhile, I'm damn sure we had sex around then. Did I hallucinate that?

"Who's your boyfriend? Who is it calls you? It's not Mick is it?"

"What are you talking about?"

"I've seen you do it, Tharcia says there's someone. I told you once I'd split if you wanted him to come over but you said no."

First she reminds me she'd ordered me to stay away from Tharcia, which I get means don't talk to her. But then she basically admits it about talking to Mick, gets a little pensive. But the softer mood passes quickly. "Get out of my way," she says. "I want to go in."

She bangs in the door and two seconds later there's a three-way screaming match starring her, Tharcia and Rayne. Gotta hand it to Tharcia, she definitely keeps up. But naturally, she's learned from the best.

The ladies, and by now I'm using that term loosely, are into round two of personal recriminations when I hear footsteps on the porch. I open the door and let Wolfe in. The women see him and Montana puts the brakes on. He says hello in a cool way, calling her Agent Harrison all formal. Montana's face takes on a scared rabbit look, probably thinking that the 3 pm Monday meeting has been moved to right now. And the two of us missed the rehearsal.

Tharcia introduces herself and Rayne. Wolfe registers the bruise on Tharcia's face, but says nothing. The shiner is better today, or she's done a better job of covering it, but Wolfe has seen it all before.

"Shall we all sit in the living room," Wolfe suggests. We mill briefly, finally sit.

"I had come primarily to speak to Mr. Clay. However, Agent Harrison, since you are here I have questions for you as well."

Montana returns a defiant glare.

Wolfe addresses himself to Tharcia and Rayne. "I hope you ladies will treat this discussion as confidential. First of all, Agent Harrison, there is an issue that's come up among probation staff. Specifically, Mr. Yamamoto. He has spoken to me about the transfer of Mr. Clay's case to you, which finalized on Monday of last week."

Monday, I'm thinking to myself. That was two days before my acro student tried to kill me. Two days before I saw Montana for the first time in two decades. Two days before Roswell expires on my porch.

"Purely a routine matter," Montana explains this calmly enough, but her eyes look hunted.

"Indeed," Wolfe replies evenly. "In Mr. Yamamoto's words, there had been some consideration offered, privately, if you were to receive Mr. Clay's case. Exactly what would be your interest in having Mr. Clay's case transferred to you?"

"None specifically," Montana replies. "Takeo was preparing for vacation, then retirement. My caseload was light, and I recognized the name. Having known Clay in school I thought I might have some insight that could help him."

"So you did enter into an agreement with Mr. Yamamoto?"

Montana looks uncomfortable. "We discussed it briefly. It was a matter of simple routine. We swap cases all the time."

"I see," Wolfe says, finished with that thread for the moment. He turns to me.

"Mr. Clay. What of your movements the night of Roswell's murder? When we questioned you on several occasions about that night, you maintained that you had met Agent Harrison at a jogging path in San Jose. We later found through your phone records that you were actually somewhere in Felton. Can you explain the discrepancy?"

"Detective," I say wearily. "You and I have already discussed that. I admitted misleading you on that point. I was here in Felton. I had arrived home earlier, when I found Roswell."

Montana is staring traitor daggers at me. Rayne and Tharcia both try to talk once, but Rayne wins this one.

"Are you saying there was a dead guy on your porch? What the hell is going on here?"

Tharcia is nodding, she knows enough.

"Then why, Mr. Clay, did you lie about that?"

"As I explained to you Detective, when I first arrived, I had no idea it was Roswell." I turn to Tharcia and Rayne and add, "Roswell is the student jumped out of my glider. I wanted someone to be with me when I discovered the body. Someone with more credibility than a parolee. Montana said she was in San Jose, I believed her. So that was our story."

"Like hell," Montana scoffs.

Wolfe ignores her and gives me an appraising look. "So Mr. Clay are we to believe that you had nothing to do with Roswell's killing?"

"You should, because it's the truth. I didn't know the guy. Plus which I don't have any firearms. Your people searched the house. Hell, you searched the entire property far as I know. No guns, no ammo. Parole violation, see? I passed your residue test."

Blinding flash from the windows, forest outside lights up as the world's largest strobe goes off, followed close by a deafening crack of thunder. Concussion rocks the floorboards. House shakes, lights go out. Firelight from the woodstove is the only illumination. First thing comes to me: the swimming pool. Power goes out there, my income is threatened. My holiday decor has gone out and with it the alert lights, I have no eyes on what's happening in the pool. I do have a generator, but no way can I start it with two cops around. I jump up.

"Stay put everybody I've got candles." I also have flashlights by the doors so I quickly grab one turn it on, hand to Rayne who is closest. Soon I have a dozen candles placed around the room, flickering gaily. The room takes on a party atmosphere, or maybe it's a séance. Everybody is checking their phones, no one has any bars.

"Agent Harrison," Wolfe says, unfazed as usual, "what was your particular connection with Mr. Clay in high school that leads you to believe your knowledge of him could influence a criminal case that took place 15 years after you last saw each other?"

Montana jerks forward in her chair, her face threatening. "Detective that is private information. Strictly between us!"

Wolfe prods further. "Could it actually be that you have a score to settle with Mr. Clay? That you're looking for a way to get even?"

While I feel that many of the things I had done with Montana tagging along should not be discussed in any company, I can relish Wolfe drilling on her.

"Go ahead Montana," I prod, "tell us why you wanted to take over my case."

"It's only because you're such a chicken shit," she spits out. This pisses me off.

"I'm a chicken shit? You were a major Looney Tune back then. You left town without telling me. You didn't attend grad, didn't complete senior year."

"Nobody's business but my own," she says defiantly.

"It is my business," I reply hotly. "It mega hurt my feelings you didn't call when my mom died. Not even a card. I knew you were around. I thought we were friends. I thought we were more than that. Never heard from you."

"Yeah," Tharcia says, leaning forward eyes ablaze. "Who else were you involved with then, besides Stuka? Always some deep dark secret with you. Who do you talk to on the phone every night?"

"You put a lid on it Tharcia!" Montana's losing the rest of her composure.

Tharcia is close to tears, something really bothering her. "Everything is national security with you. Including why you can't accept me for who I am. You're such a goddamned Puritan."

"Are those ears on your head, or ornaments? Shut your pie hole!"

It's Rayne's turn to get into the act. "You're such a bitch the way you treat her, Hannah," she spits out. "You always think you know more but you're really such a... She's a much finer person than you deserve for your daughter. And you're evil to be dissing and hitting on her." Rayne sits back glaring fiercely.

"Go to hell you little perv. You have no business in my daughter's life, you're not welcome." Montana's about to say something more, but Tharcia jumps up.

"Mom! How can you diss my best friend like that? And why are you so messed up about me?"

Montana now looks like she's the one close to tears. She points an accusing finger at me. "You have no idea how it is to find yourself pregnant in high school, you have no idea how hard it is to raise a child totally on your own, far from home."

"You're the one dropped out of sight!" I shout.

All the while Wolfe is sitting back, head turning from one to the other as he follows the conversation. Then the detective drops his bombshell.

Turning to Montana, Wolfe says, "Now, Agent Harrison, I think I know why you lied about being in San Jose. Was it because you were in Felton that evening? For a reason? Was it because you were the one who shot the unfortunate Mr. Roswell? Did you kill Roswell by mistake, because you originally came here to murder Mr. Clay?"

Tharcia shrieks, "Mom!"

"The reason I was here, detective, is I'm still in love with him," Montana says pointing at me. Her eyes flash in the candlelight. I'm thinking lust, possibly. Love, no chance.

"Hardly convincing," Wolfe says. "You have known Mr. Clay's whereabouts since he was arrested four years ago, if not before. Yet only now you make your feelings known to him."

"Don't you dare call me a liar!" Montana jumps to her feet, stands over Wolfe. "It was a simple attempt to maintain my personal space," she says hotly.

But then I recall Montana's gasp of surprise when I phoned her after finding Roswell. I speak up. "Montana, you were shocked when I phoned you that night. A call from a dead man would surprise anyone."

Montana whirls at me, but she's not attacking, she's pleading. "Stuka you don't even see!"

"Mom! You came here to kill him?" Tharcia's face is contorted with disbelief.

Wolfe speaks up, voice forceful. "Officer Yamamoto tells me you have a *quid pro quo* agreement. What is the precise nature of that?"

"Mom! Answer me!" Tharcia's voice is pleading and incredulous at the same time.

Montana stands immobile in the middle of the room, looking from Wolfe to me and back again. Her face is a twist of wild anger. Am I mistaken, or is her hand twitching in the direction of her shoulder holster?

"Ladies, everyone, please." Wolfe has finally had enough. He stands face to face with Montana, trying to manage her down by physical presence.

Two bright flashes and a double thunderclap strike in close succession. We turn to the windows, but of course it's even blacker out there cuz we're all momentarily blinded. The door blows open, extinguishing some of the candles. I get the door closed. As the noise and shuffle die down, a car starts outside, headlights race away through lashing trees. Montana's no longer with us.

"She's gone," I masterfully state the obvious. Wolfe nods slowly, a dark expression on his face. He turns to Tharcia. Tears streak the girl's soft cheeks in the candle glow.

"Did you say that your mother hit you?" Wolfe asks.

"She did hit her," Rayne answers, giving Tharcia no room to wiggle the truth. Tharcia gives Rayne an irritated look, but nods at Wolfe.

"How old are you, young lady?"

This time Rayne lets Tharcia answer. "I'm 19. I can take care of myself. It was an accident. She was trying to grab my car keys." She's looking the detective smack in the eyeballs. I see that she can be a convincing liar.

"An accident in the middle of a screaming argument," Rayne adds.

"Girl! You are seriously getting on my nerves," Tharcia glares at her. "Put a possum in it."

Rayne glares back, but her voice is softer. "Tharcia. You have to say something. After all this time."

Looks like it's official Get Montana night. Wolfe and I look at each other. His expression tells me he sees an unpleasant course of action. Tharcia and Rayne are hugging now, doing their own private I-forgive-you routine.

"Mr. Clay, ladies. I think we're through here for now. Thank you all for your patience and cooperation. This has been difficult, but most informative."

Wolfe steps out the door. We're quiet as his flashlight bobs through the rain and dark, his car drives away. The wind has let up, the rain is coming straight down now. The house is cooling. I throw a couple of chunks in the woodstove, leave the door open to let it breathe. The orange light is cheerful. Candles flicker peacefully.

As at the end of a play, the house lights come up. In the kitchen, I put on the kettle. Some hot tea before they hit the road. It's getting late, tomorrow will be a busy day.

I'm in the bathroom looking at the cut on my calf. Tharcia appears at the door, asks if she can look at her face. Sure, sure. So we're in there both of us dealing with our war wounds. I'm watching her examine the bruise, she stops and is looking at me in the mirror. Her eyes move back and forth, from her reflected face to mine. She goes kind of frozen for a second. I look too, at both of us. And that's when everything changes.

Unbefuckinglievable.

She turns to face me. Echoing between us is Montana's explanation about leaving for L.A. before grad, about raising a kid on her own. Standing by the sink, we reach out like sleepwalkers, clasping wrists. Her face holds a look of questioning wonder.

"Where have you been?" She says it real soft.

How can I sum up 20 years? "I could start with *abandoned*."

Her fingers touch my cheek. "It would never have happened, with you."

"No." I shake my head slowly. "No."

The kettle is screeching downstairs and Rayne is yelling, *where is your tea?*

Tharcia gets this childlike grin. "Hey, can you do this?" She pokes out her tongue a little and curls it up on the edges. I'm laughing fit to bust. Wade, me and our mom could all do it. I show her.

"Mom can't," she says. Laughing, she slugs me in the shoulder and heads downstairs.

I get the tea ready and put three cups on the plank table by the sofa. The gals come in and stand by the woodstove hugging for a long time, dissipating the negative energy of the last two hours. Finally we're sitting on the couch, me between them, looking into the fire, not saying much. I'm thinking some thoughts though, I'll tell you. Like, why did Montana force Yamamoto to move my case to her roster? Why does she need to be so vague about it? Why on Earth would she want to kill me, as Wolfe accused? Meanwhile my brother and I have to push our plans to the next step. I need to talk to Wade, and it has to be in person. I'm seeing him, soon as I can get out of town without being followed. And I sure as hell won't ask Montana's official permission. It's a chance I have to take.

Most pressing question is, how am I going to deal with Mick's murder-for-hire thing, threatening not just Montana, but Tharcia? I can't carry through on that. But it comes to me, if it means keeping Tharcia safe, I have to go way outside the box. Who can I trust?

The fire burns warm, sound of rain steady on the porch, wind has dropped. Tharcia and Rayne sitting on both sides of me, quiet in their own thoughts. Tharcia leans in and her head rests on my shoulder. In that moment, the universe rights itself. I take a breath and let it out slow. After a while, Rayne leans closer. We sit like that looking at the fire as the logs burn down.

And here I sit, I should be happy. Yes I am. On the other side I should be disgusted with myself. Doing the very thing I'd conditioned myself not to. Having friends.

CHAPTER 9
WILD HORSE

OF COURSE, MONTANA DOES NOT keep our appointment. Monday afternoon I'm in San Jose waiting in the parking lot beside the Investigative Services Division on West Younger, busy place bustling with cops, plain and uniform. Mostly I'm staring at my phone. I'd left her messages, but after Wolfe's accusation and her abrupt departure last night I'm surprised at nothing. What can she be thinking?

We're supposed to be meeting the detective in 20 minutes to square up our stories about the night we found Roswell. And Wolfe's accusation about her shooting Roswell by mistake while waiting for me. Do you have a word for that? I call it *showdown*.

I have the growing suspicion that a formal accusation is coming. Possibly an arrest. I am sure that is why she's a no-show. Am I happy the is blowing her way? Not especially.

There's also a text from nrrdgrrl. She hasn't heard from her mom. Even knowing Montana, this is hard to compute. She's got an intelligent daughter, potentially a good home life, successful career. Does she intend to throw that away? She seems headed in that direction. What is pushing her?

I've also reached a decision about Mick's little 'job' for me. That's definitely not happening. And I have a different plan. I pull up Wolfe's number. When he picks up he gets right to the point.

"Mr. Clay. Will you be on time for our meeting?"

"Yes detective, but we can't meet in your office. Look for me outside in the parking lot. I'm three rows back from the main entrance."

Wolfe sounds uncomfortable. "Mr. Clay, you and I are meeting with Agent Harrison to resolve the matter of your whereabouts the night of the murder."

"I don't expect Montana will join us. Plus which there's something I need to discuss with you away from your office."

Reluctantly Wolfe agrees, and we end the call. Reason *numero uno* is security entering this County building. What I have to show Wolfe would create a major scene in the screening area, starring me getting arrested. A violation, write-up, and back to lockup. Can I trust Wolfe that much?

I stand on the sidewalk in front of the building as Wolfe exits the lobby. I wave, he heads my way. I start walking. He follows to my El Camino parked a few rows back. We get in.

"I know we're not going to see Montana today," I tell him, "and you've heard my story enough times."

He nods, looking me over carefully. "Have you spoken to Agent Harrison?"

"No. Left her messages since last night, but nothing. Her daughter hasn't heard from her either."

Wolfe's face is serious. "Same." He looks out the window and sighs, like he's being pushed into an undesirable course of action. I go on.

"Detective, you could have called us in for this last week. Why did you wait?"

He looks uncomfortable. "Actually we are investigating an internal matter that does not involve you directly. We were hoping someone would do the right thing."

By someone I get that he means Montana, and I am instantly afraid for her.

"Thank you for that. But there's something else. I need your help. You cops always ask people to come forward with tips. There someone in my past, Montana's past, who is very dangerous."

"You're referring to McIntyre?"

Good, the detective is ahead of me.

"Bang on. So here's a tip I received yesterday morning from a couple of gangsta types tricked out like DEA suits. Open the glove box. Stick with me on this. I have no choice, it threatens Montana and her daughter. Look in the envelope."

At this point I am not scared I am merely terrified. With this, Wolfe can take me down for a violation on the spot. He's watching me intently, jacket open, has an easy reach for his weapon. Doesn't entirely trust me, but I'm sitting here trying to come across all relaxed, both hands on the steering wheel. That's when I notice the plainclothes dude a couple rows over, making like he's checking his tire pressures. Cool. I'm glad Wolfe is cautious. Wolfe takes out the bulging manila envelope. Looks inside.

"Mr. Clay, you realize it's a parole violation for you to have a firearm."

"Of course I realize that, Wolfe. This is a lead for you. This was handed to me by Mick's people. I'm supposed to shoot that guy, in the photo. Look it over."

Wolfe takes everything out of the envelope. Looks at the gun and clip inside the Ziploc bags, looks at the photos, reads the information on the back of the Carruthers photo. Looks at me.

"Councilman Carruthers. And you got this material how, Mr. Clay?"

"Coming out of the glider school yesterday morning, this poser DEA car was sitting there. They were gangsta, work for McIntyre. I recognized one. They push me in the back, hand me a phone, and I'm talking to Mick McIntyre from his cell at Lancaster."

Wolfe studies me thoughtfully. "What was the nature of your conversation?"

"He offered me 45 large to take this gun and shoot this guy."

The detective looks puzzled. "Why would he ask you? Surely he has his network."

"My question exactly. I'm no shooter. Look at those photos, McIntyre's enforcers say Montana and Tharcia get hurt if I don't follow through. There's been two attempts on my life already, this smells like another trap. Could be Mick all along."

"And why would Mr. McIntyre want to kill you?"

"Detective, your guess is as good as mine. Heard a rumor he has an appeal coming up. Could be worried about my testimony." This can cut both ways. Once detective Wolfe starts digging into my involvement with Mick, that thing with the dope run could bring me the wrong kind of help.

"Very well, Mr. Clay." He raises the envelope. "Of course I need to take this."

Whew. No violation. "That was the idea."

Wolfe nods. "Did anyone see you talking to McIntyre's lieutenants?"

"We were parked in front of the flight school. Someone might've seen."

Wolfe gets out, I get out. We're talking across the roof of my car. The plainclothes cop starts to walk closer, hand on his belt. I'm sure he's not the only cop out here watching Wolfe's back right now.

"One last thing, Mr. Clay. You may be interested in knowing something about your friend, Mr. Roswell."

I snort. "Not my friend, if you would be so kind to acknowledge that."

Wolfe laughs dryly. "Indeed, Mr. Clay, I use the term loosely. This Mr. Roswell we now know to be one Peter Drake, a former Navy pilot, with a carrier group. He's 43 years old, left the Navy as a Lieutenant J.G. with a Tail hook rating."

Now Wolfe says something that shakes me up, the name of the aircraft carrier Wade served on four years as a jet mechanic. As in, the one this Peter Drake flew from. I should know the name, I'd addressed enough packages to that ship.

"So why was he trying to kill me?"

"That, Mr. Clay, is something we would dearly like to know."

"As would I."

"Indeed."

Wolfe glances at the open bed of my El Camino. My beater bike is there, my bolted-in tool chest. Nothing really incriminating, but a search would raise too many pesky questions. I'm grateful when he turns to leave. The detective's posture as he walks away is that of a man with a heavy load. I remove the battery and sim card from my phone. Where I'm going I want no snooping.

I'm 35 miles outside of San Jose, heading up California 580 toward Altamont Pass, when I finally take a deep breath, watching the mirror for a tail. Way too spooky, being around all those cops downtown. But Wolfe is cool. He knows things are happening. Neither of us understands why I seem to be in the center of it.

But I've had this sinking feeling in my gut the last half-hour, and finally my noggin serves up the reason. Wolfe said Roswell is actually a retired Navy pilot named Peter Drake. Wade called his pilot friend Pete. *Ay caramba!*

But if it's the same guy, why would he come to my place and not Wade's farm, where the plane is? My paranoid brain reminds me that Drake's stunt would be a great way to shake a tail. If so, who was chasing him? And how did someone magically catch up with him at my front door, after his elaborate deception? Makes no sense, nada.

Next thing due to happen though, is a new parole officer. Cripes. I'm sure of it. Montana's already off the deep end, Wolfe more than hinted at an internal investigation. I'll be reassigned. Best for me would be going back to Yamamoto, but he's set to retire.

So then it will be the full shakedown from question one, complete review of my crime, prison records, where are you employed, all that shit. They'll find I was fired and put me on a treadmill of mindless job interviews, all the suckhole companies who say they'll hire a rehabbed drug dealer. I reassure myself I'm not gonna be here for that.

When I find myself watching all the wind turbines driving down the other side of Altamont Pass, I start thinking it's time to be sharp. Little burg out here a few miles off I-580 I know very well. Ranch and farm country, livestock, crops, open spaces.

So first I drive randomly through dusty streets making sure my tail is clean. Park the El Camino in a residential area couple blocks off the main drag. Unlock the toolbox, load up the saddlebag on the bike. Forensic clean up. Check I have my disposable phone, beater laptop, handheld GPS in the saddlebag. Place I leave my car was selected because it is less than 50 miles from the nearest corner of Santa Clara County, permissible under my parole terms. Where I'm headed is a different matter.

On the bike now, a trail leading away from the houses along a fence line, directly into the boonies. Barren moonscape out here, starting to get warm even though it's mid-November. Have covered the route in two hours before. Beauty of it is, unless you're in an airplane or on another bicycle it's very tough to track someone coming through here fast. And I like fast. The dry arroyo is my freeway. The old river bottom twists back on itself like a snake but it's worth the extra distance to stay hidden. Of course, if I stayed down here I'd miss the farmhouse, go right by it. My GPS and a small stone cairn tell me when it's time to climb the steep bank and there it is, three miles away shrouded in trees. Wade's place. I pull out the burner, dial a number from memory.

"Is Betsy there?"

"Wrong number." My brother's voice, telling me it's all clear. We click off.

Old house in the shade of tall oaks, obviously a good well on the property. Big barn a ways off, screened by trees. Something in there I can't wait to see again. Lean my bike against the wall. Couple of cats appear out of the woods and stampede toward the porch, smarming around my ankles when the door is opened by a tall guy in jeans and a work shirt with a three-day beard and a grin full of white teeth.

We're all hey bro and big hugs, he's a little taller, his beefier frame showing the four years he has on me. Intelligent eyes, familiar grin that usually hints some devilish plot. Were inside, he's offering coffee, beer, scotch, raid the fridge. Old place, this farmhouse, hundred years old likely, the smell of aged wood, furniture oil. Wade keeps his place neat. We both picked up that gene.

Wade Clay, my brother, ex-Navy man, now goes by another name. Has very good fake ID, stopped using his real name for anything that would leave a trail, such as phone, utilities, mortgage, driver's license. Everything's in his ex-wife's name. Lucky for him she's a sympathetic soul and they parted friends. Wade has been living this way for 18 years, has a son who's twelve, goes to school on a yellow bus that passes this place. Every school day, Wade watches it go by.

Why does he do this, you wonder. We always joked I'm not the only one in the family with mental issues. Wade came back from the Navy quite paranoid, reading Marxism and verging on agoraphobia. Doesn't want to go out, see people much. It must be another family gene, I hate being watched. But I can function in the world. He cannot.

At his kitchen table I'm pulling stuff out of my saddlebag, sorting through everything. First things first, I slide a plastic sandwich bag full of bills across the table. Swimming pool money. It's what keeps Wade going, keeps our project alive. A project that I'm totally hot to see right now. But that's not what keeps him out here. After Mom died we sold the house and agreed he should use the money to buy this farm. He's been a lot better, living out here in the middle of nothing.

Wade grins. "Looks like the grow is doing okay. Those two hotties still work for ya?"

"You should drop by sometime," I grin. "They are outrageous." Wade dropping by my place. Imagine. And he'd shudder at the real story of the Desmond twins.

"I'm still waiting for our buddy to show up," he says. Then he sees the set of my face and his expression changes.

"What?" His look is intent, knows something's up.

"Wade, there might be bad news." I give him a rundown of the glider flight, my jumper, finding Roswell bleeding on my porch, the shit with Montana. And what Wolfe told me this morning.

Wade groans, sits back in his chair, closes his eyes. "They said his name is Pete Drake? How big a guy was he?"

I give my description of Roswell the day of our flight. Mostly I remember the back of the guy's head, but I am sure of his stature and so forth. Also that he was a sharp pilot. Wade watches me closely as I speak. Now he is shaking his head, not in disagreement but in disbelief, saying no, man, no.

"Wade, they did ID him with fingerprints. Peter Drake, a Navy Lieutenant, Tail hook. You guys were on the same battle carrier."

He stands and paces the floor, yelling curses at the walls. "Pete you wacko, you insane little shit!"

Pacing, he turns to me. "Pete was always grandstanding. One of the best FA-18 pilots we had on board, flew a low pass over the deck one day inverted. Absolutely no fear."

"Wade, when we were up in the glider, Roswell... I mean Drake, asked me questions about Mick. The dope deal I got busted for. If he is your guy, how would he know that stuff?"

Wade looks sheepish. "Sorry little brah, I regaled him with some stories about you one time. Some shit slipped out. Bragging on you, I guess."

"Well he must have done some research after that, because he was telling me McIntyre has an appeal coming up. How would Drake know that name?"

Wade looks even sheepisher.

"Wade, he, and you, if I may be so bold, put me square on the police radar. I don't care if he's your friend. He did try to kill me."

"No, man, he's just a showoff. Way macho. He prolly figured if you were such a hot pilot..."

"Face facts, dude! Sure, I knew what it would take to save the glider. Most pilots would. But doing it is way risky. There are a dozen ways I could have failed... lost my grip, hit my head, taken too long. He wanted to murder me and make it look like an accident."

Wade looks embarrassed and sad. "Well, then why? He and I were buds aboard ship."

"You ask why. How about money? He knew about the plane, you were asking him to deliver it. What were you paying him?"

"Um, thirty five thousand. Part of that is already paid."

"Thirty five thousand. And your buyer is paying what, a million or so?"

Wade has always been evasive about the price he's expecting. He doesn't meet my eyes. "Yah, around that."

"Well think about it. Drake surely knew what a plane like that is worth. Killing me would mean you keep everything. Then he comes here afterward, takes the money, and kills you."

Wade looks shocked, seeing I have a point. "Naw, he wouldn't do that."

I stand up in front of him to better press my attack. "Suppose you're found dead. What kind of investigation would there be about you? You're a literal nobody! Way you live your life, there is virtually no info about you. No trails anywhere. Police would be stuck. Drake could have walked with all of it. Hell, he could have flown the plane somewhere else! To his own buyer!"

"It would be hidden," Wade protests.

"Torture and threats, dude. He knows you have a son. You paid him some already?"

"Gambling debt. He owes me from back then."

This is too much. I wave my arms and take a turn around the kitchen. "A gambling debt!" Dammit to hell, man! You are so naive about people! "From what, fifteen years ago? How much?"

"Seventeen grand."

I am sick in my gut at this point. I step up and put both hands on his shoulders where he slumps in his chair. "Wade, dude, grab a brain. He already wrote off that seventeen in his head. He never planned to pay you. So he stood to gain eighteen grand, while you pocket one or two mil."

Wade winces at my guess, rubbing his chin, looking dubious. But I see he's disappointed at himself. He doesn't trust anyone, doesn't trust the system. Yet he trusts an old Navy buddy who doesn't pay his gambling debts. Why? Because he looks up to thrill-seeker pilots.

"And Wade, why would he go to my place? He assumes I'm dead, right? So why go to my house? How about to search my stuff, find anything that would help him."

"Help him what?"

"Find you and the plane and cut you out of the deal entirely."

Wade looks like his plug has been pulled, slumps deeper in the chair. He has barely the jam left to reply weakly, "Nah, dude, no way. We were best buds."

"And why did he have the Roswell ID? He had this fake logbook and FAA glider rating in that name. Not his own. That took a lot of time and effort to create. Why would he need that? Covering his tracks."

I fix him with my most menacing stare. "I'm saying he planned my murder. And yours too."

We're silent. I can wait. Let him think about it. At minimum, Wade's coming to the certainty that Drake is dead. A key element of our plan is missing. No pilot, no go. I see he's thinking that. But I have new intel for him, when he gets caught up.

Now Wade is grinning at me, laughing. "Hey brah, you are totally twitching."

Well okay, I suppose I'm that obvious. "Can we see her now?"

Wade laughs, getting up. "You're hungry for that old bitch aren't you?"

Outside we're walking the graded path into the trees. Tall barn doors slide back a long way, wide enough to clear the wings and four-bladed prop of the vintage World War II fighter plane waiting there. I stand outside looking, so hungry for this moment over all the months and years. Wade is flipping switches by the door. From high rafters powerful floodlights blaze, glistening on graceful metal skin of what we liked to call 'our airplane.' A North American Aviation Mustang P-51B pursuit fighter.

There's a history to everything. For several years before prison I'd been living in a Hollister farmhouse, care-taking, because it was close to the gliderport. The owner had died and his kids back east were squabbling over what to do with the place. None of them came. To them, Dad was a looney who loved old airplanes and they were into their east coast careers, families. There was a semi-trailer parked in the barn, covered with dust and bird droppings. I'd been curious, and opened it up. Found the Mustang's fuselage, wings, tail, engine, all in pieces. Told Wade and he went majorly ballistic. It was a fixer-upper, a project plane, but most of it was there.

That was how things stood until I got busted. Wade went to the farm to gather my gear. He looked in the trailer and became completely obsessed. In spite of being an agoraphobic paranoid, he managed to drive the trailer to his farm. It was an extreme move for him, but he was hot for the Mustang and pulled it off. Yeah, he stole it.

As the forlorn Mustang's unusual past surfaced, we began to understand the value. We didn't plan a rivet-by-rivet restoration, we wanted a flyable project plane. Wade's buyer seemed to think it's an important part of history, and wants to put it back the way it was 70 years ago. That's why there is no paint on this bird. So many of these types have been modified as air racers. Wings shortened, radiator scoops removed, modern electronics in place of the original. There are more of those now than authentic restored ones.

Many postwar P-51s became bare-metal racers. Widely available at war-surplus prices in the late '40s and '50s, the combination of a 12-cylinder Rolls-Royce engine and dogfight reflexes made P-51s natural pylon-shavers. Far as we know, no one is looking for this one. At least not around here.

During the last four years, Wade's skilled work as an aircraft mechanic, his fanatical attention to detail, my income from the swimming pool, my aircraft parts business, have slowly brought this ship to flight readiness. At least we hoped it was flight-ready. It's seldom put a wheel outside the barn.

Walking around it now, the Mustang looks wicked, seeming bigger than the trainer I rode in on Sunday. Gazing up at the massive prop I recall the day Wade and I cracked a rafter in here mating that heavy thing to the propeller shaft. I find it flat-out daunting to imagine sitting in the cockpit and making that propeller turn.

A long workbench under one wing, a line of familiar boxes. They'd been sent one at a time by little old me under cover of my vintage parts business in Felton. The last components we need to make her flight-worthy are here.

We're clambering up on the wings, looking down into the open cockpit, pointing at things, discussing, flipping switches pushing buttons wiggling this and that.

"Wade, I've been thinking."

He looks at me with a cockeyed grin. "Oh God here we go. You thinking is always dangerous."

I give him half a laugh. "Sunday I went for a joyride. There's an F6 trainer at Hollister. I've got video on my laptop. Sean's start-up sequence, all his control moves on takeoff, the landing approach and touchdown. I've seen it a dozen times. I've flown the simulator a thousand times."

I stop and wait, until he's looking at me steady. "I can do it."

Wade is shocked. "You think a fricking glider pilot is going to get this monster off the ground? You don't know anything about power flying."

I'm shaking my head. "I've been flying the sims. Wade, we are behind schedule, and I could get arrested any day now. You say your buyer's ready? All the parts are here. I'm on a collision course with this detective. With Mick's enforcers. The parole system. Montana. I'm out of options. I've got to disappear right now!"

We don't exactly settle it, at least not that minute. We start taking parts out of boxes, talking while we work, checking off changes and adjustments to be made. I'm relentless, slowly convincing my older brother that I in fact know what I'm talking about.

Wade's face becomes thoughtful when I tell him Sean had given me the controls of his Mustang trainer, and what he'd said after I set her down.

And it's probably unfair of me, but somewhere in there I pull out my most convincing argument. Argument? Nah, call it a guilt trip. Wade couldn't stay after Dad died. Had to go back to his fleet, his life on a United States aircraft carrier as a jet mechanic.

But this was about Mom. I'd stayed home taking care of her, teaching flight lessons and working a skunky job driving auto parts around the Bay area, while she got sicker and sicker, gradually to the point she could no longer take care of herself. We hocked the house for home care, then hospice. It was hard. She turned real bad and Wade tried to make it home, but he was two days late. I wouldn't ask him this, but I'm sure he hasn't forgiven himself. What I do know is, that's when he got respect for his little brother.

We work. By late afternoon I have this major itch on. I wanna see the thing run.

"Com'on Wade," I say for the umpteenth time. "Get your tractor over here. Let's pull her out and crank it up."

While having a beer break we'd watched the cockpit video I'd made in the trainer. Wade agrees it looks simple enough. Complicated, yet straightforward, requiring quick hands and finesse to not fuck it up and die immediately. I'd written a checklist. Finally I am done talking, walk over and climb on the tractor, park it just in front of the Mustang's high nose.

"Okay, okay," Wade relents. "You go out there and spot me. We'll point the tail toward the field."

We could not start a 1600-horsepower engine inside the barn. The prop blast would blow everything around in there and maybe knock down a wall or two. If it caught fire the whole barn would catch and no chance of saving it. Outside is best. I'm standing here signaling and shouting to Wade on our walkie-talkies as he eases the wings through the barn doors with about a foot clear on either side. We get her turned, tail pointed toward a plowed field. We tether the main landing gear to the tractor, parked behind the plane. The tractor weighs 1100 pounds, the plane has parking brakes and won't get away from us. I hope. I have no idea how strong she'll pull, 1600 horses is a lot.

We climb up on the wings, I step into the cockpit, open my laptop, Sean's video and my startup checklist where I can see them. Just for good measure I have the Mustang's maintenance manual on my lappy. It has a startup checklist too. I start through the steps.

Finally I engage the starter, switch both magnetos on, and the whole airframe shakes as the prop swings around. I count off six blade passes, then flick the fuel boost pump switch, the electric primer, push the mixture lever up into NORMAL position. Two loud smoky bangs from the exhaust manifolds. The Merlin catches with a roar, sputters to a stop. In the abrupt silence we both get it that Wade standing out there on the wing is not a good idea. Number one, he's right in line with the six exhaust ports on that side of the long nose, and the prop blast could pelt him with stones. He climbs down. Also, I remind him over the handheld radio, he needs to grab a fire extinguisher.

He's standing near the port wing now, we exchange a couple of observations via radio.

"It wanted to catch," Wade says. "We pressurized the oil system, but the thing hasn't turned over in months. Why not crank until you think it's almost flooded?"

"I can push it a bit."

I roll the canopy closed. I start the sequence again and this time count eight blade passes. Fuel fumes around the exhaust manifolds shimmer like mirage heat as the huge prop turns. One manifold barks. Another, then another. The engine catches stuttering rough but keeps running, tach comes up near 1800 RPM, the whole thing shaking.

The sound smooths out, it's beautiful, viciously loud, a musical din. Blue flames knife from all 12 manifolds. Wade is aiming the bell of his extinguisher around but there's no panic. I bring the RPM up to 2500, switch the magnetos from one side to the other. There's very little RPM drop when I do that, a good sign. I hear the sharp whip-cracking sound that tells me the prop tips are supersonic. I bring it back to idle.

We let her run for 10 minutes like that. Sight of that giant prop blurring by the windscreen fills me with foreboding. Wade puts on his motorcycle helmet and jumps up on the wing again all thumbs up. Eagerly his eyes scan the control panel looking at temperatures, boost pressure, oil pressure, any number of things that can spell success or disaster. Finally I shut her off. My ears are ringing. I make a mental note to find industrial earplugs to go under my radio headset. This thing is just plain loud and I won't be talking on the radio anyway.

We jump down and were hugging each other hooting and hollering. For the moment we're ignoring the small matter of the 900-mile night flight with a pilot who has no power experience. Certainly never with a 1600 HP engine under his hand.

With the tractor we pull the bird into its coop. We're silent, looking up at the magnificent ship. Recalling my hands-on flight and landing with Sean, I'm sure I can fly this thing, but my stomach is reminding me that when I release the brakes and put the throttle all the way forward, I'll be completely over my head. No test flight, no instructor in the back. My first powered flight ever will be my first solo.

I can land her, because I can land a glider. It's the takeoff that will have my full attention.

It's near dark, the barn doors are closed, everything's cleaned up. We're feet up on the coffee table, telling stories over beer, chips and guacamole. Wade wants to know how I got hooked up again with Montana.

"Man, it came out of nowhere. All of a sudden she's there in my life. I didn't know she was around, hadn't thought of her for years. Then bingo, she's my parole agent."

"And the day you fly with Pete, you get home and there he is dead. Your detective says Montana was close by. And she's lying about it."

"I've gone over it in my head hundreds of times. She denies it, totally shrugs it off."

"It was a dark and stormy night," Wade is chuckling. "She wants to kill you?"

"She's hooked up with someone gangsta though, gotta be Mick, telling her what to do."

Wade considers. "Well, he asked you to shoot a guy once, it's conceivable he'd tell her to do the same. But why you why now?"

I shake my head. Why me indeed? Same thing Wolfe wants to know. But something is nagging at me, something bugging me about going through with all this. Besides

possible death ruin and disaster. Wade says his buyer is
ready. But what if I don't go?

I mean yah deliver the plane, but what if I don't run to
this new life I've scoped out? After all the dreams of it. So
perfectly planned, it would be a shame to not see it work.
I'll see more of Wade that way. But is getting away from the
system worth having a life like his? And, I remind myself,
now that Wade has hinted at the take from this deal, my
chances of hiring a high-powered attorney are looking
damn good. If I can just not kill myself in the next week.

I take a different tack. "Wade, what if you come out in
the clear? What if you give up your secret existence and just
came out as yourself?"

He laughs. "Think about it Buckaroo, it's been so long,
this life is my real one. I file taxes, have a twelve-year-old
son I love. Only thing gonna change is my hidden income.
But then I won't have this airplane ruling my life. And," he
grins, "we will have the money."

I sigh. He has a point. But me? I don't have a fake life
that's become my real one. What if I stick it out, face things
as they are, work through them, live the life of a reformed
felon. But then there's Wolfe digging into my past
connections with Mick. And Montana. If she doesn't kill me
first, she'll rat me out. She's on the run and dangerous.
Deep down, I'm hoping Wolfe can reel her in.

Conversation orbits around the flight, plans for
delivering the plane. Wade is explaining how he has it
worked out with the buyer.

"I set it up to avoid Pete handing over the plane in
exchange for cash. Traveling home with cash is too risky.
And tell you the truth, I was worried about Pete being alone
with it. So what you're going to do is circle the landing area
first. There will be one guy standing by a motorcycle near a
long dirt strip. Smoke flare at the last waypoint. You will
land about a mile from the guy, then call my burner. When
he sees you he'll call his people out here to meet me with

the money. After I count it and they've left, I'll tell you. That's when you taxi over to the guy with the motorcycle and shut her off. You get on the bike and you leave."

"Wade, since you mention cash…"

He gives me a grin, his favorite devilish one, like when his poker hand has all the cards.

"A paltry two point three," he says. Wade always did like fancy words.

"Two point three, as in…"

"Million," says my big brother.

Holy hell, I could hire two attorneys. Takes a few minutes to adjust to that, then I'm asking questions about all the ways things can go wrong. Paranoid or cautious, don't care what you call it. "What if they try to take the money back from you after I've given up the plane?"

"Well I'm meeting them a long way from here, and I'll be on a trail bike out in the bush. All farmland and game trails from here to there. When I have the money I'll tell you. When you shut off the engine you'll tell me. That's when I ride away."

I think for a second. "What if they came up with a way to just trap the plane when it's on the ground?"

"Look, these are old dudes, a group of pilots. They don't want any trouble just want the plane. That's what your fly-by of the landing area is all about. We picked this area north of Gallup because it's remote. The buyer is well connected in aviation circles. There will be only one person there, with a motorcycle. They want the plane bad, brah."

"I trade the P-51 for a motorcycle." Doesn't sound so appealing. And Wade had trusted Drake. Wade insists it's not like a drug deal, just a few high rollers want a special airplane. The only risk is, this buyer might be a front for the party it was stolen from, if it was stolen before we stole it. We don't even know if that's true, it was in that Hollister barn so damn many years.

163

"Okay so after I'm away on the bike then what?"

"You are coming back here, right?"

"Yeah, that's the idea. I'm thinking what I do is ditch the bike, hop on a Greyhound somewhere. Bus around a day or two then come back and get myself over here."

"Hell why do that? You'll have your new ID. Why not just bring the bike back, or rent a car? Call me and I'll pick you up."

There's more. We'd thought and talked about this in every detail for years. There are challenging parts of not being found. Can't do anything the same as you used to. Can't hang out at the same places, can't buy the same booze, can't work the same job. Flying gliders will be out for me, especially since so many people know me in that circle, former students will recognize me, especially around contests. If I want to fly, it will be power, or nothing.

But do I want a life of always being that careful? I think back over all the precautions Wade and I had put in place over the years. For instance I never bring a phone here that has batteries in it. Only prepaid dumb phones. No snoopy phone companies watching my every move, it's not just my paranoia says they do that. And there are apps that let anybody track your smart phone. Live with it.

I never drove here in a car, always rode a bike through the arroyo. Would've done it at night but then you need lights and you become more noticeable. Daylight is best. The life I'm going to manufacture will make me older. So what, I'll look young for my age. Every move I make has to be completely unexpected.

How else could I work my life, with my half of two point three million bucks? Just thinking of that, I feel lighter. There are people I'd regret leaving behind. Stacy. The twins. And Tharcia. How do I know who she is, if I take off?

Next day I'm on the bike, heading back through the dry riverbed, the drive home. Somewhere along the way I flip the burner phone, carefully wiped, into a restaurant dumpster, minus its batteries and totally bent. No connection.

At home, the telltale lights inform me the swimming pool is unoccupied, everything's clear. I put my phone back together and look through messages. Wolfe wanting me to call him immediately, from two days ago. Three messages from Montana. Two from Tharcia. The twins. Couple calls from people were at the party saying thanks for a good evening, and can we do that again.

So first person I call is Montana. Amazingly, she picks up.

"Where the fuck have you been?"

"Yes, Montana, and it's great to hear your voice too."

"Don't get cute. Why didn't you call me? Got something important."

"I left you messages. Now you're the one in a big rush. So now you're finally going to admit you wanted to shoot me?"

Her voice is now all syrupy sweet. "You blockhead, of course I don't want to shoot you. Wolfe is delusional. How could I know Roswell would be there?"

Her *non sequitur* stops me cold. She knows nothing about Drake. But it also means that someone from Mick's network was trying to kill me, and Drake walked into the middle of it. She'd asked about my evening life, so I think she's behind it. Which means the last thing I want is to be anywhere near her.

"So what's up?"

"Well you're right about one thing, I did talk to Mick. He says he can help you. He wants to give you a fresh start. He told me about his proposal, and I found out something about your guy."

I'm damn glad this is a phone convo so I can go quietly apoplectic where she can't see.

"Wait a minute," I say with forced calm, "Mick talked to you about my weekend research project?" It worked for *Bullworth*. Let's see if Montana gets it.

"Yes and you need to meet me. Movies, Tuesday night. We'll drive there together."

Just like in high school, she wants to help me kill someone. On a date. What a modern couple. I don't want to get into more detail on the phone so I just ask her when and where. It's the Century 21 on Winchester in San Jose. Fine.

I dial Wolfe. "Detective, it's Clay. I just had a very interesting convo with Montana."

"You mean you've seen her? No one here has seen her for two days. Her daughter says she's been home only once, picked up some things and left."

I fill Wolfe in on what Montana had said. It confirms what he's deduced about the link between her and Mick. Telling him makes it more real, and I feel sick. I ask if he found anything about the pistol, any prints on it or the photos.

"Nothing on the weapon, there's a partial on one of the rounds from the clip. Lots of prints on the photos, the baggie, we're looking at everything."

I am sure nothing in any of that will trace back to Mick. That would be the Holy Grail. That's when it dawns on me, what I want.

"Detective, is there any way to take Mick out of circulation? Disconnect him from his little empire?"

Wolfe is silent for a few moments. "That has been discussed and it's being considered. What we are lacking now is the means. There are certain legality issues. You know he runs a network from inside. It's a corporate pyramid structure, modeled after the Cosa Nostra."

Does Wolfe think he's telling me anything new? Chill, dude. I was inside for three years, an unwilling part of that. Imprisoned gangbangers are pushed to complete their GED's and learn everything in the prison libraries about the law. All paid for with taxpayer money. According to Mick, the only reason I didn't become part of that is I went to the San Luis Obispo Country Club instead of Lancaster. But if Mick is so effing powerful, why didn't he pull me over there? He's the one incriminated me in the first place. And I know why he did, to cover his own fuckup. That will come back to bite him hard. The fact that I don't yet know how is a mere detail.

"But what would it take to totally nail him? Cut off from his setup."

The detective is silent for a minute on the other end. "Evidence is the problem. What I know of this case so far is he has loyal people. An unrelated crime could do it, if we can find anything on him. An angle he is not prepared to defend."

Wolfe turns back to the current situation. "Be sure you talk to me before this evening. Working something out over here."

I say sure fine and hang up. Montana knows all about the proposed hit, and Mick's apparently coached her to make sure I go through with it. It sounds way fishy. Mick threatening me with the lives of two people he actually cares about. And Montana stepping up to make sure I do it. Wolfe fiddling in the background with arrangements he won't disclose.

I'm in a bind, and there are few options. Only way out is through Wolfe. The best plan I can sort out unfortunately depends on him. Has he become *simpatico* enough so I can trust him? Given what I must set in motion, will he work with me, or in trapping Montana, will he also snare me into a violation that sends me back to prison? Smack into the hands of Mick's crowd on the inside.

CHAPTER 10
BAD MOON RISING

ONE O'CLOCK THE FOLLOWING afternoon, I find out what Wolfe is working on. He plans to capture Montana and bring her in, under arrest or willingly, pick one. Sounds to me like she's going to be charged. Presents me with a moral dilemma. Do I warn her because she's a friend, at least a former friend, or do I keep my yap shut? Phone to my ear, I'm sitting feet up on a cardboard box in my living room. Wolfe is walking me through the details.

"No, Mr. Clay, it's critical that you meet her somewhere away from Councilman Carruthers' home. Under no circumstances are you to get close to that location with Agent Harrison. Understand?"

"*Capisc.*"

"Do not obtain any kind of firearm. You are not to be armed. My men will be counting on that."

"Absolutely," I say. Last thing I want is some amped-up cop thinking I need subduing with deadly force. I'm hoping it won't come to that. Thinking I should practice my dead possum pose.

"Detective, it sounds like you plan to arrest Agent Harrison, am I right?"

"We would prefer that she come in on her own. I've left her messages to that effect. We have secured her office and my team is searching there now."

Thing I'm wondering is, what is going on with Montana that pushed her to such a ridiculous extreme as a police sting created especially for her?

"Let's change the schedule on her," Wolfe continues. "Call tonight and arrange to meet her in the parking lot of Spartan Stadium. As close to 10 PM as you can make it. Park next to her driver's door, do not get into her car. We will be on you with telephoto lenses."

Yeah, I say to myself. Telescopic laser-dot rifle sights is probably more the story.

"And Mr. Clay. We want absolutely no heroics from you, is that understood? This must end peacefully."

All I can do is mutter into the phone, yah sure, and hang up. I don't care if he's done or not I've heard enough. Hero, schmero. If Wolfe and his cop buddies had any idea how inconvenient this is for my plans they would give me a hero badge just for putting up with it. I turn my phone off. I've had more crap than I can deal with today. So for a mindless chore I busy myself getting rid of excess debris around the place and generally making it presentable. Am I worried about tonight? Hell yeah. I know that Montana wants to finish what she started the day I walked into her office, only there won't be any mistakes this time. Because this time she will be holding the gun.

So about eight-thirty that evening I call her. She actually picks up. I come right to the point.

"I looked into this, I have it wired. I'm taking care of it ahead of schedule. I'll let you know how it works out."

"You utter imbecile," are the first words out of her mouth. I can tell her teeth are clenched when she says that. "You don't have a prayer of pulling this off without me."

"Actually, sweet cheeks, my chances of survival are better on my own, without you in particular."

"Not so fast. Where are you doing this?"

"You nuts? You wanna talk about that right here on the phone? Why don't you just send a few tweets about it?"

"Then we have to meet."

"It'll have to be before 11. After that I'm busy."

"You mean tonight? You're doing it tonight?"

"Shut the fuck up. You're out of it. See ya." I punch off.

What works on Montana is ignoring her. She absolutely can't stand it. My phone chimes. Of course it's her. What did I tell you?

"Not so fast," she picks up where she left off. "I got some info you're going to need. I can meet you after 10. Down the street from his house. You know who I mean. Construction project. Look for my Jeep."

"Big N-O to that, sweet life. Gotta be no later than 10. Be at the Spartan Stadium. Parking lot. See you there wise ass."

I hang up. She is thinking to hit Carruthers at his house. Spartan is only 10 minutes from the Councilman's place. Wolfe and I discussed that, I'd looked it over on Google Earth, and driven by slow with a video camera. High walls around gated homes in that neighborhood, but there is one good vantage point that allows a shot where Carruthers' limo lets him off at his door. A new home under construction up the street. Vantage point and good cover. Of course, as Wolfe says, I am not to go there.

I send Wolfe a quick text: *it is set 10 pm at spartan*

I'd had messages from Tharcia but hadn't called her back. I get her voice mail and hang up. Couple minutes later a text comes back.

nrrdgrrl*:* hang on 5 min

Sure. So I go back to what I was doing, which is heating up a frying pan for scrambled eggs. Finally decided I'd rather die on a full stomach.

Phone rings.

"Hey Tharcia."

"Hey Stuka what shakes?"

"Getting ready to take a trip."

"Going to lie in the sun somewhere?"

Now she mentions it, that's not so bad an idea. "You might say that. Sunny Mexico. Sunny Senoritas."

"Funny you don't seem the Mexico type. I could see you piloting a float plane among the islands of British Columbia."

"That has some appeal. How's school going?"

"It's okay. Mom's been weird though and it's hard coping with that."

"Weird how? What's she doing?"

"Hasn't been around. Clay, I'm worried. Couple days ago she was here while I was at class, took a ton of her stuff, left things in a mess. It's like she moved out. Wolfe has been calling me."

I recall the sign on Tharcia's door, *Actual Parent Wanted*. "What's life like with her usually? You guys do stuff?"

I hear her sigh, can almost see her frustrated expression.

"We used to. She was more involved with my stuff when I was in high school. Now at State it's different, she's preoccupied. I want a home life. I want to hang out with her."

"Well she's around, right? You see her every day?"

"Besides right now? She's always been this driven career girl with a major nightlife. She leaves the house before seven, I might not see her until late in the evening.

Sometimes after I'm asleep she kisses me goodnight. Like I was two years old."

"She have a second job?"

"No. We've never lacked for money and stuff. She's just always busy. When we talk, she's telling me how to do my life. How to not be homo. She totally doesn't get me."

I recall the tension in the room between Montana, Rayne, and Tharcia the night Wolfe came by. "When did you let her know you're gay, baby?"

Wow. That baby thing just slipped out. She doesn't seem to notice. Either that, or it's okay with her.

"She says I'm only experimenting. Doesn't even admit the fact," Tharcia says sadly. "Looks at Rayne and my other girlfriends as a bad influence. Like it's all them trying to perv on me. Nothing about who they are as people and what my preferences are. Not like it is any part of who I am."

"That bites," I agree. "Gay was not on the radar when we were growing up. It was all hetero."

"But you got me right away," she says. "Me and Rayne. Rayne was way jealous of you at first." Sound in her voice is gratitude, and something else. She goes on.

"Your vacation. Where are you actually going?"

"New Mexico." I omit the fact I'm flying there in a stolen airplane. "I'm taking a cycling tour of Monument Valley, Arches, Wild Horse Canyon. I'll be up there a few weeks." Oh, I can be such a great liar where's my Oscar?

"You're gonna bike through the Utah desert in late November? You'll freeze your cojones."

"Hah, listen to you, a ladylike journalism student, making reference to a total stranger's body parts. You got a license for that?"

"You're not the least bit total," she laughs. "Although you are a bit strange."

Maybe because her voice sounds like Montana's, I get a flash from the old days with her, after we first got together with Mick. Things were easy, all kidding and light banter, fooling around. Until the time I found them kissing at the shooting range. The sullen way Mick looked at me. I passed it off at the time, but I recall his expression. Irritated, inconvenienced. He was looking at me as a sexual rival. For Montana.

"O hey will you be in town tomorrow at all? I have a break between afternoon classes. I'll treat you a coffee."

"Sure. What's that retro soda fountain place in the mall, on Second street?"

"You may be thinking of Johnny Rocket. It's on First though."

"Yah. Let's meet there. Tell your Rayne girl if she can make it."

"Stuka?"

"Mm?"

"Did that thing really happen?"

I know what she's thinking. The mirror thing.

"You know it did," I say.

"Made me happy."

Sound of her voice saying that makes me short of breath. "Times two," I manage to say. When I punch off the call it's more than definite with me. I'm not leaving.

I'm so nervous I get to the stadium way early. So I cruise up Tenth Street and drive up 280 to Saratoga and turn around, too fidgety to wait in the car. I get back still 20 minutes early, so I hang all tense outside the stadium gates, up a side street with the lights off. That's when I see something that wakes up a stray memory. A car. Of course it's a thumper, but the exhaust leak is familiar, from the night of the blues jam at my place. After Mick's enforcer took the gun from my head and walked off, I heard a car drive away. This one sounds the same, as it departs the stadium parking lot.

All is still. Can't wait any longer. I drive slowly into the lot. There's a vehicle small and distant in a back corner of the vast lot, lights out. I take a deep breath and head that way. I pull the El Camino next to her Jeep, my door by hers. A cigarette butt burns on the pavement.

"Took you long enough," she says by way of greeting.

I am well past being disturbed by anything Montana says. She is running down some weird track now. Me reacting to her bent vibe will be merely distracting.

"You check the layout?" I ask her.

"What is this, my job interview?" She sounds insulted but that's OK, I want her unsettled. Even knowing that Wolfe will be monitoring things, I am scared out of my Sunday School wits to be around Montana in her current state.

She goes on, staring at the clock on her dash. "I know exactly how to get in there and where to stand. He gets home eleven-ish from the City Council meeting. Fairly dependable. We have thirty-five minutes."

I know as much from talking to Wolfe. Except there are some details planned for this evening that Montana won't guess. I just hope nobody gets hurt. I'm still thinking I should warn her, somehow.

She speaks again, all in charge. "Let me see the gun."

"What gun? You said you would have a gun." Complete bafflegab on my part.

"You loser," Montana hisses through clenched teeth. "The piece Mick gave you."

"You must be confused. That's a parole violation, remember? You are my parole officer."

I had no idea what Montana and Mick had talked about. Chances are it was in code, on the phone, so the possibility of misunderstanding was always present.

"*Agent, not officer!* Shit, I knew you would screw things up."

"I can always come back next week."

"What? No way, has to be done now."

"Mick tell you what would happen if I don't hit this guy?"

"Yah you are toast."

I silently hand over copies of the three photos, Carruthers, Montana, and Tharcia.

She looks from one to the other. "What is this?"

"You should know, gangsta bitch. In case I didn't feel like going through with it, Mick takes out you and your daughter."

Montana laughs. "He would never touch us. You're making it up."

"Think about it. My probation is due to be over in a few months. You saw my file. I'll be free. Mick is asking me to violate parole, commit a felony, for a few bucks. And here you are, my parole agent, ready to write me up."

"Oh Stuka I would never." She doesn't sound convincing at all. She could have arrested me if I'd produced a firearm.

"And," I go on, "just in case I'm not interested, he threatens me by hurting you guys. Which is really stupid considering what he already did to Tharcia."

She seems to ignore that. "Well it's a good thing I came along, you moron. If you need something done right..."

"You down with Tharcia getting hurt?"

"That's not going to happen, schmuck boy. Mick won't hurt his own daughter. You however are another story."

"So I was right, Mick is Tharcia's dad."

"Play your cards right Stuka and things will go well for you. We want you in the network."

Oh great news, now she's making a deal with me. Rubbish. I know that Mick wants me wiped off the board because I threaten the appeal of his conviction. If Mick wants that, Montana wants it. She looks at her phone. "Time. We have to go. Follow me up there and park where I show you."

I check my phone. It's way too freaking early. "Not so fast, we're not on a schedule are we?"

"I've got a gun you can use," Montana is saying, looking around at the empty parking lot. "I'll give it to you when we're in position."

I'm thinking that her actual plan looks more like this: She shoots me with her service pistol, takes the other gun and pops Carruthers, maybe she'll miss but take a shot anyway to prove I'm evil, then press that gun into my cold dead fingers. I'm doubtful Tharcia will swallow such a story. Montana underestimates her daughter, as she does most everyone.

The parking lot is quiet. I know Wolfe is out there somewhere. Just to pass the time, I begin to nag her. "This takes me back to that time in high school. You loved me then."

"Don't flatter yourself."

"Well I loved you. Idiot."

"You're joking." Her tone is derisive but I know her inner narcissist wants to hear more.

"I did, Mon. But you were more interested in hanging with Mick."

"That's not true," she says defensively. "He was always trying to help both of us. Just like right now. He respects you Clay. He was impressed with your getaway after the diamond thing. But it was a mistake for you to double cross him."

Diamond thing? I never heard about any diamond thing. I try to sound nonchalant.

"Double cross him? Which getaway?"

"Mt. Baldy dummy, your fake car crash."

"What the heck is this *diamond thing*?"

Now she laughs at me. "Oh, you were so stupid. Completely in the dark. Mick planned that robbery in infinite detail. Except you were supposed to show up in a car to take your package. Not on a bicycle. You didn't tell Mick where you put your stash. That's why he fingered you and made it look like a drug deal. He fooled the cops on that too."

My mind is racing, trying to integrate diamonds with my money run after Mick's drug deal. This is scary now, her being careless with such secrets. Why? Because the way she sees it, 20 minutes from now I won't be telling anyone anything.

Montana's still talking. "It was only good luck that you got away. You weren't supposed to. You startled the guys at the drop. They handed you the wrong package."

Wrong package? So what was in the package I took? It means someone else took a handoff, someone I didn't know about. There could have been a mix-up.

"Nah, it was cash. That's how Mick set it up." I try to keep my voice even.

"You moron. Mick knows where you put them, we don't need you anymore."

She's talking nonsense. I told no one. No one could find where I hid it. *Them?* And it isn't what I've always thought. "Why didn't Mick just ask me?"

"By then he had been arrested."

"I mean when we were at the restaurant."

"Because you didn't show up."

Oh crap. Mick has been feeding her the feces on what happened that day. She's an important part of his network? No way. Time to change direction. "You're a player in Mick's organization? Hah. Mick is only interested in your fat ass."

"My ass is not fat!"

"Only language he understands is spoken by your butt."

She glares at me, teeth gritted around her next words. "Mick wasn't interested in you. It was me all along. Mick loves me. He's stoked at how powerful I have become. He played you until he had me. You were so lame. Then all he wanted was to get rid of you. You had no skills, it was hard to fit you in. He only wanted me. You won't believe the plans we have, when he gets out. It's only you and that fucking Wolfe made me move ahead faster."

I'm incredulous. How many women have said that about jailbirds? Rescue chicks with low self-esteem, thinking they can save the dangerous bad boy. And how many other women is Mick conning right now? It gets lonely in there. I know it does. Guys make plans with women they have never met.

"Well I hope I'm around the day you discover you're just another pelt on his trap line."

"You numbnut. You can't imagine the power I have in his organization."

"Oh I'm sure. You send him homemade porn to keep him warm at night?"

The way her face hardens says I'm not that far off.

"I wonder how much he makes selling those," I say sarcastically. "You're probably the poster pussy in half the cells at Lancaster. Parole Agent Porn Queen."

"He needs me and he loves Tharcia. He loves his little girl."

"Then why didn't you two stay together?"

"Complications," she spits at me.

"Complications?"

"None of your business, bozo."

"Let me try my luck. Let's say the complication is Mick. Abusing your nine-year-old daughter under your own roof?"

"What! You are out of your mind!" She says the words, but there's no conviction in her voice.

"So Montana, then why did you two split up? More precisely, why did you move out of his house to a motel, then to a nice house in San Jose? A house you couldn't possibly afford?"

"It wasn't like that at all."

"Fuck you, mother of the year. I can give you the name of your daughter's shrink."

And now I see Montana do something I have never seen her do before, not even as a girl. Hands to her face, she begins to sob, heaving gasps of air pulled from a lifetime of self-loathing and inner rage.

I don't care how she feels. I am beyond furious. "Tharcia came to you afraid and in pain. What did you do? Told her to shut up. You got in Mick's face, but you didn't really separate. Ten years later you're still hooked into him, still sucking off his power. And you deprived your own daughter of help she needed by telling her not to talk about it. Mick had to keep you and Tharcia quiet. Child abusers are the bottom-slime in prison. If that got out, his network would cave in and grease the guy. That's why you are valuable to him. Your silence keeps him operating."

"Please Clay just shut up shut up shut up."

"So I get it now. It was a diamond theft. Mick thought he'd get me arrested, or killed. Expected I'd be shot dead by the cops up Mt. Baldy. But when he figured out I'd hidden diamonds, Mick brought the heat on me so I'd be inside, where snitches die. Inside, where I couldn't make a deal for the hiding place. Of course he didn't want me on the outside screwing you. But he doesn't care who bangs you, really." That's when I get it... I'm alive purely because no one knows of my hiding place. And after all those years in prison, I finally know what's really hidden there.

"Shut the fuck up Cicero." Now that were on a safe topic she sounds more normal, if you can call it that.

But as wacked out as she is, I still feel the need to warn her. "Okay, I admit it. I stashed the diamonds somewhere else."

Her eyes are on me all intent. "Where?"

"Split this scene and meet with Wolfe tonight and I'll tell you. Whatever happens, those diamonds will be in your future." I am totally faking. With all the lying and mix-ups, I can't be completely certain what I shot up that tree on Mt. Baldy four years ago. It's an educated guess.

"You are demented," Montana says. "Mick retrieved them. I already have a share."

"A few maybe. You know what a liar Mick is. He got me busted because he doesn't know."

"Bullshit."

"I talked to him the other day, remember? He doesn't know where they are."

I can see it's not working and Montana is getting restless. My first big clue comes when she pulls out a dark pistol, twists a long silencer to the end of the barrel. She slaps a clip into the grip and sights over her steering wheel.

"So why did you shoot Roswell?" I ask her. "Think it was me?"

The question catches her off guard. "I never do my own work," she tosses off, intent on the pistol. She realizes what she'd just let slip, but she doesn't care anymore. She's been lying for so many years, she's relieved to have this pretense gone. In the dimness her face changes, as though she'd grown a pair of pointy horns, a smile loaded with sharpened teeth.

"It was supposed to be you, schmuck-boy." Her voice is defiant and relieved at the same time. It's out. Something she's wanted to say to me for years: *I want to kill you.* Once more I give thanks to the gnarly traffic on Highway 17. And to Drake. For being a greedy double-dealing son of a bitch, he took a bullet meant for me. You're welcome, dude.

I press the attack. "So you threatened Yamamoto so you could take over my case. Is he the only guy you blackmailed? Wolfe thinks not."

"You're talking to Wolfe?" She sounds hurt, betrayed. Really ironic coming from a major traitor.

"Oh, Wolfe and I are best buds," I remark confidently. She's holding the gun directly on me now, no further pretense. It's all Mick, pulling her strings. I have one consolation. At least before I die I know exactly how it was our last year in school.

She was all about him, totally a bad-boy's girl. Eight years older, he completely outclassed me. Montana went right over to him from the day the three of us met, hungry for his power. I was only her training wheels. And I realize why she wanted to be the shooter that time so long ago. Showing Mick she could play by his rules for the power he could give her.

"Get out of the car," she says with ice. "Walk around slow."

I get out, holding my hands in view. This has veered off Wolfe's instructions, I was not to get in her car. But we hadn't discussed this gunpoint thing. She opens her door and stands, tracking me over the Jeep's roof with the pistol. Her face is serene now, prettiest I've ever seen it. Angelic. She looks happy. She's saving her relationship.

"I could kill you simply because you stole from me," she says out of nowhere.

"Huh?" I reply eloquently. "Stole what? I've never taken anything from you."

"My jewelry. From my bedroom. You were there alone when I went to work. Who did you sell it to?"

She is raving. But now I know why it's so important to her. Her diamonds are real. *Pink diamonds?*

"So Mick didn't know anything about Roswell," I say, dragging my feet to kill a little time.

"Nobody in our chain knows who he was. He just wandered up your porch while my guy waited for you."

"You're such a fool. Could've been my UPS driver. You're so incompetent Montana. Is that thing even loaded?"

"It's loaded. As you'll find out the hard way when we get up there."

"Oh you have a schedule? And by the way, is that the same pistol that killed Roswell? Wolfe already has you as a Roswell suspect. He'll connect the dots, you'll be in the shitter."

She laughs. "You don't know the half of it," she spits back. "Mick will take care of me."

"Oh I'm sure Mick will get you adjoining cells with a shared bath. And what does Tharcia get? A mom she can see on visiting days? Pat downs on Christmas and Easter?"

"Mick helped me a lot. Helped us a lot. It's how I got through school with a kid. You idiot."

I'm at the passenger door now. "It's locked," I tell her with a crooked grin. I'm nervous, fingers trembling, but I manage to crack, "You're so smooth."

She reaches for the lock button, not taking her eyes, or the gun, off my face. Door clicks and I climb in slow. The pistol, in her left hand, is still on me. A lunge for the weapon is out of the question.

"Mick is wrong about Tharcia by the way."

"What are you talking about?"

"She's not his daughter."

"She is. I am sure of it. A woman knows."

"Tharcia knows who her real dad is now. And so do you. You're just stringing Mick along on that one."

Montana mutters something unintelligible. Her phone ping-pings. She pulls it out and glances at it. "That idiot is so getting on my nerves!"

I can guess who it is. "Wolfe wants to stop you from doing anything dumb. He might be out there right now, waiting. Guns on you." Hint hint. Come on Montana, *connect*.

Her pistol wavers slightly. She drops the phone into her purse. She'd like to finish me now but her plan needs my bleeding corpse at Carruthers' house. She's thinking she can wave all this away by appearing to save the Councilman's life.

Suddenly from out in the night, a bullhorn crackles. "Agent Harrison, lower your weapon."

Montana jumps at the sound of Wolfe's amplified voice. Her face is a hunted mask. She curses, looking around the parking lot. There's nothing to see. Her phone pings again but she ignores it.

"It's over Montana," I tell her quietly. "Put it down now. Think of your daughter. For once. The diamonds I'm holding can be yours!"

Her eyes turn into slits. "You fucking traitor. I regret I ever knew you." I can see in her face that the least she can do for Mick right now is be sure I am dead.

"Agent Harrison," the bullhorn blares. "Lower your weapon or we will fire."

Montana hesitates a split second. She screams out, "Mick!"

She floors it. The Jeep takes off across the deserted parking lot. She's concerned with aiming for the distant exit, not so intent on me. Waving randomly in my direction, the gun is almost within reach. I tense up to lunge at her, anything to get that murderous barrel off me!

Sirens and squealing tires, five police cars charge into the parking lot from behind the darkened stadium, sweep toward us fast in a comet of flashing lights. The cars fan out in a line, all we can see are blinding headlights and sparkling blue and red.

With a curse, Montana brakes and swerves hard left. I select that moment to pop my door and roll off the seat, hoping I don't get mashed by a pursuing car. An evil *pffffft* slices air as I exit the Jeep. A slug hits the asphalt behind me and whines angrily into the night. I hit the hard pavement rolling and the chase moves away, the wailing cars converge on her Jeep. About a hundred yards off they get her hemmed in. There's a crash. I hear Wolfe on the bullhorn, voice commanding.

I am kneeling on the asphalt willing her to stop, give it up, think of Tharcia. But incredibly, she is out of the car wielding the pistol, silhouetted in headlights. Her arms jerk upward and she's falling to one side before the shots reach my ears. She hits the ground limp as a sack. The arm with the pistol flops out awkwardly. *Montana what were you thinking?*

Then she doesn't move at all.

I'm on the ground, staring across the parking lot in empty disbelief. One of the cars rushes toward me. Two hooded men jump out, all in black with assault rifles. They draw down on me and loudly do their get on the ground thing. I stay down, looking across the littered surface to where Montana lies, a shapeless lump surrounded by milling cops. One has a foot on her wrist, the hand that holds the gun. I know that hand will never move again. This hooded cop is searching me, cuffing me. I'm led roughly to the cruiser.

I'm in the back of an unmarked car. Wolfe was here for a moment. He didn't speak, only shook his head sadly. Cuffs are gone. I'm cold and I'm shaking. Tears streak my face but no sound comes. For Montana, for Mick's corruption and her lost promise. She could've been great, if not overcome by her lust for power.

What hurts is the daughter. For the living hell Mick brought her. She had differences with her mom but never suspected how far off center she'd become. This ultimate betrayal will cut that girl like fire.

I resolve again, for the hundredth time in the last four years, to find a way to make Mick pay. He cost me three years of my life in a state lockup, a permanent blot on my record, most of my friends. A chance with Stacy. And now, indirectly, the life of a woman I once cared about. My demands are small. I want Mick crushed.

We are downtown. I'm not in the lockup yet, haven't been processed. They did take all my valuables and put them in a large envelope. But Wolfe left me alone in this interview room, which is a big step up from joining the gaggle in a holding cell.

Good thing is, it gives me some time to think, which is a bad thing. What keeps cutting a groove in my brain is how to tell Tharcia her mother is dead. What about the circumstances? Do we say, your mother was fleeing a police intervention, pointed her weapon at some nice officers who blew her head off? The thought brings revulsion. I will do everything in my power so Tharcia never hears that story.

Hidden players out there pulling my strings. My paranoia's in the red zone. Wade's friend Drake. Greedy fool. And Montana, her guy chain-smoking on my porch waiting until I come home so he can put a bullet through me. Mick, a child abuser who's running a mini-cartel from inside Lancaster, setting me up to do some pointless political hit so Montana can pop me in the process and make herself look good. I'm out of the way, hero badge for her. But she was wrong about my stash. They will never find it But now I'm sure what it contains.

This depressing reverie is interrupted when Wolfe comes in with another man who carries a small box. While Wolfe wears chinos and a sport jacket, this man wears a dark suit, diamond stickpin in his tasteful necktie. Hair gray at the temples, erect posture, bushy brows, he stands to one side. I get up. Who's this guy, the District Attorney? Did he get out of bed to read charges on me in the middle of the night?

"Mr. Clay, this is Harlan Rich from the D.A.'s office. We have a situation here." The two men exchange glances. Rich clears his throat.

"Mr. Clay, we understand you've been helpful and cooperative. But we have an issue of departmental confidence whenever one of our people is injured." My heart holds its breath. Is he about to say Montana's okay?

"Whenever we lose an officer, there are certain, ah, procedures to be followed." The two exchange guarded looks. "We think it's best, Mr. Clay, if we filter, or *shape* some of the events that took place this evening. For the press. For friends, even for the family."

"So are you cooking a story to tell her daughter?"

Wolfe clears his throat. I can see he's having a very bad night. "Mr. Clay, it's a matter of departmental morale. What happened tonight, the official story, is that Agent Harrison was pursuing one of her parolees. There was gunfire. An officer was wounded, and Agent Harrison sadly lost her life in the firefight."

I look at these two in disbelief. Then I think there might be a helpful practical matter.

"Does she have a life insurance policy? Is there anything for her daughter?"

Harlan Rich picks it up. "Mr. Clay, the Department takes care of its own. But there are realities."

Realities. Like what, Catch-22? "Does she have any family?"

"She has an aunt, in Los Angeles. We haven't contacted that family yet, but were on it."

Vaguely I recall a sister. Catherine?

"Has anyone told Tharcia?" I ask, at which point helpless anguish invades my chest. Wolfe's face reflects the same. He'd met Tharcia, the night Montana fled.

"We have not," Wolfe says, shaking his head. "We were hoping..."

Rich picks it up. "It is preferable for you to accompany detective Wolfe here, and our Trauma Intervention Specialist, to inform the daughter."

That fills me with icy dread. I can barely nod.

"Detective, do you have Agent Harrison's effects?"

From the box Wolfe removes two clear baggies. One contains Montana's purse. The other holds smaller articles. Her cell phone, a pair of reading glasses, keys, her red leather wallet, a small address book, lipstick, makeup, that sort of thing. No fancy jewelry.

Abruptly I remember the night long ago when police came to our house with a bag like that, containing my dad's valuables, collected from the wreck of his car. Too real.

"No!" I blurt out. Both men look at me in surprise. "Don't show her that. Not yet. Please not yet." I can only plead with my eyes.

"We need to go now," Wolfe says. I follow them out. He stands with me at the glassed-in cubicle as a cop slides toward me an envelope containing my wallet, phone, car keys, change, all the stuff I'd had on me. Apparently, I'm not being charged. I look at Wolfe, he simply nods.

Joining us in the jail parking lot is a diminutive woman who calls herself Ricky Emmanuel. She explains she's a TIS, trauma intervention specialist. She works everything from family services to officer emotional trauma response. On the ride through San Jose's dark streets she's asking me what I know about the victim, and about Tharcia. I'm so close to tears my answers are incoherent, Ricky asks me in a soft voice to please repeat. She's already found out I'd lost my folks, have a brother I never see.

"I haven't seen Montana for almost 20 years," I tell her. "We ran into each other recently by chance. I became friends with her daughter and some of the daughter's friends. I don't know any adults Tharcia is close to."

"Have you spent any time with the daughter?" Ricky asks.

"Some. She and her girlfriend were at my house one evening, the night Montana ran. Wolfe was there. We've talked on the phone several times, I spoke to her at their home some."

Ricky looks at me closely. "So Mr. Clay, how would you describe your relationship with the daughter?"

"Friends. Family friends. Well, I was friends with Montana. Agent Harrison. And Tharcia is..."

Then I can only shake my head, holding up a hand as if to push the whole thing away. Ricky's hand rests on my arm. Turning into a quiet street we pull up in front of the house. Rayne's gray pickup is in front, Tharcia's little gold sedan is in the driveway. Montana's Jeep, of course, is nowhere to be seen.

CHAPTER 11
HOT PINK ICE

CRUISING MONTANA'S STREET this cool Saturday, I'm surprised at the many cars. Can't park on her block at all. I'm walking along, slacks and a black leather jacket, fresh haircut for once, looking through branches of bare winter trees to cloudy sun overhead. Car door slams behind me, a woman's high heels clip-clip along the sidewalk. From a block away, I see a couple in somber clothing walk slowly toward Montana's house.

Funny. Being away from someone for a long time you have no idea what their life has become, who it has touched. People talking on the porch, front door standing open. Voices, music from inside, tunes we danced to in school. I edge my way through the door, excuse me, pardon me. Small tight smiles.

Kitchen counter's loaded with food, fruits, meats, salads, casseroles, desserts. Finger food. Bottles of wine, soft drinks. People elbow to elbow balancing plates, wine glasses. The box of Godiva chocolates I brought gets wedged in somehow.

No sign of Tharcia. Rayne's in the kitchen with a knot of young people, Tharcia's school friends presumably. Twyla is there, talking to a woman I'm betting is Montana's sister, what the heck is her name? I see Ricky, the trauma intervention specialist, talking to some others, maybe parole cops. Couple school classmates I recognize say hi with their eyes.

I work my way through, Rayne sees me, her face is veiled in weariness. She hugs tight, I feel in her the tension of carrying so much pain for her friend.

"Clay," she says, pulling back to look at me. She looks wiped out. "It's so so sad. How senseless."

I nod glumly. This is going to be hard, staying connected with the cover story Wolfe pasted on top of the reality at the stadium. Agent Harrison, intervening in a difficult case, ends up shot to death.

"She was a true professional, a real giver," I say. How the hell do I not vomit?

"I just met Tharcia's aunt," Rayne tells me. "Do you know each other? Catherine, do you remember Clay?" She touches a woman's shoulder, who turns from her conversation with Twyla, looks at me.

"Is that Stuka?" She gives me a brief smile, puts out her hand. There's a resemblance, it is almost spooky to look at her.

"This is so difficult for me, you can't imagine. One day I'm taking my boys to soccer practice, next day I'm flying in to bury my sister and help poor Tharcia."

I nod, reading her face. Trying to remember. I'd seen her occasionally at the family place when I came on my trail bike to pick up Montana.

"How is Wade doing, is he here with you?" She's interested, more than merely curious. She and Wade knew each other in school, makes her a couple years older than Montana.

I shake my head. "How is Tharcia doing?" I haven't seen her since I came in.

"Holding up," Rayne says at my elbow. Catherine's reply is cut off when Twyla pushes through for a hard hug. She starts sobbing like she'd been saving it. Annoyance on Rayne's face.

Catherine gets re-started. "Tharcia is a mess, poor dear. I don't know what I'm going to do. Somebody needs to take her out of this wretched situation. But I can't handle my boys as it is, plus now a girl in college. Oh, I suppose she could transfer or something, but I don't know how Jonathan and I can cope with it."

Twyla pulls back, with a tissue dabs at streaked eyeliner. "Talk to you?" Doesn't wait for an answer, she's towing me through the crowd. I have time for an 'excuse me' glance for Rayne and Catherine. We're headed out the door, to the sidewalk. Twyla faces me, holding the lapels of my jacket in clenched fingers. In the cloudy autumn light her hair is radiant copper. I notice for the first time she has green eyes.

"Stuka I have so needed to talk to you." No explanation, she just looks at me, letting the line hang as though it means something. I shake my head.

Twyla pulls on my jacket until she's pressed against me. "It's been so hard for me, Tharcia is such an angel. You'll know when you see her." She's in her own world. I ease her away.

"You have to do something for me, it's mega important."

"What's up?"

"I need you to give her something."

"Tharcia?"

She nods.

"Why can't you do it yourself?"

She looks toward the house. "It's just too. Embarrassing for me. I did something evil bad. Oh, Stuka I'm so sorry." She's pulling me in hard as though her sexual touch will bring forgiveness. I gather her wrists and push away.

"Alright. What is it?"

Her lip quavers as she pulls a small tan envelope from a coat pocket. Inside, the necklace and earrings from Montana's night table. What she'd been wearing when I first saw her downtown. The stones glisten pinkish purple in the winter light.

"Twyla, what the hell are you doing with these?"

"I saw it on her night table. Couldn't resist."

"What were you even doing in Montana's room?"

"It's just me, Stuka. Sometimes I get a little bent. Will you help me? I just can't face Tharcia right now, not with what she's going through."

"What were you doing in Montana's bedroom?" My voice is harder now.

"Tharcia's mom sometimes goes out late."

"So?" Then I truly get it. "Did you give me something that night?"

Twyla looks down at her cute shoes for support. She nods. "You are so hot, Stuka."

This little nut job actually drugged me. Then helped herself to Montana's jewelry.

I am absolutely beyond pissed. Talking through clenched teeth. "You might not know this but I could be drug tested any time. If I fail I go back to prison. Tell me, would that be worth it for your little thrill?"

Now she can't look at me at all. She lets go of my jacket. Her face sags. "I didn't know."

Now I'm grabbing her elbows, shaking her. "That was you, wasn't it, when Montana left."

She's pulling away, not meeting my eyes. I let go. She's looking at bare trees down the street, nodding unhappily.

"I don't want you around me ever again. Tharcia deserves better friends."

She glances up, shocked at my words, but it's the hard look on my face that nails her. Stumbles back as if I'd shoved her, turns and starts unevenly down the sidewalk, like a sleepwalker.

I take a deep cleansing breath of the cold autumn air. The sun is pushing through clouds, blue shadows in the street. Turn to the house, people are leaving, I can see across the living room now. Ricky is there, studying two large poster boards covered with photographs. I stand with her, both of us looking at the pictures. Tharcia must have done this. It's a whole lifetime, Montana as a young girl, a teenager, sometimes with men, many with Tharcia. Couple photos of Montana with me on my trail bike, Tharcia's high school grad photo next to her mom's, the raven and the blonde. Tharcia and her mom with friends, a younger Tharcia with her mom clowning, laughing together, running in the pumpkin maze out by Hollister. No photos of Mick. I'm getting a major lump in my throat.

In the doorway, Wolfe comes in as a couple plainclothes cops are leaving. They talk briefly.

Something familiar on the coffee table. The high school yearbook from our grad year. I flip through, wondering how Montana even got it. She'd left school early. No signatures and messages in it, but I do remember some of our classmates. Seeing them now makes me smile. And the senior photos, image of the kid I was then, not smiling, just maintaining.

Tharcia walks out of the hallway with two friends. Group hug, tearful kisses. They are leaving. Tharcia sees me, comes over. I hold her. Her face looks drained, but she seems more together than some of the method actors I've encountered today. Pulls me through the hallway, into Montana's room. We sit on the edge of the bed.

She laughs, a small sound in a tired face. "It is so strange. Sometimes I completely run out of gas for this. Like it's still there, but at a distance. For a while sometimes

I can't even feel it. Insulated. Then it comes crashing back in."

I pat her hand. "It never stops, just changes. Only thing you can hope for, peaceful equilibrium. Someday."

"It is so weird, the way some people act about it. Like they want me to move on, get over it, get closure. Like I'm supposed to be in a hurry to feel good."

"Yah I've seen that too. People are afraid of grief."

"I'm thinking it takes one to know one," she replies, holding my gaze.

"You got that right."

From the small bathroom, the first line of a current rap song. Tharcia gets up. "I've had that thing on the charger. Ricky brought Mom's stuff."

She comes back with the phone, were sitting there watching it ring. Caller ID shows a restricted number.

"It's been doing this."

My mind is suddenly going a mile a minute. "Have you answered any calls on her phone?"

Tharcia shakes her head. I'm getting an idea.

"Babe, I get the feeling it's someone we want to talk to. Would you take a chance? Don't answer. I'll be right back."

I return quickly with Wolfe in tow, close the door and explain what I've guessed.

"I think it's Mick calling Montana. Tharcia has seen her talking to him, I think I have as well. If he will talk to her on speaker…" I let my meaning hang.

"What do I say?" Tharcia asks.

"He probably doesn't know about Montana. It will shake him up. Because it's you, if you say it's you right away, maybe he won't hang up. Maybe we can find out what's going on with them."

Wolfe agrees. Tharcia is noncommittal, unhappy enough as it is, without talking to a man who mistreated her as a child. But she knows we need her for this now.

She sets her mom's phone on the bed. Pushes the speaker button, then callback. I'm amazed it even rings, sometimes you can't get back to a disposable phone. We wait. I pull out my own phone and start recording video, Tharcia, the phone on the bed, for what might be said. Wolfe does the same. It stops ringing, voice comes on the other end.

"Hannah, that you?" Voice is unmistakable. Tharcia's face confirms it.

"Micmac?"

If a silence can express surprise becoming comprehension, this one does. I visualize a man in a cell hearing a voice he hasn't heard for years, trying to understand how this can even be.

"D-girl, that you? How'd ya get your mom's phone?"

"Micmac it's me. I've got her phone. Mom's dead."

Tharcia begins crying uncontrollably. Wolfe and I are motionless and silent. The distant voice comes through the speaker.

"What are you saying D-girl, what the hell happened? Are you okay?"

"She was shot, Micmac."

Mick's voice spills over into hardened anger. "Who's mixed up in this?"

"It was just random," Tharcia chokes out. "A random thing. Family violence with her parolee. The department is giving her honors."

"Did that chickenshit boyfriend get it too?"

"What, Micmac? Nobody else got shot."

"Has he been hanging around her? I'll kill the suckah." Mick has picked up the scent, doesn't care about Tharcia, her pain, about Montana, only interested in making his own ego comfortable.

"Who are you talking about?" Tharcia fakes it well.

"Ah, someone you probably wouldn't know. Did she find her jewelry? She told me someone jacked it!" Wolfe and I look at each other.

Tharcia looks confused. "I don't know. Nobody here would take it, just costume jewelry."

"Not fucking fake shit. The most precious thing in the world."

"What is, Mick?"

His next line is calmer, not quite syrupy sweet but verging on it. "You, Diamond Girl. You are the most precious diamond in all the world. When did this happen?"

"It was Tuesday night. In the parking lot at Spartan Stadium."

Mick is silent. "Hey baby are you on speaker?"

Tharcia is shaking her head. Her eyes dart pleadingly from me to Wolfe, asking. *What do I say?*

Mick's voice comes, a grated snarl. "You greasy little twat." The connection goes dead.

Tharcia recoils from the phone, mouth open in shock. Shaking her head, her expression hardens. She screams.

She keeps right on screaming. Unintelligible sounds of wounded anger and betrayed trust. She's stomping her feet against the hardwood floor with her fists clenched. I stand and pull her in. She grips hard, screaming into my chest and shaking with rage. People are trying to push into the small bedroom. *What's wrong what's wrong?* Wolfe does a good job of traffic control. He lets Ricky in. And Rayne. They sit on the bed, trying to help Tharcia get through.

I turn to Wolfe. He's checking his phone, his recording.

Wolfe says to me softly, "What are these jewels?"

"Montana was wearing them. Then last week she started accusing everybody of taking them."

"What were they? Where were they last seen?" Wolfe wants to know.

"She said in here, on her night table. A necklace with some colored stones. I saw them, she accused me too. Matching earrings."

"I have to get downtown, go over this recording. Mr. Clay, not a word to anyone." I close the door after the detective, Twyla's envelope an ominous weight in my shirt pocket.

Voices at the door. Followed by Ricky, Tharcia goes out, people wanting to say goodbye, final round of hugs. I am hoping that Tharcia can tell the trauma specialist what Mick did to her as a child. She must tell.

I sit alone, looking around Montana's room, how neatly kept it is, her beautiful things. Never thought of her as ladylike but now I see she has refined taste. Nothing here I remember, it's been too long. True what they say, you can't go back.

Then I see it, something that couldn't have been here before. Gracefully shaped, glazed maroon with gold leaf decorations, a crematory urn sits before Montana's dressing table mirror. To think of all that vibrant life burnt to nothing in a jar.

In her adjoining bathroom I turn both taps in the sink. For the noise. Then I'm twisted over, speared by the pain of it, unable to make sense of anything. No matter how conflicted she was, how contrary, how bent on evil outcomes, I know I could have loved her, for the way I knew her then. Not what she since became, with Mick.

Only a few folks in the living room now, couple gals helpfully putting away food, hugs and tears at the door.

Tharcia is urging people toward the porch, still gracious though clearly exhausted. Finally the place is empty. Front door closed, we park on the sofa. She curls her feet under her, fingers twirling a strand of her hair.

"I remember what our house felt like after Mom died. It was hard to be there." I watch her face. "You said one time you wanted an adventure."

She gives me a disgusted look. "This is an adventure?"

I shake my head. "Something you said when we first spoke. We can have a mini-adventure right now, if you're up for it."

She's thoughtful, looking around the empty house. "I wouldn't mind getting out of here for a while."

"We can go flying."

"You mean in your airplane?"

"One of the school gliders."

Soon we're cruising out Highway 25 toward Hollister Airport. She looks more comfortable in jeans and a fleece-lined black denim jacket, baseball cap with a Red Bull Racing logo. Bulky black leather satchel at her feet, Montana's school yearbook clasped in her arms.

At the gliderport she's interested in everything. I sit her in the front cockpit and show her the altimeter, the variometer, what the controls do, the towrope release. On the runway hooked up behind the tow plane, we wait as a Piper Archer shoots a landing on the intersecting runway. Sun is out, afternoon is warming. I signal the tow plane and we start to roll.

In the decent headwind, the glider lifts off before the tow plane does, I hold us about five feet off the runway as we gather speed. She's laughing in the front, looking around, thrilled to be gliding effortlessly over the ground. It's bumpy on our ascent, there are thermals around, though it's a cool afternoon. We drop the tow at twenty-five hundred feet and head for a gaggle of six gliders circling a couple miles off the end of the runway. Unusual for Hollister in winter weather, but hey it's lift we'll take it.

We join the gaggle, circling with them, all turning counterclockwise centered on the invisible column of rising air. In a left bank, we can look across the spiral at other gliders. Colorful. Through their canopies we see the other pilots, passengers. I see a gap and cut across the thermal's core, gaining altitude. Five minutes and we are above the others, Tharcia's looking down at the floating carousel of graceful long-winged planes. Dirt roads and patchwork fields far below.

She lifts a hand behind her head, smooth fingers wiggle at me above my control panel. I hook fingers with her as we go higher. Cloud above us, concave on the bottom where the thermal tops out. I bank steeply and for half a circle our high wing cuts graceful vortices through the cloud. We make a swooping dive across the valley. We're picking up speed, losing altitude, feel the bumps as we again find lift. She shouts out a happy woohoo. We spend ten minutes in that thermal, working back to cloud base at six thousand.

Small cumulus clouds mark other thermals, we spend another 40 minutes like that, hopscotching between updrafts, soaring quietly above the tapestry of fields and fall colors far below. Finally it's over. We fly a normal landing pattern and we're down. The look on her face climbing out is gratitude, relief. Anything for a brief respite from the pain she's carrying.

Driving out in my El Camino, I remark she probably wants to be getting home. But she surprises me.

"No. Your place. Please. You don't mind?"

We're quiet on the drive, which works for me. I am picking apart my impressions of the call with Mick. Poor lost little Twyla and her thieving mischief. Driving into the setting sun. I pull out my phone. Try the twins but it's their voice mail.

"Hey you guys, want to talk to Carla. Something I'd like you to see." No idea if they are around, in the swimming pool, whatever. I have a hunch.

It's full dark when we stop in front of my place. In the living room I build up the fire. I notice Tharcia's forlorn expression. The universe is dealing out crap hands to everyone. Tell her I'm taking a shower. She brightens, asks can she have a tub bath.

I wave my hand toward the upstairs, sure sure, then get a call from Darla. They are available and can come by in an hour. No details on the phone, which we all understand, but there are inquisitive spaces between Darla's words. Bring a loupe, I tell her.

Halfway up the staircase, Tharcia stops to listen.

"Who is coming over?" Like she's had enough people for today, ready to chill.

"Good friends, old friends. They know things might be useful. High school buds." Her expression says she's not wild about it.

Anyway later we're all clean and warm. I'm putting out hummus and salt crackers. Tharcia asks about the twins.

"You're serious?" I smile at her. "We go back to grade school. How much you wanna know?"

She smiles a little. She's tired, but ready for any mild distraction, take her mind off her mom for a while. I take a swig of my beer and settle back on the couch. She's curled up at the other end, in my sweatshirt and an old terry bathrobe that's way too big. Her inquisitive gaze sends me back over the years.

"Before we go there, I need to ask you something."

"Sure."

"You already told me a little about what happened with Mick. What I want to know is, how you came back from that." What's on my mind is, where did she hide the wreckage?

Tharcia takes a deep breath, not looking at me. "It seems like this should be easy, I have told it so many times."

"You don't have to tell me if you don't want."

"You should know." She gives me a long look. "First of all, it wasn't the worst kind, not what people usually think. It was mostly not contact abuse. It was like peeking at me in the tub or in my room, exposure, spankings. He spanked me in front of a man and a woman. It was degrading."

I shake my head slow. This is disgusting. "Your mom was out?"

"Mostly. But sometimes she was in the house. Rayne was one of my babysitters. She was fifteen. She saw my bruises. Neither of us knew what to do, I was scared. When we moved to the new house, Rayne got her driver's license and sat with me when Mom worked late. She took me to a survivor's group without telling anyone. I learned to meditate. My meditation teacher didn't have to know anything, didn't ask. He just taught me how to be silent and watch my thoughts. That was hard. Sometimes I relived everything, without wanting to.

"I started working on letting go the guilt. Rayne got me books. By the time I was sixteen I was able to get a counselor. It was only then that Mom got involved, because she had to sign things. She told them I had a hyperactive imagination. My counselor said the other parent can be in denial. Mom had to swear she wouldn't bring boyfriends home.

"But Mom herself didn't help directly. It was a taboo subject. Especially about any connection with Mick. Now Mom's gone she can't control me anymore."

"So Rayne was your babysitter, and there are records with your counselor that these things happened?"

"I know what you are thinking. Rayne saw everything. She swore not to tell. But I'm not a victim anymore. Not for a long time. I am a survivor. Recovering was a decision I made."

We're quiet for a while. "I decided something else," she says with firm conviction. "I am ready to go after Mick."

I look at her. What I am feeling is pride. "I'll help in any way I can."

She gets up and sits next to me, leans her head on my shoulder. I put an arm around her. There is no way to describe what I feel at this moment. She looks at me.

"But hey you were going to tell all about Carla and Darla." She is ready to change gears. So am I, but I sure feel better we had this conversation.

"Ho ho. That is a saga. Carl Wilton Desmond. A guy I've known since we were second graders in San Jose. Best buds for years. Me with my interest in airplanes, war history, and electronics. Carl liking sports, astronomy, geology. We did all kinds of wacky stuff, sleepovers at my place or his, camp-outs in the neighborhood with the other kids, hikes up in the hills, major bike rides all over the Valley and the coastal wetlands. Went to the same YMCA summer camps three years running. We managed to get in the same cabin, which helped a lot with us playing tricks on everybody else.

"We found out from his dad that both of us were geeks. Meaning anything from computer hacker to a carnival performer. It also means peculiar or dislikable, or overly intellectual.

"Carl decides he prefers being known as overly intellectual, while I'm attracted to the idea of being peculiar. Carl's twin sister wanted to be a geek too, but it was our boy's club. Girls, who needs 'em?"

Tharcia tries to make a stern face here but she's amused anyway. I go back to my story.

"Carl was a star on the football team, despite his slim build. He was one of the most precise place kickers in the history of our school. Carl drifted from being overly intellectual as a geek, to one who is highly peculiar. My geekiness had migrated first to electronics, such as radio-controlled cars and model airplanes, then to more normal kid stuff, such as getting the perfect haircut, the coolest shoes and jeans, and finding out I could say certain things to any girl and get a nice kiss. If I gave her my soulful look."

"Catch-dawg."

"Yeh. Carl and I had a severe falling out. He came in his sister's room and found us under the sheets. The parents were away that weekend and we thought Carl was out on his bike. The look on his face was utter devastation. He didn't seem to notice me, he just started shrieking at his sister, saying, *Darla, you said you would never. Why? You said it was only me.*

"Darla is pleading with him, like, *Carl honey, it's not like that, it's not the same. It's not like with you at all. I love you baby.*

"Wait a minute." Tharcia's voice brings me into the present. "They are twins? Fraternal right?"

"Exactly," I tell her. "But they looked identical, even back then. They would cross-dress each other to prank people for a laugh. Of course Carl changed his name slightly since moving out of the house, adding the 'a' on the end. Carla and Darla. They're about the only people I still know from high school days. They knew Montana too, sometimes we would all hang out."

Tharcia is thoughtful, "They were here at your party. I spoke to them, they seem nice. Thought they were lez together. You sure Carla's a guy?"

"Am I ever. But what's this about 'I love you baby', spoken from sister to brother? That was way weird even for me. Turns out the two of them were sleeping in each other's beds since childhood. Being twins, they had strong bonds.

When puberty struck they discovered sex together. And the sibling affection became something else."

"Sibling rivalry begets sibling revelry," Tharcia cracks. Her one-sided grin surfaces for a second.

"Hah. You made an actual joke. So then Carl knows he hates me, which leads to me getting jumped by the football team a couple weeks later. There was also major split between the two of them at the time. Darla was branching out and experimenting as kids will and Carl was still hanging onto their childhood. It was a sad time for him. Puberty basically sucks for everyone. Who invented it?"

Tharcia nods knowingly. "Worst time of my life."

"Roger that. After grad I briefly connected with them. Darla came to my mom's funeral. She had become the most beautiful refined woman, and we still felt the same friendship. We sat up late and had drinks, but never got involved after that."

"Oh Stuka, I remember you said about your mom, but you never told much about it."

"Yeah. I was the same age you are now." For a few beats we lock gazes sending that one back and forth.

"So imagine my surprise after renting this funky house, and in the neighborhood come across a little shop with *Dollhouse Furniture* painted over the door, real cute little place, very colorful, and inside is this lovely chica that just has to be Darla. Long dark hair, slim build, nice boobs, lovely skin. I say her name, she shakes her head and smiles. She says, Darla's out, may I tell her who called?

"Then I can only stare like a dummy. This sweet looking woman lets her jaw go limp for a moment, and blushes. She's flustered, not knowing what to say. Finally she stands up, extends her hand, introduces herself as Carla Desmond, with an A."

"Wait, hold up. Did she do something? Surgery? I have a friend who..."

"She went part way. Carla is still a he, with boobs and hormone cream. Anyway the voice, the grip of the hand, the dark steady eyes, I'm looking into the face of a best friend from school days, a time portal back to another life. Carla's wearing jeans, which fit her slim hips very well, a long-sleeved silk blouse that drapes nicely over her breasts, no bra for sure I can see her nips.

"Then it's my turn to blush, trying like crazy to recover. Skipping over the very obvious Topic Number One, namely his/her gender identity, I ask what they've been doing since high school. Carla says she heard about my folks. Such great people, so sorry and all that."

Tharcia nods sympathetically.

"She tells me about the dollhouse furniture biz, which they'd just set up. Wanting to do something artistic."

"O hey." Tharcia says, "how was it going from calling her a he to calling her a she?" You know what I mean."

I chuckle. "I made a few mistakes. Anyhow we talk a while, I get that after he graduated from Berkeley in gemology, and Darla got her degree in theatrical set design, they wanted to do something together. Carla suggests I come by their house. And then I get the rest of the picture, it's them living together, no third parties need apply."

"What? Like boyfriend girlfriend?"

"Yuppers. They are maxed out in love."

"Their kids could be genetically damaged!" Tharcia is already beyond the sibling incest part, she's more worried about any kids.

I laugh. "Haven't exactly discussed that detail. I do know they love each other. So about Carla's gemology thing. She studied geology, then gemology, became hooked on valuable and rare stones. She makes money now buying and selling gems and minerals worldwide. But like with lots of enterprises these days, it's not enough.

"They showed me around their house, showed me a closet grow op. I told them if they want to make some money doing that, they need to see my swimming pool."

"You have a pool here?"

"Old pool, uphill, out of commission on an adjoining property. House there burned to the ground years ago, killed the entire family. The site was cleaned up and left. No one goes there. It's a decent-sized lap pool, four feet to eight feet deep. I put a top on it, disguised it, and built a sizable grow operation inside.

"The twins went mildly nuts when I showed them. I'm doing 20 times the production they were trying for. Guess you'd say my geekiness had leaned over to plant horticulture. Along with the mini law degree I'd studied for at the Colony."

"You have a law degree?" She looks puzzled, like I'd skipped a page.

"Figure of speech. Many cons in lockup study law, for appeals and such. Spend enough time in jail with guys who know things, you can practically memorize every fact about any topic. My minor was growing pot under lights. Anyway, that is how we come to be in business together."

"So why are they coming over tonight? To talk about old times?" She sounds a little snarky, not like her usual centered calmness. Bit of the old Montana leaking through. I see she's been rubbed raw.

"It's about the jewelry."

Tharcia gives me an ah-hah expression. "Major freak-out at the homestead over that. Mom accused me of borrowing them, she accused Twyla and Francie, everyone who had been around our place. Twyla cried and ran out. Mom backed Rayne against the wall and screamed in her face. She thought you took 'em."

"It was Twyla," I tell her sadly.

"What! How do you know?"

"Twyla comes up to me today and gives me these." From my shirt pocket I hand over the small tan envelope with Montana's gold necklace and earrings in it.

Tharcia sees, and breaks down in tears, clutching the envelope hard.

"Is this them?" I ask her. She manages a nod. Of course I have no tissues in the place, fetch a roll of paper towels. "These are heavy duty," I tell her helpfully.

The beauty of her face as she laughs through her pain is stunning. I kneel by the sofa and pull her in. She is cursing into my shirt and clutching the envelope. "Twyla, you little klepto dump." She looks up at me. "Don't ever get mixed up with her, she's poison."

"Believe me I already got my first clue."

Tharcia is just calming down when a car stops by the porch. She pulls away and runs to the bathroom. I hear the latch click.

They don't knock, just kick the door open and barge in, their usual boisterous hellos. Darla has a paper bag with bottle necks showing, Carla has a cardboard box that's folded shut on top.

"Hey sweet cheeks," Darla comes close for a full contact hug. I am feeling neglected so hug her hard and give her a kiss. She kisses me back, just enough for old time's sake.

"Leave my sis alone, you perv," Carla cracks. Scenes from our childhood.

I'm not in a joking mood. "We just came from the memorial," I tell them solemnly. "Tharcia is here." I tilt my head toward the bathroom.

The twins are immediately all serious and whispering. "Oh we didn't know. Is that the daughter?"

I nod. "Well," Carla says, "we'll do our thing and get out of your way."

"No, it's fine. You guys met her at the jam night?" Both of them say yes.

Carla's at the kitchen table removing things from the box.

"Clay you want a G and T?"

I think. "Sure, a slow one."

Darla digs out some ice. Carla has her tools ready. "So where is this stuff you want me to check out?"

I pat my shirt pocket. Whoops. I gave the bag to Tharcia. I tap on the bathroom door. "T, did I give you the jewelry?" Door clicks and a slim wrist extends the envelope.

"You OK?" I whisper. I get a glimpse of red-rimmed eyes. She closes the door without a word, expression unreadable. Whew.

Carla takes the envelope, slides the three pieces onto a dark velvet cloth. Sharp intake of breath when she first sees them. Darla and I sit with her at the table. Carla's totally silent, looking carefully at the sparkling rocks. I hope I'm not wasting her time with this, but the pinkish stones cast back fierce light.

Carla has a small microscope, and she positions the pieces so she can see each one in turn under the powerful lens. I can tell she's thoughtful.

"Clay," she says cautiously, "where did you get these?"

I try to keep my voice low. "Montana had them."

"She have any others like these?" Carla is looking at me with wild eyes. I try to think.

"She might. Tharcia would be the one to ask."

Carla is intent at the microscope. Her fingers tremble. Finally she sits back and looks at both of us. Her face is pale.

"It's a good thing you didn't try to get these evaluated."

Darla and I look at her blankly. I shake my head. "I don't get it."

"Besides having serial numbers engraved on each one, these diamonds are beyond hot. Completely over the top."

"Pink diamonds? Montana said they were costume jewelry."

"Star Eyes, can I see?" Darla is busting to get a closer look. Carla slides the microscope in front of her.

"Diamonds absolutely," Carla says. "I think they are Argyles."

"Argyles."

"The Argyle Pink is a type of diamond from an Australian mine, the Rio Tinto. People aren't much aware of colored diamonds. Know how Montana got them?"

"They were given to her," Tharcia says from behind us. "A boyfriend."

We all turn at the sound of her voice. Carla goes to Tharcia and hugs her. "We are so feeling you on this girl. It is beyond hard. She was such a lovely soul."

Darla steps over and does the same thing. "We knew her, when we all were kids." Tharcia comes to me to be held and for a time we're all quiet.

"Why do you say they are hot?" I ask. "I don't know anything about diamonds."

"There was a major theft," Carla says. "In 2003, an Italian gang got inside the Antwerp Diamond Center and emptied most of the deposit boxes. Almost all were full of gemstones. There were many Argyles. The loss was in the hundreds of millions of Euros."

"You said hundreds of millions," Darla observes cautiously.

Carla nods. All three of us are riveted as she goes on. "The thieves dump some trash down the road including half a sandwich. The saliva DNA leads authorities to a few suspects. At least one's in prison, but may be out soon. None of the jewels have ever been found. May have been lost. Could have traveled all over the world."

"Including here," I throw in just to cover the obvious.

Carla nods, "Including the USA. These are the first I have heard of, and I'm freaking touching them! There are all kinds of theories, like movie stars have them, Arab princes, et cetera. But you couldn't wear them on the red carpet or anything public, would have to be a private party. A very exclusive one."

"But the ultra-rich play to a select audience," Darla reminds her.

Carla nods. "There's rumor in gem circles that mentions a theft years after the Antwerp robbery. Supposedly, some stones had come into possession of a certain film actor living in Malibu canyon. Sources suggest a private sale at the star's home. A number of set diamonds and raw stones was later being transported to a secure storage facility in Claremont, California."

Do my ears prick up when I hear Claremont? You damn well betcha.

"There's a deception," Carla continues, squinting again into the microscope, "a Brinks truck was hired to return the jewels, but the stones went by private car with two armed guards. Some say a servant or bodyguard was bribed for the information. The car was to arrive at the storage location after the Brinks truck left. But a team of robbers hits the car before it arrives, taking the jewelry. One of the three thieves is shot and dies later that day. The others escape in different vehicles. One left on a bicycle." Tharcia throws me a sharp glance.

We play musical chairs, taking turns at the microscope. Tharcia just cries when she looks at the image of perfect, pink-toned facets, saying *Mom, why why why.*

"They are incredibly rare," Carla continues, "so they would pass as costume jewelry for most people. The pinkish cast looks like cubic zirconia, a synthetic crystal. The Argyle Pink Diamond is the most concentrated form of wealth on earth. Because of that one mine, Australia produces double the diamond output of any other country."

"So you are saying," I'm groping for a coherent thought, "that no matter how valuable, Tharcia could never sell these?"

"Not to say it's impossible, but someone would have to be well connected. This pink ice is beyond hot."

I'm stroking my chin. Then I start to grin at everyone, at Carla in particular. "Well, wise ass. Why you suppose we called you?"

CHAPTER 12
CHANGE OF PLAN

WADE AND I HAVE AGREED that I will fly the Mustang to New Mexico. Full stop. Which means I have a lot to sort out. There are a lot of supplies, equipment and logistics to deal with. I've spent a ton of time with sectional charts of the airspace from California, Nevada, Arizona, and New Mexico. I know the route I want, I'm checking the weather daily.

I've been playing with the flight simulators on my laptop, reading everything I can find online. I phoned Sean and asked about some of the maneuvers we made on our flight. I have read dozens of NTSB accident reports involving the P-51, researched blogs by and about WWII pilots who flew the Mustang. I've done everything except take one off and land it on my own. I am as ready as I can be, without advertising what I am contemplating. Will flying a stolen aircraft to New Mexico violate my parole? Bet on it.

I'd made one *banzai* run to Wade's place, to go over the plane again and work through our various contingency plans. What if I crash on takeoff, what if it won't get off at all, what if I have to bail out... how do we handle those possibilities? And last but not least, what are the steps for the payoff if I should, by some remote chance, actually succeed?

That possibility cheers me. And I realize with greater certainty that I've pulled away from the idea Wade and I have worked out over several years... switching my identity and vanishing from a life that revolves around being a convicted felon.

The complication that trumps them all is Tharcia. Between her mom's death and the fact that we could be related, she's been hanging onto me for dear life. And she has awakened a part of me I never knew existed, a part I genuinely like.

My phone goes and who do you think it might be?

"Hey Tharcia, how's by you?"

"It comes and goes. I dropped my classes."

"Really! Actually I am not surprised, you need to decompress."

"Yeah. The term's half gone and I've missed a week already. I'm all skitzy, crying one minute, normal the next. Ricky helped me with that, she's an angel. My adviser suggests I wait until Fall term next year then start back. Doesn't matter if I am a year behind, no jobs out there anyway. I've got a lot to sort out. Are you back?"

Only a week since Montana died. Seems like ten years, so much has changed.

"Yah. Got in last night. What about your scholarships?"

"Well, I lose out on this year, the money is spent. I might be able to get one of them reinstated when I enroll next year."

Her voice trails off. Then, "I thought about you Stuka."

"Missed you babe."

"Yeh."

"Wolfe leaving you alone?"

She sighs. "Not really. I am meeting him at Mom's bank."

I am immediately on alert. "What for?"

"Wants me to open her safe deposit box for him."

"What! Does he have a search warrant?"

"He says he does."

"What time is this going down?"

"Quarter after three."

"Have you spoken to your attorney?"

"I don't have one. Think I should?"

"Listen, let me come by and pick you up. We can talk on the way. What bank is it?"

"Union Bank on First. I'll be here Stuka, thanks."

At ten till three I get the weirdest feeling, realizing it's the first time ever I knock on Montana's door without expecting her to be there. Tharcia steps out. With her long blond hair, black beret, and camel hair overcoat, she looks the part of a classic gangster's moll from an old time film, such as *Casablanca*, or a Raymond Chandler character.

The house is different. Things are gone from the walls, lighter-colored rectangles where pictures, paintings, an embroidered saying once hung. The tank with its colorful fish is gone. Rooms are bleak, hopeless. The *Actual Parent Wanted* sign has vanished from her bedroom door.

"What's going on?" I ask, gesturing at the empty walls.

"Can't stay here. Can't stand how this feels. Been staying at Rayne's apartment."

"Where will you go?"

She shakes her head.

"Stuka, why does the detective want in Mom's safe?"

"It's about the diamonds. They could help put Mick away for good, and ice his network besides."

"You mean Mom's jewelry?"

"Yah. They might be connected to something Mick pulled off."

"So what do I do?"

"There might be more diamonds or other jewelry in her safe box. What Carla said about those robberies. If so, Wolfe will take that as evidence against Mick. Which would be a good thing." I hope to steer her away from discussion of evidence against Montana, although she's bound to see that. I'm coming around to the fact she will find out what her mom was up to, but I firmly believe it should be me that tells her. And hopefully not too soon.

"If there are no diamonds in the box, give him your mom's jewelry. Say I gave them to you at her memorial, from Twyla. You put them aside and remembered today. Otherwise keep them and say nothing."

"Okay." Her face is soft, tearful.

"Tharcia?" She looks up at me.

"Tell me the truth. Are you attached to them?"

Looking around the barren room, she thinks about it. In this house she'd grown from a nine-year-old girl into a mature woman. I can sense her disbelief in the way it came crashing down.

"I have other things that are more important. Mom was attached to those, I'm not. But Stuka, if they are stolen, and from Mick, those aren't memories I would keep."

"Good. Tharcia, what does she keep in her safety deposit box?"

"There is the house deed in it, insurance policies, legal stuff. I found her key after Wolfe called." Her eyes fix on mine. "Stuka? My mom was bent, wasn't she?"

I look back at her, not surprised she knows, wondering how she will handle the details, finding her mother was a gangsta mole in the Santa Clara County parole system. So I soft pedal, tell her about my meeting with Mick's enforcers, the hit Mick ordered, the threats against her and Montana.

"Mick may have been forcing her to help him. If he threatened you, she would find it hard to resist. Those guys play mean, with guns."

She nods unhappily.

"Get her jewelry and we'll take off."

She returns with the small manila envelope. I give her a hug. "You are going to be okay. We should go."

"Stuka, there's something I need you to help me with."

"Sure. Anything."

"What do I do about Mom?"

I get an instant flash of the crematory urn on Montana's dressing table.

"The ashes."

"Yeh."

"She ever say anything to you about that?"

"She said at sea, one time."

"I'd be honored to be with you."

Downtown, we wait in front of the bank. Wolfe walks up with a man in a dark suit. With them is Ricky Emmanuel, the trauma lady from County. Inside the bank, Tharcia and a clerk retrieve the deposit box and bring it to a private cubicle where we all stand, expectant. Tharcia opens the box.

There is a collective gasp. Aside from the usual paperwork, the deed to Montana's house, her will, insurance papers, some old photos, there are several fat bundles of hundred-dollar bills. There is also a roll of black felt. Tharcia carefully unrolls it on the table. In separate small clear bags are six pink diamonds. There are four pieces of set jewelry, a bracelet, a necklace, and two pendants, all featuring the same exotic stones.

The man in the suit looks them over carefully using a loupe and a special light. He nods at Wolfe.

"Ms. Harrison," the detective says, "we must seize these jewels. We believe they are from a theft in Belgium in 2003. We must also seize this cash."

Tharcia looks straight at him. "How did my mom get this?"

Wolfe shakes his head. "We think it was Mick McIntyre."

"So my mom was mixed up with him?"

"It is too early to tell. We need to trace these diamonds back. They may have been stolen more than once."

Meanwhile sirens are going off in my head about the day of the Claremont job. Montana as good as told me but I have to go down there, see for myself. We leave the bank; Tharcia is silent as the two of us walk to my car. Exiting onto First street heading for 280, I know what I have to do.

"Tharcia, there is something else. Remember about the chase up Mt. Baldy? I think it's diamonds I stashed up there, not money."

Her mouth forms a round O. "You said it was a drug deal."

"I thought so until recently. Those diamonds in your mom's safe. That has to be part of the take from the Claremont job. Which means they are from Mick. The stash I left up there might be diamonds too."

"Hah. Does that mean there is an adventure in your future?"

I smile back at her. "Yours too, if you play your cards right. Is tomorrow too soon? What is your lady love up to?"

So early next morning Tharcia, Rayne and I depart in a pounding rainstorm for a run down Interstate 5 in Rayne's Dodge crew cab, south across the California Mojave, over grapevine pass to the 210 then to I-10 and east, toward San

Berdoo. In Claremont we get off on Mountain Avenue and go north, uphill, toward Mt. Baldy village.

From a roadside pullout we look down a rocky slope. Four years ago I'd gone over the edge here on a trail bike. Riverbed at the bottom was dry then, but it's been raining here and snowing on top so there's some runoff.

There is no trail, unless you're a goat. Rayne is a bit hesitant but I tell her since she's hanging out with Tharcia she's a thrill-seeker by definition, which wins that argument.

We fill backpacks. We have no idea if we'll get stuck down there, it might take more than one day. Each pack gets a compass and flashlight, some compressed granola bars, water, binoculars, rain gear, saws and knives, a branch lopper, sleeping bag, and a first aid kit. It won't look like overkill when we need it. I have a pocket GPS unit. We're dressed for the weather down to our waterproof hiking boots.

We step over the side. After 30 minutes we're jumping small streams in the riverbed. Moving beneath trees down here, I'm following the GPS and watching for landmarks, one tree in particular.

I find it easily but when I do I am not very happy. The tree has broken about 50 feet up. The top 25 feet of it toppled and hung up in a neighboring pine, forms a slender bridge between them. With binocs I see tangled bungee cord and the outline of something that could be the small dry bag I'd left. Why is it still here? Stupid Mick. I could have come back for it easily. But I wasn't in his long-term plan.

"You're sure that's it," Rayne says, holding the binocs.

"We're at the coordinates. Not much doubt."

"But wait," Tharcia says, peering through the binoculars. "I don't think you have to climb the tall tree. Go up the smaller tree. I think you can dislodge the broken top."

I look again, follow what she's thinking. "Might work. Could use the loppers to cut the broken part away, let it fall."

Then, I wonder, what does it do? Maybe it breaks off and falls to the ground. Great. But if it doesn't snap off, what we're after could dangle out of reach.

"How about this," Rayne says. "Tie a rope on the broken part, then we break it free by pulling from down here."

Well she's got a brilliant idea, only hitch of course is the execution. No better ideas come, so I start to climb. The rain has let up but everything's slippery cold and wet. I've got the loppers and the saw and about 200 feet of line, my stupid looking bicycle helmet, which helps with pushing through the branches. Loppers and saw dangling from my belt, constantly getting tangled. Anyway after about 10 minutes I'm up here staring across at the bridged treetop. Small rubber dry bag only 15 feet away. I'm dying to know what's in it.

The broken tip of the other tree goes right by my face but it's only two inches thick here. Marginally strong enough to hold me. So I want to get the rope around a cluster of branches about 10 feet out where the grip will be secure. The three of us will be able to pull it down.

I am having no luck getting a loop out there, taking a breather and looking things over when branches shake below me. I look down and there are Tharcia's baby blues peering up through the pine needles.

"What you think you're doing? Are you demented?"

She laughs. "Why miss all this fun? Think of me as a silent observer."

"Hah, as if you could ever be silent."

"I have my quiet moments."

"For instance?"

"When conjuring the Devil."

"Lunatic."

Now she's squirming up through the branches next to me and we're eye to eye in the pine needles. Raindrops sheet her cheeks. All she has for noggin protection is the soggy Red Bull baseball cap.

"So what are we doing Captain," she asks, looking at the fallen treetop. "Hey is that it, is that your bag?"

"Yuppers. I'm trying to rig a line to this, then climb down and we all pull on it. Want to get the rope tied farther out."

"I already have a better idea," she says confidently.

"Hit me with it."

"Tie the trees together real tight so this part can't fall. Then one of us climbs out there and unhooks your bag."

"Not bad. May I suggest a safety harness first?"

We talk about it then finally I start to work, using some of the rope to lash the broken top to the trunk we're holding onto. Branches slap me in the eyes as I work.

"Speaking of ideas, I had one the other day," I tell her, trying to feed the line around a branch.

"Like what?"

"You were saying you don't want to live at your mom's?"

"Yeh. Feels too strange. Mean and sad."

I take a second to yank a knot tight. "Well, there's a room and bath at my place, any time you want it. Room for Rayne too. I'll throw in the services of a certain cat."

"Stuka! That is the coolest ever." She's quiet for a minute. "That's close to Cal Santa Cruz isn't it?"

"Um, twenty minutes."

"Killer," she says, from a foot away.

I can't tell you how happy that makes me. I go back to lashing the two trunks together, look up when it's tight, and get a real shock. Tharcia has worked her way out along the broken section of the other tree. The whole thing is sagging like a bow. She's ten feet out, the tree I'm in is leaning toward the other one. Her legs are dangling down and she's inching along.

"You lunatic," I yell out. "At least you should have a safety line. Get ready I'll toss it."

"Cool your jets, Clay. Told you I'm an experienced rock climber."

"This is a tree, you nutter, there's a diff."

Tharcia laughs it off. "Also Rayne's down there she'll catch me. You roped that nice and tight I presume."

About this time Rayne notices what Tharcia is up to and yells bloody murder from below. Tharcia's reply is a looney laugh that echoes among the trees. I'm prying my mind away from disbelief as Tharcia, 15 feet away and suspended over the clearing on the sagging broken trunk, she's using her knife to cut my dry bag loose.

"Okay if I just drop it?" She's holding the bag in one hand now.

"Should be all right."

The bag and the tangle of bungee cord falls free and plops on hard earth 40 feet below.

Jeez, watching it drop all that way is too graphic, with Tharcia dangling out there. "Can you get turned around okay?"

She says oh sure, spends a while maneuvering, the whole thing bobbing and swaying. I am not going to describe how she does this, but only a woman's hips could manage it. My hair's standing up when she gets turned around, working her way back. Ten feet away, now eight feet. Something in my mind is starting to ask why that tree trunk broke in the first place when with a loud crack it snaps in two, five feet behind her.

She doesn't scream. But the section she's clutching swings down and disappears into branches below, Tharcia clinging to the slender trunk. My lash job twists and groans but holds tight.

"Tharcia! Are you all right?"

She's not saying anything. I'm climbing down as fast as I can. Can't see her. Soon enough I'm there, and Tharcia's draped over a branch and gripping it like a lover. Her mouth is open she's gasping for air. But her eyes twinkle. I get close and hold her jacket with both hands.

Her face is scratched up and her hat's gone.

"Knocked the wind out."

Meanwhile Rayne down there is screaming her head off for somebody to tell her what the fuck just happened. She hollers she's coming up. I yell down no don't she's okay got winded can't talk just wait.

Eye to eye with her as she's catching her breath, I ask the question I have been holding onto. "Tharcia? Did you say anything to Ricky? About Mick."

At first it seems she's about to cry. But a worn smile lights her face.

"Everything, Clay. I told Ricky everything."

"Sensational. Would you..."

"Testify?" She looks at me, all courage and resolve. "That a-hole is going down."

Ten minutes later were sitting on the ground congratulating ourselves for still breathing. Rayne, after totally loving her up, launches into a long string of profanity. Threats and imprecations. She has a point, it was a risky move. Tharcia smiles tiredly.

I pick up the dry bag. The Velcro separates with a loud rip. And then I'm holding what's become for me the Holy Grail, the zippered fanny pack I'd carried up the mountain in a car, down the mountain on a bike, shot up a tree on bungee cord, and which Tharcia has just retrieved by damn near splattering herself.

I open the zipper. Inside there's an opaque blue plastic bag that's taped shut. Feels like money packs. But instead of the bundled cash I'd visualized every day of my life since then, it's only newspaper. In the bundle is a roll of black velvet, secured with rubber bands.

I unroll the velvet on the ground. Inside, each in its own small transparent sealed baggie, are fifteen cut and polished pink diamonds.

"Stuka." She's kneeling next to me looking at what's on the black cloth. Rayne's close too, and for a minute were just staring at them. I feel like my plug's been pulled. Fifteen Argyle diamonds, not in settings, just perfect cut pink stones. I don't know carat sizes, but a couple are phat wedding ring size, larger than those on Montana's 5-stone necklace. Diamonds that Carla told us are beyond price, but hot as they are, have no value.

Zero.

But a small voice comes, reminding me that the world being how it is, there has to be something we can buy with these. Emotionally I'm on overload. I start shaking, my insides convulsing like I wanna puke my guts. But that's not it. Sure, I've waited four years for this moment, but it's Montana. She was devious and scheming. But.

"I miss her, Tharcia. I do."

Men aren't supposed to cry, according to rules somebody made up. Tharcia's arms come around me, then Rayne's. They're rocking me. I feel like wanting to be sick, but that's not even close. Unsteadily I roll up the velvet with the diamonds inside. It makes a small bundle I can zip inside a jacket pocket. I wad the dry bag and the other stuff into my pack, get busy collecting our gear. The rain has stopped. Slowly we make our way up the wet hillside to Rayne's truck. We leave the mountain clean.

Hours later we've left I-5 and we're heading across 152 toward Gilroy and San Jose. I put the batts back in my phone. Looking through my messages, something completely throws me off. From Montana's phone, this morning. Blindly grasping at hope, I punch through and listen. Brutal disappointment. Should not have even hoped, she's been gone over a week now. I'm cursing too fluently to hear what Detective Wolfe's message has to say. I replay it.

"Mr. Clay, forgive me calling on Agent Harrison's phone but I must reach you at once and you may be screening my calls. We need to see you at my office as soon as possible. It is imperative you contact me immediately."

Still fuming, I dial the number. His, not Montana's.

"Mr. Clay, is that you?"

"Wolfe you have no idea what you put me through."

"Of course. I am very sorry, Mr. Clay. It was unavoidable. Some issues have come up around Agent Harrison. It is vital we talk in person as quickly as possible."

"What is it?" I snap. His apology is probably acceptable to a sane person, but right now I am enraged at his deception.

"How soon can you come? We have made an arrest and have information about Agent Harrison's activities. I believe you can fill in some gaps for us."

"Will it shorten my parole?"

"Mr. Clay, I can make no promises but…"

"I'll be there in two hours," I snap, and kill the connection, cursing.

So by six o'clock I'm touring the uninspired institutional hallway, wondering distractedly how the people that work here can keep their sanity in these inane surroundings. I find Homicide and the sign-in sheet. I don't have a chance to sit before Wolfe sweeps through the waiting area carrying several thick manila folders, a uniform cop in tow. Wolfe introduces us. Firm handshake both ways and I'm now a valuable witness.

Unbefuckinglievable.

I walk quickly after these two, Wolfe stops at an interview room and the cop walks on ahead.

Inside, another shock awaits me, it's Deputy Parole Officer Yamamoto, my former owner. The guy Montana snagged my case from. Odd seeing him in an interview room instead of his office. Dressed as usual in a tweed jacket and black jeans, Yamamoto does not look happy. He glances at me and then away.

"Mr. Clay, Mr. Yamamoto, I'm sure you know one another," says Wolfe. My guidance counselor is entranced with the texture of the table between us.

Wolfe jumps right in. "Mr. Clay, let me bring you up to date. Since the night of Agent Harrison's tragic shooting, a number of facts have come to light. First of all we have, thanks to Officer Yamamoto here, the answer to your question. As to why were you transferred to Agent Harrison."

The hefty Japanese looks like he'd rather be anywhere else, preferably smoking an unfiltered cigarette.

"Um. Yes," my former case officer says. "This activity goes back over two years. Hannah, Agent Harrison, was in the habit of requesting certain cases from me. Well, not only me, but other parole officers in the section."

"Is this usually done, Mr. Yamamoto?" Wolfe prompts.

The officer shakes his head. "It is not unheard of, but not prevalent. I am getting ready for retirement, and did need to offload casework in preparation for that."

"The numbers," Wolfe prods.

"Yes. It was much more frequent. In the last two years, a dozen of my cases went to her roster, at her request. She acquired cases from other officers as well."

"Mr. Yamamoto," the detective says, "how would you characterize the cases that she requested?"

"As we've seen in the last week, they are similar offenses, usually drugs and smuggling, extortion."

"Thank you, Mr. Yamamoto." Wolfe flips through a file folder, hands me a sheet of paper with a list of names.

"Mr. Clay, please review this list and tell us what you see. This represents roughly fifteen percent of Agent Harrison's caseload."

On the list are sixteen names, with dates, institutions and crimes. I'm only a few names down the list when I glance over at Wolfe. His eyebrows lift but he says nothing. I continue reading. Finally I get the idea.

"Nine of these are familiar. My name is on it too, but you know that. I know six of them from the Men's Colony, San Luis Obispo. Others by association or hearsay. One of those dudes I saw going into her office last week."

"I see," Wolfe is nodding. "And how would you characterize this group of people?"

"All of them have some drug activity, dealing, running, transportation. Two may be smugglers. And there is something else."

"Please continue, Mr. Clay."

"I'm thinking that most of them worked for McIntyre."

Wolfe says, to Yamamoto, "Then all of these are cases Montana asked you to transfer to her roster?"

Yamamoto nods. "It is also significant that all of those men have had their parole chores lightened in a, shall we say, informal way."

"What do you mean?"

"What he means, Mr. Clay, is that while these men were attending regular interviews in Agent Harrison's office, they were not adhering to the terms of their parole."

"I have reviewed five of these cases so far," Yamamoto continues, "and the record-keeping is questionable. Some home addresses are incorrect, employment records don't check out. Several of them had arrests or trips outside their designated area. Ankle bracelet alarms that did not lead to parole violations. Certain technicalities are quoted in Agent Harrison's write-ups."

"Technicalities that would..."

"Allow these men to walk all over the Parole System," Yamamoto says firmly.

"With Agent Harrison's willing assistance," Wolfe supplies.

The three of us are silent, looking at each other.

"In short, Mr. Clay, what we are seeing in her case roster..."

Now it's my turn to finish Wolfe's sentence. "We're seeing part of Mick McIntyre's gang network."

Bingo. Montana was Mick's proxy gang boss.

Wolfe goes on. "We are in the process of connecting Agent Harrison's phone records to these people where possible. There is a pattern. We have searched her vehicle. The night she died, she had nearly fifty thousand dollars cash hidden in it. She had her service revolver, issued by this department, along with two clean heavy caliber pistols. One suppressor, which is not legal even within law enforcement teams. Any ideas, Mr. Clay?"

I look from one to the other. "Tells me she could be managing a network of gangstas. Perfect setup. She can meet with them openly, here in her office, without suspicion. They could pass information or cash freely."

"Parole Agents," says Yamamoto, "as opposed to DPOs, or deputy parole officers, have wide latitude geographically, and broad discretion in how they carry out their work. It is possible she was enabling McIntyre, on the outside, by giving parolees in his network a free pass."

My turn to ask a question. "I have one for you, Officer Yamamoto. Have any of these dudes been written up?"

"First of all, yes. We have five parolees in custody, pending review of their status. There may be more."

"Meaning five of Mick's guys went down?"

Yamamoto nods, so I ask, "But why were you so cooperative with Agent Harrison?"

Yamamoto now looks as he did when I'd first entered the interview room. Embarrassed. "This is difficult. I was protecting my retirement, which is due in two more months. At my last annual merit review, Agent Harrison caught me in a small infraction. Or claimed she had. Minor, but potentially damaging. I could not be sure, but it was easier to transfer the few cases she requested than face an official inquiry. I was supposed to say nothing."

A few more minutes of this and that, and Yamamoto makes his exit. I'm looking at Wolfe thoughtfully.

"Money," I say. "You found cash on her. Plus what was in her bank box. Any trail from that?"

"In her office safe we also found records. The diamonds we found in her deposit box also confirm she is well connected to Mr. McIntyre."

I get up to leave. Wolfe motions me to wait. "We have been looking into many of Agent Harrison's cases. Including yours."

"They have reopened my case?"

"When you were arrested, it was based on Mr. McIntyre's statements. There was no evidence that connected you to the diamond theft."

"That is what I have been saying all along, detective. I transported a pouch of money." I say this on autopilot, but for the first time ever I know I am lying.

Wolfe nods. "We searched your house, the farm where you were living. The drug dogs found nothing. Three weeks later, a quantity of cocaine was found among the evidence that was collected."

I jump to my feet, hotly enraged. I'd been held on a variety of charges for nearly a month, before they charged me on possession with intent. "How come my public defender didn't find that?"

"Mr. Yamamoto pointed us to an individual in the evidence section. Records may have been falsified. It would not be easy to spot."

"What was Montana telling you?"

The detective's expression is grim. "She made a racket that we should search again. She was vague, she was casting doubt on the search protocol. Mr. Clay, it's possible that she or someone else corrupted evidence."

"So you're telling me Montana was behind that?"

Wolfe nods. "Not conclusive yet, but it may be so."

He lets this sink in. It was Montana who arranged for me to spend three years in prison. Why? To protect Mick from me? No, to protect her power. If he goes down, she goes down. I was too dangerous.

"There is another matter," Wolfe goes on. "We made an arrest the night Agent Harrison died. Near Councilman Carruthers' home."

"Really?" I am surprised. "Coincidence, or connection?"

"We have someone here I'd like you to meet. He was found holding a Glock-40 with a suppressor in a vacant house across the street from the Councilman's home."

I am shaking my head. "Detective, that hit was a fake. Montana was setting me up."

"We thought so too. But there was room for doubt, so we took the precaution of placing a team there."

"You have him?"

Wolfe nods, starting for the door.

"Detective, there is something I need to ask."

"Please."

"The daughter. Tharcia. Will she be taken care of?"

"How is that any of your concern, Mr. Clay?"

"At the least, she is my friend's daughter. At the most, we have become friends."

"In a very short time, it seems."

"I want to know if she will be taken care of."

"Scarcely a concern of yours, Mr. Clay. I am sure the system will find a home for her."

"She's of age, Detective. Can she collect Montana's life insurance? Can she keep her house?"

"Those are things you should discuss with Ms. Harrison, if she feels it appropriate."

Oh crap, is all I can say to myself. The system. Oh crap.

"Please come with me now, Mr. Clay."

I follow down the hallway to another interview room. Standing by the door inside is the uniform cop I'd met on the way in. Inside, seated at the table, is a wiry long-haired dude in an orange jumper. His hands are cuffed behind him.

"Mr. Estevez, please look at me," Wolfe says.

For a moment nothing happens, then the eyes come up and fasten on Wolfe. They shift across to me. The instant flash of recognition is unmistakable. It's enforcer88, the dude who pressed his heavy pistol to my head the night of the blues jam. The look that passes between us carries a silent conversation that goes like this:

You with them, or you with me?

None of your business.

You gonna rat me?

None of your fucking business.

You gonna get wasted.

Like hell I am, pee wee.

What I know beyond doubt is I'm looking into the flat cold eyes of Drake's killer. The man who waited at my house to kill me. Montana's shooter. Wolfe opens the door, I follow him out. We stand in the corridor, close enough to whisper.

"Dude was at my party," I say in a soft voice. "Called himself enforcer 88. Delivered a message for me to call Mick. Pulled a gun to show he meant it. Drove away in a noisy V8. I heard the same car at Spartan Stadium just before I met Montana. Leaving the parking lot."

The way Wolfe nods, looking at me, I see the tumblers falling into place in his head.

"This guy might be the one who shot Drake. Don't tell me he's on Montana's case roster."

Wolfe nods. I'm catching on.

"Anything else you can think of? Any detail at all?"

"There was a cigarette butt smoldering beside Montana's jeep when I pulled up."

"And Agent Harrison did not smoke. I'll review our crime scene report."

"Oh, also the fake DEA suits followed me to the gliderport and delivered the gun and the photos. When I talked to Mick about the Carruthers hit."

Wolfe nods grimly, straightens up. "Mr. Clay this has been most valuable. Thank you so much for your cooperation. And once again, I do regret calling you from Agent Harrison's personal phone."

I sigh. "Had to be done, I suppose. But there is something else."

"Yes." Wolfe looks tired, ready to pack it in for the day.

"Montana's daughter. She's prepared to testify against Mick for child abuse. She was nine years old." My throat is tight, I can hardly get the words out.

Wolfe looks disgusted. "Who knows about this?"

"Ricky. Tharcia made a full statement to Ricky Emmanuel, and a Child Protective Services counselor. She'll testify. She has witnesses."

Whatever elation Wolfe might have felt at the clear opportunity to disconnect Mick McIntyre from his organization is held firmly in check as he says, "When next I see young Tharcia I shall give her my deepest condolences, and my thanks for her courage."

The detective turns on his heel and strides down the linoleum corridor. I head for the exit. It's long after hours, cleaning crews are moving through the offices. Bone weary, I walk the empty parking lot to my El Camino, absently musing about where I now find myself. My former girlfriend had lived her dream, found the power she'd always lusted for by hooking onto Mick's coattails, and had perverted the County parole system in doing so. She'd stuck me with a false rap that sent me to prison, after her boyfriend's plan fell short. She'd tried to have me killed, and in the process, mistakenly prevented Drake from doing so. An accomplice in the evidence section suggests that further traces of the late Parole Agent's activities will be found. A thorough house cleaning will follow wherever she has touched.

A house cleaning that is now underway, I remind myself with muted pleasure. Parts of Mick's network, the cases Montana controlled, are now headed back to prison.

Did Montana want to kill me? She did fire off a round in my direction. But it was Mick pushing her buttons, always Mick. His upcoming appeal, his anger over losing fifteen diamonds to his own arrogant stupidity. But what he did to Tharcia years ago is about to attack him in a way he cannot defend. For her willingness to go public about that terrible experience, Tharcia is the hero in all of this. At least, she is for me.

A cold morning two days later. Carla, Darla, Rayne, Tharcia and I board a motor yacht in Santa Cruz Marina, and make our way to the center of Monterey Bay. The sun fights through the morning overcast. Winter swells are heaving mountains.

Far offshore, Tharcia and I lower to the water a small, gaily painted wooden boat. Into the boat Tharcia empties Montana's ashes from a clear bag. Among the loose white fragments of what was once a human being, she places two diamond earrings and a gold diamond necklace. Although everyone knew Tharcia's intention in advance, Carla cannot suppress a tortured gasp.

Tharcia's lips move quietly as she says goodbye. She places on the ashes a small envelope. Gently she thrusts the boat away. We watch in silence as unseen currents start the tiny vessel on its unknowable journey. Everyone manages to hold Tharcia at once as the tiny craft sails from view among the massive swells. Our boat swings about, motors for the harbor.

Tharcia and I sit aft, watching our wake, pondering the voyage of the tiny boat, of the life that had culminated in this reality.

I lean closer. "How you doing babe?"

"It's black, Stuka. I have no family and no home. My mother's house, not my place anymore." I hear the ache in her voice. "Stuka, was she happy?"

Tough one, I have to think. "I saw happiness in her. Don't know if she let herself own it."

"Her pulse was with me since before mine began. It is silent now. She showed me what it means to be a woman."

"Yah. There are things every day I would like to say to my mom and dad."

"I don't have to fear her disapproval anymore." She's quiet for a bit. She looks into my face, voice tinged with uncertainty, "Was she proud of me, Stuka?"

I wrap her in my arms. "You know she was Tharcia."

"I'm so glad." Her voice is muffled in our heavy coats.

"Hey, what do you think of Christmas in Hawaii? You, me, Rayne, the twins."

"Anywhere. If we can all be together." Way she says it, sounds like the only family she has.

"Doesn't have to be now. Anything to get away."

She turns to me. "Stuka, what you said. About me staying with you?"

"I remember." A long moment sings as we hold each other's eyes.

"Can we go home now?"

CHAPTER 13
THE COLONEL

GETTING TO WADE'S FARM is as usual, except I need to leave my car behind. Tharcia drives me and my beater bike strapped with a wacky assortment of gear through bare dirt fields to the Salinas Greyhound station. She knows the full truth about my 'vacation.' The only goodbye we can manage is a breathless hug. Neither of us speaks. Her face is pale as she turns from me.

The bus drops me and the bike somewhere near Altamont. The ride out the arroyo is uneventful except I surprise a pair of coyotes enjoying the last of what could have been a rabbit. They stare after me as though calculating their odds, but do not follow. I like coyotes.

The air is colder as I approach Wade's farm, the uneven dirt track across the flat now too faint to see in the waning daylight. But far across the desert floor, the bright rim of a full moon among distant clouds is a reassuring beacon. We'd chosen this night so moonlight would be an advantage.

When Wade gets a look at my bike he has to laugh, all the junk and the big Army pack strapped to it. A couple black garbage bags complete my ensemble.

"Where is your supermarket grocery cart?" he cracks. "Oh right, the brake locked up on you."

"Well it's all necessary stuff," I remind him, and I'm right. Parachutes, main and reserve. Day pack and hiking boots for when I'm traveling out of the landing area. Step-in coveralls, Nomex underwear for warmth and in case of fire.

Ski jacket, bicycle helmet. A laptop to display the pilot's manuals, checklists, procedures we had developed; it's without wireless capability to avoid detection. And the five GPS units I'd insisted on. Wade congratulates me for being more paranoid than him. But he shrieks with hilarity when he sees all but one of them is rigged with its own little parachute.

"For tail-shaking, see? Every couple hundred miles I throw one out. It floats down still broadcasting its location. Nobody can connect the dots from here to the landing site."

"I'm getting you professional help," Wade replies with a grin. He beckons me after him and strides off toward the barn.

Now here I depart from my long planning. I leave the fake ID at Wade's. I do not dispose of my real ID or my phone, as I had long planned to do. I'd had other tail-breaking strategies too. Such as putting my real phone on a bus for New York or sending it somewhere by UPS to throw snoops and followers off my scent.

But that was before everything changed. Now, all of it seems foolish. What I need to do is survive the flight and come home. To my real home, and to the life I will hold onto tight, if I'm alive tomorrow morning. If I'm not, tough luck.

We're standing between the open barn doors looking up at the Mustang. Under bright lights, the bare metal gleams silver. There is no paint on her, no tail number. Officially this aircraft does not exist. Wade has been busy, he has much to tell me.

"You have 240 gallons on board. I only put 25 gallons in the fuselage tank, burn that off first, for stability." That old balance thing again.

"The wing tanks are full. Keep your speed below 300 or you'll run out of fuel. Your burn rate is about 60 gallons per hour at that speed, which gives you an extra hour in the air in case you have trouble locating the landing zone. The hydraulics are perfect! Look at the pistons in the landing struts, three and a half inches. Just like spec!"

Wade is clearly proud of himself. Can't say I blame him. This Navy jet mechanic has done a superb job.

It's a long time till our planned 3 a.m. departure, but there's lots to take care of and time passes quickly. Of course we have to do things like eat and talk story. Wade loves World War II history. One of the officers on board his Navy carrier got him hooked on old warbirds. I remind him that's one of the ways he takes after me, Stuka.

Wade had traced this P-51's deployment to the Mediterranean theater. It's a B model, meaning it was built in Inglewood, California around 1944, along with about 2000 others. He thinks it had flown with a fighter group of the 15th Air Force. Not many Mustangs were shipped back from Europe after D-Day, many were scrapped at their air stations or sold off locally. He is excited about the fact that one of the four 15th Air Force fighter groups was a Tuskegee unit.

"So there's a one-in-four chance that our plane could be a surviving Tuskegee Airmen ship," Wade explains happily. "But I don't have to trace that down. My buyer is confident that he can authenticate it completely, using the Air Force records. Every so often he asks for a photo of some detail, or about the condition of some part, which way a certain handle faces, what color the knob is. He's not telling me what he makes of that, but I am confident he'll be happy."

"Dude, how do you communicate with him?"

"I Skype him from someplace reasonably far from here, using a fake IP address. They might know it's my Skype ID, but never my location. Who I am."

Yeh right, just call us the Paranoid Brothers.

Through the last couple years, proceeds from my grow operation have gone almost entirely to buying parts for the Mustang. I'd been on the hunt for P-51 parts ever since

Wade hinted he had a certain semi-trailer in his barn, before I got out.

In prison, I pitched my business plan to parole examiners as preparing for a career in vintage aircraft replacement parts. Told them there was a ton of money in it and I could employ other cons once it got going. A con job about con jobs. After getting out I bought components from all over the country, and Wade made things from scratch. When that effort added up to a complete fuselage and a wing, I spent a week out here with Wade and a couple of chain hoists mating wings and fuselage, setting the ship on her landing gear, hanging the prop. That was the first time she'd looked like an airplane, though a lot of work lay ahead.

"This aircraft is not going to be restored, at least not by us," Wade reminds me for the umpteenth time. "Best I could do was make her flyable." Both of us know flying her out is the only way we can deliver such a thing. And the value of a flyable plane is greater.

I'm in the cockpit finding places to secure all my gear. The laptop is open on my lap, where else, and we're going over the instrument layout again.

"I got the rear radar warning checked out," Wade says with pride, pointing to a tiny light. "This here's an indicator for when there's an object on your six. The light goes red. Right here's the on-off toggle switch."

"You know it works?"

Wade grins. "I turned the system on, pointed a Skyped laptop at it, then drove the tractor around the field behind the plane. The light goes off and on. It picks up the tractor within 500 yards of your tail."

He's beaming with pride, but I worry about what I might do if a tractor comes within 500 yards of my tail in flight, but I'm sure he doesn't mean that exactly. We move to other things, checklists and procedures. Canopy release drill, how to un-dog the hand crank if I want to roll the canopy back. Such as to toss out a GPS unit over desolate terrain, which gets Wade laughing again.

We begin the preflight in the barn to get the engine primed, all switches set for takeoff. We want to minimize the time the plane is out on the strip, visible from the road. However I insist on making a taxi run. I need some idea of how she handles on the ground, throttle, brakes, rudder, tail wheel, before I bring the engine to takeoff power. It will be loud enough just in taxi and run-up. The nearest house is two miles away across plowed fields. It will wake them up, but farm people are used to loud machinery at night. We're hoping we don't attract company.

So what we do next is take the tractor across the road to the improvised airstrip. With Wade driving as straight as he can along the edge, I operate a spreader full of white lime. That white border down the length of the runway on pilot's left will be my only indication of being pointed right on the airstrip. I'm not using the Mustang's lights for takeoff.

As we turn around at the far end of the field, I glimpse the power poles. I'll need at least 50 feet altitude by this point so the tall landing gear will clear them. Otherwise, the mission will be over promptly and I'll be smashed flatter than a whole-wheat pancake. Heading back, I make the line's final 100 yards double width.

Soon as I'm off, Wade will hook the tractor to his disc plow, and spend the next hour obliterating the runway. We'd discussed even if I auger in on takeoff, he's to ignore the plane and destroy the runway first. Won't be any help possible for me if that happens.

Where the Mustang stands proud in the wide doorway, we hook the tractor to her landing gear. We've done the walk around, now I'm in the cockpit. The feeling I'm trying to push away is similar to the stark terror I'd felt first time I slid into bed with a naked girl.

We continue the preflight. "Ignition off." Wade calls out, looking at his own checklist from where he stands in front of the prop.

"Ignition off," I echo.

"Mixture at Idle Cutoff."

"Idle Cutoff." I move the mixture control to the marked position. At this point I have to climb down to help Wade pull the 4-blade prop through three full rotations, and it's not easy. Even in the cold night air we're sweating when we get that done.

That's as much as we can do in the barn, so we get on the tractor and start to roll. I watch behind as the Mustang follows obediently, nose high. She has this small air scoop under the prop spinner that looks to me like a laughing cartoon mouth. I can feel the spirit of this proud relic leering down at us on the dusty tractor, as though saying, *What are you pretenders about to do?*

With minimal use of lights, we tow the plane across the road and onto the hard dirt surface. The moon is behind cloud, I don't know if that's good or bad. I'd sure like to see the strip better. Even in the quiet nighttime dark, I have the creepy feeling we're shouting at the world for attention, and are being watched. The white line we'd laid down points out into blackness.

I'm in the cockpit buckled up tight. Thermal undies, coveralls, down jacket, boots, two parachutes, motorcycle helmet, all making me feel hot, clumsy and uncoordinated. Not confidence inspiring. A red darkroom light illuminates the cockpit. On my laptop is the startup sequence Wade and I had worked out. We assume our priming in the barn does not have to be repeated. Canopy still open, using hand signals as well as the walkie-talkies, I raise the starter switch cover and hold the switch at START. My fingers tremble.

A high-pitched whine is quickly replaced by the sound of the starter, straining to move the big prop. The whole plane jumps. I count six blade passes, then switch the magnetos to BOTH. Flick the fuel boost pump switch at the left of the starter, then the electric primer to the right. I bring the mixture lever to the RUN position.

The whole airframe twists and shudders. A few loud bangs from the manifolds, then a fuel-scented roar and the blades become a blur out front. Orange flame jetting from the twelve exhaust manifolds lights up the wings. She smooths out.

Unbefuckinglievable.

The oil pressure needle jumps and starts to rise. If it's not at least 50 pounds within the first half-minute I'll shut her down. There would be no point in continuing. An engine without oil pressure will not survive takeoff.

Wade is standing down below with a fire extinguisher. All kinds of black smoke I smell rather than see is belching out both sides of the long nose, blowing past the cockpit on the tornado from that prop. I sit here letting it idle at 1200 RPM until the oil temperature hits 40 degrees C.

Following what's next on my screen, I make sure coolant and oil switches are set to AUTOMATIC, and move the mixture control to RUN. Move the prop control forward to the INCREASE RPM position. This part would go better if I had two right arms.

I hold the stick back to keep the tail wheel locked straight, check that flaps are in the UP position and oil and coolant shutters are open. I release the parking brake and the taxi roll is on. Engine RPM at 1200, I maintain my clearance to the white line on the left of the strip. When the line becomes double I've only got 100 yards of runway so I slow, release the tail wheel, and press the left brake. The wheels skitter on the dirt as she pivots around. Heading back toward Wade I leave the tail wheel free, try some S-turns using rudder.

An electric thrill runs through me, replacing the dread I've felt the last two weeks. This thing is alive! Just as when flying with Sean, she's wonderfully responsive to the controls. Now I can't wait to get her off the ground and do some flying. Man, I wish the moon was out.

I do a fair job of swinging the Mustang around at the other end. I see Wade standing there, clothes flapping in the prop wash. With her nose pointed at the far end of the runway, it's time for the engine checks. If these don't go right, we might still wind up towing her back to the barn. I ease up the manifold pressure, tach rises to 2300 RPM. Magneto checks show no serious drop when I switch from left to right and back to BOTH. Simmonds regulator, supercharger, switches for carb air, radiator air, a dozen more things from the checklist. They all go well, but my breathing is still high in my chest.

I drop the RPM to idle. Set the flaps to 15 degrees and watch them move into position. There's nothing more to do now, except advance the throttle to full manifold pressure. I pull my headset away from one ear. Damn, that engine is loud! With the walkie-talkie, I yell at Wade.

"Hey man you rule. This is huge."

"It sounds great," he yells over the radio. We can hardly hear one another above the engine. "You take care little brother."

"Talk to you at dawn." I switch the handset off, toss it to the ground. I crank the canopy closed and make sure it's locked. Dude, it sure is hard to move in this cramped cockpit with all the gear I have on.

I check rudder trim for about the fifth time. Needs to be set at 6 degrees right for takeoff. Stick aft of neutral to lock the tail wheel. Forcing myself to inhale, I ease the throttle up until the manifold pressure gauge shows 40 inches boost. The airframe trembles.

I release the brakes.

Damn thing tries to leap out from under me! Quickly I increase boost to 55 inches and the roar is deafening as she begins to roll. At that moment the high winter moon finds a hole in the clouds and the dirt strip appears in faint silver light. I anticipate the nose wanting to swing left and add some right rudder to keep her straight. It's too much. When I back off the rudder, the Mustang fishtails a bit. As I fight to catch it, the acceleration is so strong my seat harness feels loose. Airspeed shows 70 MPH already, and the tail is ready to fly. I ease the stick forward and the fuselage comes level. For the first time I can see ahead and I'm lined up OK with the runway and the chalk line. At 95 MPH it's rolling straight and true on the main wheels.

But wait I am slowing down!

Engine RPM is *dropping*. With this crescendo of noise and action in the cockpit, white line whipping by to my left, I have no time to process this at all. I reach for the throttle and find it's crept back toward idle. I shove it forward fast. Bad move. The abrupt engine torque tries to twist the plane over and one wing goes airborne so I have no choice but to ease back on the stick to get her off the ground where it's safe to roll level.

I have no idea where the white line is anymore, or the runway. Or the telephone lines. I'm off the dirt at 115 MPH. I nudge a little more back pressure on the stick, hoping it's not too soon, and with great relief I feel a mighty hand beneath me lift the plane upward into the dark. I pull back a bit harder and feel my body get heavier, gritting my teeth as she rises, expecting the worst. Those power lines are somewhere out there, waiting.

But nothing comes. Indicated airspeed 170. I throttle back to 46 inches boost and the RPM drops to 2700. Just like the books all said! I set the flaps to zero. Unlock the landing gear lever and pull it toward me. Whirring sounds and unfamiliar thumps underneath the ship. The ride smooths out, gets quieter, speed picks up to 225. Frantically I scan the instrument panel looking for anything out of place but there's nothing. Good God what a feeling. This thing is flying!

I am wishing I could say something to Wade right now. I can imagine him whooping and hollering back there with tears in his eyes, practically shitting himself as his airplane, the one he worked on the last five years, becomes a darker shadow where night-clouds chase a winter moon. I am somewhere between ecstatic and scared out of my wits to be flying her, in all her din and uproar. Mostly I am beyond busy, looking back and forth between my laptop and the instrument panel, checking dials and readings and control settings over and over.

Outside the canopy there's moonlit farmland and a scattering of distant lights. Watching the GPS strapped to my knee, I turn the ship toward my first waypoint. Steady in the turn, my mind has a chance to replay the last few seconds of takeoff. *What did I do wrong?* Oh, of course. Had to be throttle creep. The friction setting on the throttle quadrant had let it slip back toward idle. A little thing like that, and I almost lost the ship in the first 20 seconds. Three hours to fly. What the hell else will wait to bite me?

But I survived my first power takeoff.

I tighten the friction lock until the throttle stays in position. My job now is to hit the correct altitude so I can follow the terrain to my first waypoint. Whatever navigation gear the Mustang has, I'm using something far simpler and better, the GPS. Using sectional maps covering from here to Gallup, I had laid in a series of waypoints and altitudes that will carry me on a terrain-hugging course, avoiding major traffic lanes all the way to an empty desert north of Gallup.

Basically I'll fly south toward Fresno, down the San Joaquin Valley, over the mountains well south of Tehachapi, low over the country north of Interstate 40, often following railroad tracks at 200 feet. To further fool any snoopy radar, I'm planning 60 miles of my route through the Grand Canyon, below the rim. I look at the small GPS unit on my knee and wonder at the leap of faith it took to trust my life and this historic aircraft to a little chunk of plastic and circuit boards that cost less than 80 bucks at Best Buy. Life of the modern airplane smuggler.

I get relaxed enough to think. Something Sean had said on my joyride comes to me. It's been said that Reichsmarschall Hermann Göring, commander of the German Luftwaffe during WWII, remarked, "When I saw Mustangs over Berlin, I knew the war was over." It's a fact that the Mustang helped ensure Allied air superiority in Europe by 1944, the year my dad was born. Dad! How I'd love for you to see me flying this.

By the time I've covered 300 miles, the moon is behind me. Her light fills the cockpit, illuminates the silver wings I ride on. My eyes continually scan the panel. Engine coolant in range, oil temperature and pressure in range, RPM steady at 2250, indicated airspeed 322 miles an hour. My ears are ringing behind this V-12 engine, but she sounds fine far as I can tell. The engine note has been consistent since I leveled off, not a stumble. I can only imagine how the real World War II Mustang pilots must have felt, returning after eight-hour missions that often included a lot of shooting, being shot at, and demanding aerobatic moves. Many of them were teens and twenty-somethings when they got started. Unstoppable youth. I'd like to meet a real Mustang pilot someday. A dying breed of real warriors.

I'd ridden in a perfectly-restored B-17 bomber years ago. The four radial engines on the wings set up such a racket that the only possibility of conversation inside the ship was headsets and intercom. I had imagined being a 19-year-old kid at 22,000 feet above the lights of some German city at night, such as Dresden, watching a thicket of artillery explosions around him as the bombardier guides them on a precisely straight and predictable course to the release point. Sitting ducks to all the firepower below. I'd imagined going down in one of those things after it was crippled by flak, a cramped straitjacket of screaming metal, nearly impossible to get out of. War. What a monstrous sin.

For a few moments I take my mind off the airplane, change hands on the stick so I can flex my fingers inside the heavy glove. Now I'm happy for the bulky clothing that seems to take up half the cockpit. The temperature out there must be near zero.

One second, everything is going along all normal. Next instant, my world tilts on its axis. Doesn't seem like much, just this one ruby indicator light on the panel. What had Wade called it? The rear radar warning light. Here I am, over an expanse of low cloud that's typical of Nevada this time of year, which means that down on the deck it's dense fog.

The ruby glow holds steady, which means only one thing. There's another aircraft on my butt. I crane my head around, looking behind as much as I am able. Nothing in the dark sky. I bank sharply to the left, the light goes out. Turn back to my GPS course. Light's out. Hold my breath. No, dammit, it's on again, shining fierce and steady from its place on the panel full of other lights, switches, dials, indicators. If it's an aircraft, then they have visual on me, or radar. And I can't see them. I lower the nose and advance the throttle, increasing speed. The light stays on. The cloud bank is coming closer. I see from the GPS I have enough altitude, just then the light goes out. I level off, a few hundred feet above the clouds.

I watch the panel, the light stays dark. I'm just starting to breathe easy when I become aware of a presence outside the canopy. There off my port wing floats a sinister dark shape, red position light shining steadily. A row of six blue flames along the nose. Someone stalking me!

My mind goes on full turbocharger mode. Who is here? Mick? The Air Force? My new parole officer? Who the hell can be out there? I know I've probably lit up radar scopes somewhere along the way but I've been so low much of the time I would be hard to follow. Except by another aircraft.

My first reaction is to bank hard away from the dark shape beside me. I increase speed slightly, which gets me busy changing rudder and elevator trim to keep her flying clean. Banked 70 degrees and pulling around 5 Gs, I'm aiming for a 360-degree turn that will shake them and put me back on course. *Who is out there?*

Well, apparently it's a damn good pilot. Before I'm a quarter of the way through the turn, the fricking red light comes on steady. Shit oh dear! Back on my desired heading now, the light's still solid. I sigh. Learning evasive maneuvers in the dark with an unfamiliar aircraft is out of the question, so I have only one viable option. I hope it doesn't lead to disaster.

I lower the nose and enter the cloud. Now this really is the shits. Without the ability to see a horizon, human senses can't tell if a plane is right side up, turning, diving, or what. The GPS can show my speed over ground, position and altitude, but it knows nothing about the Mustang's attitude, whether it's flying wings level or not. But built into every one of these warplanes is a wonderful device called an artificial horizon.

I use it now.

Keep my heading with the GPS, keep her level with the instruments. I hate this I hate it and hate it. Every sense is screaming to let me out of this damn blanket so I can see the horizon, the moon, the sky. But I fix my mind on the GPS trace, the artificial horizon, and oh God the altimeter! I clamp down on my spinning brain, which is telling me I'm in a steep bank again. I set my sights on twenty minutes. Just that much. Stay hidden for that long, they won't be able to find me again. The ruby light stays dark.

My mind drifts again, following the instruments by reflex. Somewhere in the last few days I'd told Tharcia and the twins about my former plan to drop out of sight. What it meant, why I wanted that. How long I had longed for a new life, a clean life. And that suddenly, finding a new life was the last thing I needed.

The twins got their shorts in a complete twist, what about the grow, the jewels? What about us, you blockhead! I hadn't realized how hurt they would be. But Tharcia's reaction was a model of serene confidence. She simply said, "That's not what you are thinking anymore, Stuka. It isn't." Looking into her eyes, all I could do was shake my head in time with hers. No.

"I will find you," she informed me.

But immersed in unending cloud my mind somehow finds its center, and I stop being afraid. I think back, knowing I could have died five or six times in the last two weeks. I did not. Why? Simple answer, it ain't time yet. Montana, enforcer88, Drake, Mick, the almost-bungled takeoff tonight, any of those could have finished me. There comes a vision of my life stretching out ahead, long beyond this night, spent with people I love. It ain't my time yet.

Two hours later I'm flying in clear air, alone above New Mexico. Daylight creeps toward me over the desert, hills and valleys take form below. Following the GPS, I hold a straight course as I approach the final waypoint, watching for the marker. There it is! Stretched across the empty desert, a long trail of pink smoke points toward sunrise.

The landing area is just as Wade described it, just as it looked in the satellite images. I circle back, line up on the smoke and follow it in. For the hell of it, knowing this is my only chance ever, I up the manifold pressure to 55 inches and bring her in low across the valley floor at about 390 MPH, enjoying the blur of speed close to the ground. As I draw closer I make out some shapes: a man, a motorcycle, a pair of fuel drums. Am I mistaken, or is the man standing at attention, holding a rigid salute as I make my pass?

Man, motorcycle, fuel. Well, okay, just like the plan said. All that remains is for a pilot who has never before flown a power plane to now land one. As in, set down a rare and valuable war relic without erasing it from history.

Is it going to be that simple? I have landed gliders many times, and this is a landing. When I landed with Sean, he was taking care of all the checklist crap, rudder trim, and other controls. I find myself wishing I could talk to Wade, about how things are doing where he is. But the cockpit noise and all the tasks ahead of me put that out of reach. An edge of orange sun flames a distant sawtooth of snowcapped peaks.

I pull up the landing checklist on my laptop.

I'd practiced several landing sequences during the flight, using the flaps, all the touchdown steps, feeling the incipient stall in a nose-up attitude. The Mustang definitely talks to you approaching stall, but is stable and predictable. The only thing I hadn't tested is the landing gear. No way would I risk a gear malfunction mid-flight.

I take a deep breath and let it out slow. I see from the direction of the pink smoke that I'll be able to bring it in straight upwind on the ancient lakebed. Lined up from about four miles out, I set prop and throttle and slow to 150 MPH, pull the gear lever toward me to unlock it then shove it into the DOWN position and lock it. Thumps and bumps, more slipstream noise. The indicator tells me that tailwheel and mains are down and locked. Airspeed is low enough to dial in full flaps. They're hydraulic and take about 15 seconds to extend. I can see them move from the cockpit.

No rush. I can take time to get this right. There are 50 gallons of fuel left on board. The trick is, according to the P-51 pilot's manual, to hold her off in the 3-point attitude just above the runway, let her lose speed and settle in. I pick my aim point near the smoke trail.

Well, the first time I don't like it so much. I feel the stall coming when I am still fifteen feet up, so I apply power and do a wide slow circle. I am ready for the engine torque this time and there's no excitement. This circuit takes a while because the manual says not to make any turns until the flaps are up. What do I know? So I follow the book, which also says raise the gear for go-arounds but I am not about to take any chances with the hydraulics and am flying slow enough.

Lined up again, flaps extended, it feels better coming in, but I stall from two feet up and she drops out from under me abruptly. I'd expected more of a cushion from ground effect, but there you have it. The Mustang's V-12 engine alone weighs twice what a loaded glider does, so I bounce her in. Slowing from about 130 MPH, it slews sideways but I chase it with the rudder and manage to catch it. Speed drops. I get the tail wheel on the ground with no drama. Get her slowed and swing around so I can look through the spinning prop to where the guy with the fuel is waiting.

That's when I get it. I am down and the Mustang is still flyable.

So the drill is to sit out here while I check in with Wade. I let the RPM drop to a bare idle, set the parking brake. Quarter mile away I see the waiting man, fuel drums, and motorcycle. Nothing else moves out here in the desert. Unbuckle myself and notice I'm really glad for the ski parka. Must be below freezing out here. Locate a phone in one of my many pockets. Wade picks up quick.

"Clay?"

My answer is a wild yah-hoo that I'm sure can be heard in Gallup. We have a hard time making ourselves understood because of the noise from the engine, but this is the gist of it.

"Dude, we are down and we are in one piece."

"Jeez man I been about to turn blue here. You see our guy? You're down?"

"That's a big affirmative. Did your wife give birth?"

Wade's wild joyous outburst rivals my own. "Dude I am about three miles away, they are headed in the opposite direction, and I have the baby in the carriage."

"Okay, Papa. See you at the hospital."

"Adios."

Now there is nothing to do but taxi in. It's over. What hits me right now is aching sadness. I'll never have another chance to fly one of these, at least not in the form of a real adventure. No Mustang owner in his right mind will let me twist a switch in his precious warbird.

As I approach, my reception committee is making arm signals, like he wants me close to the fuel. But of course. Fill her up so he can fly her out.

He has the drums perfectly spaced, and carefully I line up between them, moving slowly as they pass out of sight beneath the wings. He is in front of the wing where I can see him, and raises both fists to his chest, crossed at the wrist. I push both brake pedals hard and cut the ignition. My ears ring in the sudden silence.

I'm looking at the laptop, returning levers knobs and switches on the Mustang's panel to their proper places. There's bumping on the starboard wing, and this old dude is scrambling up beside me, pressing the emergency release at the forward edge of the canopy. The canopy slides back. A very cold breeze enters the cockpit.

"You Pete?"

I have to rewind mentally to dig out that name. This guy standing on my wing in the aviator shades is exhaling clouds of tiny icicles. Underneath the puffy blue ski parka, he's got on an ancient leather flight jacket with a patina of fine white cracks. Blue uniform shirt and khaki trousers cinched by a frayed cloth belt and a scratched brass buckle. Faded jacket patch says 456 or it could be 458. One of those peaked cloth caps on his head, garrison cap they called them. Sweat stained. Now I recall who Pete must be.

"Pete couldn't make it today," I tell him.

"So who the hell are you?"

"I'm his den mother."

Guy laughs, white teeth. My instant name for him is The Colonel. More I look him over, the more I get it. He's a relic, pushing 90 years. But he can still boost himself up on a Mustang's wing. Because he's here to fly this bird away it's gotta mean he's one of the few remaining originals. It hits me he has more stories about flying warbirds than I shall ever dream.

I stand on the seat and start tossing my stuff to the ground. The soft stuff anyway. Whatever's breakable I hand to the Colonel. The cockpit's cleaned out, he leans in, looks everything over, puts a few switches the way he wants them.

He looks at all the layers I'm wearing. "Cockpit heater not working?"

I shrug. Details. That refinement wasn't in our scope.

Standing with him on the ground I see the image of my zany getup reflected in his dark glasses. "This was your ship?"

The Colonel shakes his head slowly, eyes tracing the Mustang's nose, the exhaust ports, the knife-edge wings, remembering way way back.

"No. We believe it was my flight leader's plane. Some of us got together to bring her home. He would have liked that."

I nod. "He will like that."

We're underneath, fueling her up, using only the wing tanks as the Colonel prefers, turning hand cranks to transfer fuel into each side. We're in the middle of this and my ears start twitching. There's a majestic roar growing closer in the distance. We both look up, and I flat out drop my jaw. It's another Mustang, don't know the model, passing low, close and very loud, all painted up in Army Air Force trim like it's still 1945 and screaming across the desert fast. My sweet Lord.

Colonel looks up and nods. "You dumped your escort," he says with a grin.

"Ah. That's who that was."

We get the fuel in, this guy is not waiting around, wants to be in the air. He shakes my hand, says thanks, tells me the bike's full of gas, climbs up the port wing and starts getting himself ready in the cockpit. No checklist for him, he probably memorized it 70 years ago.

No fire extinguisher handy, nothing at all for me to do, I just stand to one side gathering my stuff, packing it on the bike.

Watching the Mustang start is riveting. She's still warm, no priming is necessary. Big prop starts to swing, the manifolds bark and shoot black smoke, then it's a solid roar and it's all I can do to scamper aside to avoid the dust plume she kicks up.

Man. Taxiing out, this guy doesn't pause, no run-up, probably does his own short and sweet version of the checklist items he thinks are important as he's rolling to what would be the centerline if this was an actual runway. Couple hundred feet away, without slowing, he points her nose upwind, looks my way and snaps off a salute. I give him what I know for a salute, couple fist thumps to my chest, lockup style.

The engine rises in pitch, she starts to accelerate. Only a couple hundred yards and she's off. I can make out the gear coming up. The Mustang flies straight out as the sound fades, then it's gone.

I look around.

I am completely alone in an empty desert. Bright sun rising, but it's still damn cold. I check out the bike. In the saddlebag there's a bottle of slightly frozen water, some cheese, energy bars, crackers. A map and a note that will get me out of here and over to Gallup. Name of a motorcycle shop there that wouldn't mind getting the bike back if I don't really need it. There's a sealed envelope with 'Rental Agreement' written on it. I stuff it in my pack.

I am just securing the last of my things when I hear them, from far across the open desert, two powerful engines in perfect unison. There, from low on the horizon they come, two sliver P-51 Mustangs in tight formation, the Colonel on point. Gear up, these guys are so close to the ground as they pass me that a single mistake and the props would touch. They must be doing 420. I am wishing Wade could see! Half a mile out, they climb in formation and bank into the bright morning. Sunlight glints on silver wings. What washes through me as the planes pull up and away is a sure and steady trophy I'll carry the rest of my life. *I flew here in that!*

For an instant the clock turns back decades, to a time when men like the Colonel and planes like these helped bring peace to Europe and the world. And for those few seconds, I get to be there. They vanish into shimmering dawn. The desert is silent again.

Tired, my blood a toxic brew from hours of adrenaline, I complete my chores mechanically, feeling drained. I'd thought about this moment many times and had always focused on the money. But in the reality of this primal sunrise, in what Wade and I have accomplished, money does not figure. We can claim a minor role in something that does.

I'm packed up and about to start the bike, comparing the Colonel's hand-drawn map to my last remaining GPS, when my phone chimes. Sunlight obscures the caller's name but I pick up anyway. When I lift it to my ear in this desert stillness there is no mistaking that voice, the soaring destiny it calls to me.

"Dad?"

RUSSELL LEE BALDWIN

Anyway, at age 14 I was pecking away at my mom's Smith-Corona on a story about two teen boys who invent time travel. Lucky I was in California by then.

But alas! Writing was subsumed in a left-brain education as a misfit mathematician. University brought a nadir of bizarre turns, during which I became in '62 a kinda-sorta rocket scientist in Los Angeles, a painter, and later a human interface designer in Silicon Valley.

Along the way I was busy exploring glass art, hard-edge impressionism, and again, writing for the hell of it. These days I like mysteries and thrillers and science fiction. Including love story subplots and one romance. And a smart machine that's seriously taking over the world.

When I hear people ask how they, too, can become a writer, I'm often tempted to say that one never becomes what one's always been.

ANGLE OF ATTACK

An Adventure in Aviation, Love, and Crime

Lee Baldwin

Copyright © 2012 Lee Baldwin

ISBN-13: 978-0-9854777-2-1

www.ingramcontent.com/pod-product-compliance
Lightning Source LLC
Chambersburg PA
CBHW022005010726
47494CB00003B/905